P̶R̶A̶I̶S̶E̶ ̶F̶O̶R̶ ̶T̶H̶E̶ BLUE CHEER

"It isn't often that a genuinely new voice enters crime fiction. Author Ed Lynskey chooses a West Virginia setting for this second title in novel-length format, and it proves a resounding success. The prose is spare, and the dialogue pitch-perfect."—Jeremiah Healy, author of PI John Francis Cuddy mysteries

"This is a New Wave Gold Medal novel, intricate, harrowing, rich in people good and bad, ripe with nasty surprise."—Ed Gorman, author of *The Day the Music Died*, *Wake Up Little Susie*, and *Will You Love Me Tomorrow?*

"*The Blue Cheer* is as well-written and well-plotted an example of the new Appalachian noir as you're likely to find. Ed Lynskey's hard-boiled narrative voice of protagonist Frank Johnson is distinctive, entertaining, and authentic.—John Lescroart, author of *The Second Chair*, *The Hearing*, and *The Oath*.

"This pure sheer first-rate mystery is the reason why we read the genre, and as long as we have such stunning grab-you-by-the-collar-and-not-let-go narrative, the future of mystery is not only assured, it's damn essential."—Ken Bruen, author of Jack Taylor series and White Trilogy

OTHER BOOKS BY ED LACKEY

Out of Town a Few Days
The Dirt-Brown Derby

THE BLUE CHEER

Ed Lynskey

POINT**BLANK**

THE BLUE CHEER

Copyright © 2007 by Ed Lynskey.
Cover design © 2007 by JT Lindroos.

Edited by Allan Guthrie.

Point*Blank*
www.pointblankpress.com

For more information, contact Point*Blank* Press.

ISBN-13: 978-0-8095-5667-0
ISBN-10: 0-8095-5667-7

Dedicated to Heather, with love,
and to the memory of Charles Williams
and Those Who Came Before

CHAPTER ONE

A sonic force engulfed the mountainside and echoed up the laurel hollows. Even the treetops quivered. I craned my neck to gaze over the cabin's roofline at a bursting fireball. The heat's explosive wave stopped me in my tracks.

Glowing red embers drifted down. The smell of scorched fabric stung my nostrils as I took a deep breath. I struggled to make sense of what I'd just witnessed.

Lately life had been a chain reaction of bizarre events. Tucked in central West Virginia, my cedar log cabin lay in that rural ghetto called "Appalachia". To others, it was a fly-over scabland. They were wrong. Just the night before, a puma's howl had set a chill at my spine and, man, life didn't get any richer than that.

Earlier in the afternoon, I'd burned up a slew of calories slinging my double-bladed axe, its solid helve jarring my palms. Aromatic red oak sat corded to the woodshed's eaves. Finished at last, I sank the axe blade into the chopping block. I balanced an armload of wood, staggered past the parked Prizm, and caught the door with an elbow. I went inside the cabin. Pieces of bark and pill bugs dribbled to the fir plank floor.

Past lessons had taught me that the woodstove drafted better with its flue open. I lit the sappy pine cones, tipped on kindling and in a few seconds, the red oak strummed into a fire. I closed the hatch and ran a sanity check: smoke detector, ash bucket, farrier gloves, hearthstone tools, and fire extinguisher. The twig broom belonged to the previous owner, a coal miner named Stubbs, a two-packs-a-day smoker whom lung cancer had forced into a hospice in Charleston.

No hard-bitten primitive, I felt grateful for the cabin's electric and running water. But my FM radio sat quiet. WAMU marketing gurus had bumped late afternoon bluegrass music off their programming.

DJs Jerry Gray and Ray Davis, both radio old-timers, no longer broadcast that five-finger picking music. That'd ticked off plenty of listeners.

A Charles Williams novel had then engrossed me until hunger won out. I'd eaten the remnants of browned venison last night, but the pantry stocked such canned delicacies as split pea, creamed corn, and minestrone, while chef's surprise came in the unlabeled tins. I was foraging for Charlie Tuna when the droning racket started up.

The noise drew nearer. I hurried out the cabin door to the dark stoop. Not yet luminous enough to cast shadows, the moon poked over a tree-fledged summit. My eyes scanned for the unseen buzz, a cross between an ATV and a chainsaw. What the hell was it? I retreated a few paces, stooping to search between the tree branches.

A flying triangle, backlit across the star-pocked sky, glided into sight. A UFO? Whoa, easy, country boy. You'll freak yourself. A blimp? The breeze batted chimney smoke into my eyes. The bogie, by now a ways in the distance, banked in a languid U-turn. The fact the bogie had robotic smarts unsettled me. Could my .243 rifle knock it down? Not unless a harder target appeared. Gnawing the skin on my thumb pad, I rejected the idea.

What was the bogie? A motorized hobby plane? No, this bogie flew too fast for kids' stuff. More than likely some Friday night yahoo cruising in his ultra-light aircraft. Such contraptions, I'd recently read in a men's magazine, flew at 100 feet high and topped 40 m.p.h. That sounded about right.

"Hey up there, hello!" I hollered between my cupped hands. "I say, hello!"

The hum continued tracking downslope. Maybe the natives could give me an explanation. Natives? What natives? Fordham County, West Virginia, now boasted fewer folks than before the Civil War, when McNeill's Rangers rode these trails. My nearest neighbors, the Maddoxes, lived three miles over the laurel ridge. Andes, the young fellow operating the fire tower on the knob of land between our places, had recently moved back to Racine University in North Carolina.

That's when the midair explosion occurred and the wall of heat hit me.

I shook my head. Who'd shoot down a manned ultra-light? Second thought told me this'd been no ultra-light. I then had a different sinister thought. Had a heat-seeking missile zeroed in on a drone and smashed it to bits?

I darted inside the cabin, my boots stamping over the plank floor. Due to the diminished winds over the last 48 hours, odds favored the land lines were still up. I rustled up a dial tone. Old Man Maddox grunted a greeting after the fourth ring.

"Johnson here. Were you outdoors earlier?" I asked.

After a cough, Old Man asked me to say again, only louder. I did. "The wife and I are fighting chest colds. We've been playing backgammon by the stove. What bothers you, babe?" Old Man used his favorite expression.

"Something blasted a bogie out of the sky. Made a big bang with lots of fireworks. Did you see anything? Hear anything?"

"Nothing, babe. Maybe a fuel tank dropped off a prop plane and detonated. Not unheard of."

"My guess is a missile took out a military drone," I said.

Old Man spent a moment thinking. "There's no airport from here to Elkton. Is Andes on fire patrol?"

"He packed off to school Wednesday. Came by and said you were away. What do you think?"

"Unreal. I can drive up and help you scout the bush, if you like. Got a couple of four-cell flashlights. Just say the word, babe."

"It can keep till morning."

"Sleep on it. Good idea. I'll drop by a little after breakfast. We'll get to the bottom of things then," said Old Man.

I hung up. I felt let down. Ages ago, my M.D., violating all manner of ethics and laws, had written me a lifetime prescription for an antidepressant. Happy pills, he called them. I'd always fought depression, always been predisposed to brooding reflections. It wasn't a true bipolar disorder. Doctors had yet to light up my brain like a Leyden jar. They reserved electric shock treatment as last-ditch heroics to rejuvenate vegetable minds. Until such time, I took a happy pill every night.

I tried to renew my interest in the Charles Williams noir, then strode over to my bookshelves. All of the Golden Field Guide Series—birds, trees, rocks and minerals, wildflowers, and reptiles—stared at me. But nature wasn't enough to distract me so I went to bed. Sleep, sure. My nerve endings, exposed electrical wires, jittered together. Screw waiting until sunup. Pulling on a CPO jacket, I trudged to the corner cupboard.

I found the Coleman lantern behind the fishing tackle and wicker-work creel. The lantern swished with plenty of gas when I picked it up. I pumped up its pressure, stuck in a lit barbecue match, and fired up its twin mantles. Hissing, they threw out compact hemispheres of light that I adjusted. I wondered what awaited me down the mountain. The fireball's mystery had gotten under my skin and I'd never relax until I'd checked it out.

My .243 lay on a deer hooves gun rack. The front drawer to the roll top desk eased out. My fingers roved inside to find a Kel-Tec P-11's polymer grips. Advertised in Shotgun News as the tightest and lightest 9 mil ever constructed, its knockdown power was impressive. I pocketed it and shouldered through the cabin door.

Radium-tipped dials on my wristwatch glowed on ten o'clock. I walked on the balls of my feet, halted to hold up the Coleman by its wire handle. My red Prizm grazed by the woodshed while my Lamborghini languished in the shop awaiting a tune-up. Yeah, right. I hoisted up the Coleman lantern, scanned a 360, and only spied my breath vapors.

A 10-point whitetail had tramped down from the higher ridges to eat crab apples fallen by the cistern and we'd bonded. I prayed he wouldn't end up tied to a 4x4's roof in three days when deer season started. I didn't spot him at the crab apple tree, however. Unlike me, the buck wasn't in a rambling mood.

I relied on my mental map to pinpoint the debris spill and crossed the twenty or so paces of my backyard down to the ring of big boulders. Jouncing from rock to rock, careful not to dink the Coleman's glass globe, I descended into denser shrubbery while I felt through my pants fabric the heat from the Coleman's porcelain-steel ventilator. Tramping down that dark mountainside, for the first time in weeks I craved a human voice, a gentle and caring female voice. Christ. Next thing I'd go soft and give marriage another fling.

My feet crunched over dry hickory leaves. Wood rangers had stapled up Smokey Bear ("Only You Can Prevent Forest Fires!") signs along the state roads. One cigarette butt flicked out a passing car window and there'd be real hell to pay.

I smelled no odor of char or ash to orient me and had doubts if anything had reached the ground. Could it be that the ejecta cascading through space had incinerated before hitting the treeline? If so, the drone had been flying higher than I'd first estimated.

Mushy persimmons swatted against my cheeks. I'd be back to pick those delicacies later. Moonlight had washed out all but a few stars. Had any of the wreckage snagged in the treetops? Feeling chillier, I strode faster. At Trout Creek, I stopped and cursed for having overshot my target area.

I did an about-face and started back uphill. A witch moth batted into the lantern's artificial light and my boot mashed down on a round, hard object. I set down the Coleman and scooped up the object. It was a steel cylinder, four inches in diameter and perhaps a yard long. A black, crusty crud pitted it.

I'd handled such hardware before but always prior to their detonation. This was nothing less than a Stinger flight motor case, Uncle Sam's anti-aircraft weapon lauded for its dead-on balls accuracy. I'd vowed never to hold a Stinger again.

CHAPTER TWO

During the mid-1980s, ages before my present so-called livelihood as a private detective, I'd worked as a master technician for a propulsion house. They'd landed a lucrative government contract to manufacture Stingers by the thousands. What a different era it was back then. Ronald Reagan ruled from the Oval Office; Communist Russia constituted an "evil empire"; and our skimpy post-Vietnam defense budget bulked up.

Never mind that a social leukemia sucked the marrow from our cities' cores. Or that the spread of AIDS had grown rampant. It was an age of go-go greed where in their retirement CEOs peddled non-fiction blockbusters on how to finance the life of your sweetest, wildest dreams. Tax-free annuities and Cabbage Patch dolls were in vogue and Lee Iacocca became a media icon.

Uncle Sam, on the sly, smuggled a few Stingers to the Mojahedin guerillas in Afghanistan where the rockets humbled the Red Russian invaders, shooting down their flying gunships with impunity. After the Russians pulled out of Afghanistan, the CIA busted their fannies to repurchase the Stingers, each rocket returned netting $35,000. How many Stingers did the CIA buy? A couple at most, if memory served. The lion's share went on the black market and sold to the highest bidder, possibly how I now came to be holding this Stinger. The CIA's $35,000 bounty was a laugh.

I can only guess that running this through my mind distracted me because something hard slugged me over the head. I saw pinwheels of light and fell into darkness . . .

The next thing I knew light flashed into my eyes and this face hovered over me. The Angel of Death? No, wrong day. My fingers registered no feeling. I smelled his witch hazel aftershave and blinked up into Old Man Maddox's scowl as, degree by degree, my senses recharged.

"Wake up, babe. Hear me?"

I hawked out a mouthful of lichens. Cliché be screwed, it felt as if some fool had planted a hatchet in my skull. "What happened?" I asked.

"So, you are still with us. Did you get a look at him?" asked Old Man.

"Who?"

"The guy who clocked you."

"What did you say happened?"

"Rest easy, babe. Your bell got rung."

"You got that part right."

"How many fingers do you see?"

"Six," I replied between zaps of light. I turned my battered head and winced at the Coleman's brightness. Quantifying time, my unconsciousness ran anywhere from a half-hour to three days, but my attacker was long gone. "Help me get to my feet, Old Man." Even to my own ears, the verbal instruction sounded garbled.

"Uh-huh, die-hard. If you go into shock, don't put it on me."

His enormous hands helped to sit me upright against a tree stump. Bile swilled up in my guts. I lifted a finger to wave at him.

"Wait a sec. Should be a Stinger rocket there in the leaves. See it?"

"Shit." Old Man took up the Coleman lantern. While he scrutinized the ground beyond my boot tops, I nursed a hope, however slim, that he'd run across the Stinger. Mumbling, he doddered back and forth in the lantern's illumination, twice glowering over at me. He polished off the search grid and set down the lantern on a rock slab.

"Find anything?" I asked.

"No. Did your brains turn into applesauce?" said Old Man.

"No amnesia, no coma, and no applesauce. What I held in my hands was the Real McCoy. A metal cylinder, oh, no longer than your arms stretched out."

"I only see rocks and roots." Old Man rubbed at his nose. "Better forget about it, babe. Job one now is getting you up this mountain."

"If we go slowly, I'll whip it," I said.

"Uh-huh."

At a young 65 Old Man could still bust up a cord of red oak. Picture football's William "The Refrigerator" Perry, then flesh out his legs and arms with a few hams. Well, hyperbole aside, Old Man was strong enough to half-drag me. We managed three woozy steps, then halted.

"At this rate, we might beat Christmas. Let's stop and retrench." Lowering his mulish back, Old Man tipped me aboard it and anchored my wrists in his hands. The firefighter's carry was a stroke of genius and we, or rather he, packed us uphill. He asked in a breathless, raspy voice, "Is your cabin door open?"

Two taps on his shoulder indicated "yes." A clammy sweat broke out on my forehead. My head felt swimmy.

"Move that shit away from me." The ammonia bottle withdrew. The tweed-covered La-Z-Boy scratched like a hair shirt.

"You keep zoning in and out. We'll take off for the ER in Elkins in a second," said Old Man.

My wrist gave him a dismissive flick. "I'll get back my land legs in a jiffy."

"No medical insurance, huh?" Old Man's tone was sympathetic. "No cause to feel embarrassed, babe. Nobody under the age of sixty-five has it anymore."

"My head is clearing. I'll be all right. I'm good."

"You weigh a ton," said Old Man, massaging his shoulder.

My hand darted inside the CPO jacket, fumbling at my waistband as my worried glance met Old Man's knowing grin.

"Is this what you're after?" He held up my 9 mil in the lamplight. "You dropped it."

Relieved, I took the 9 mil from him and laid it aside. "Go take care of your sick wife. I'll sack out here until dawn. Pour me a jigger before you go, please. And toss a couple oak logs in the stove."

"I'll stay a while yet. I woke Jan from a sound sleep. She's, um, not happy." Old Man finished loading chopped wood into the stove. Then bourbon tinkled. He brought the drinks over in butterscotch shot glasses ("Compliments of Blackburn's Auto Court, Luray, Virginia, 1956") that, along with chipped agate ware, were my late mother's honeymoon souvenirs. I didn't own much else of hers.

In tandem, Old Man and I tossed back our drinks. "Ah," he said. "Okay, what was up earlier, babe?"

I recounted in a wooden voice the evening's drama and fingering my head lump pictured an emu's egg. "Even if blind as a bat, I could read that hardware like Braille. Years of assembly line work burned it into my brain. The Stinger case part number was XYX-2309QQ. See? I can dredge up even that anal detail."

Shifting on the deacon's bench I'd bought at an estate auction, Old Man jostled his family jewels and spat on the floor. "Who'd be out here firing off these Stingers? And why? And even scarier, where did they lay their hands on the Stingers?"

"I don't know. But I'll gut the motherfucker who walloped me." Anger boiled my blood.

Old Man peeled back a cuff. "Quarter to eleven. Okay. What to do? This is my advice. Call up the authorities. A deputy should be on night duty in Scarab. Tell them the whole shmear. Don't gloss over anything. On the other hand, don't overplay it. That way, you've done your part and can forget about it."

"If it lowers your blood pressure any, make the call," I said.

Five minutes after midnight, a Mac Wiseman ballad played on the radio while the vanilla joss stick I'd lit to keep me awake had smoldered down to the wood spike.

"You like that country and western, babe. So do I. Charley Pride," said Old Man.

"This is bluegrass music. Old-timey mountain music. Has Irish-Scottish roots. All strings and no electrification or drums," I said to set him straight.

"I like mine a little mellower," said Old Man.

"Well, that's good music, too. Charley Pride is one of my favorites."

A rap at the door interrupted our chess match. Old Man lifted an eyebrow at the second knock and walked to the door. "Keep your hair on! We're coming."

So this was our public servant. A late middle-aged fart, the deputy was brawny shouldered and took, I'd guess, a 42-inch belt. Sallow skin gave him a jaundiced look. His oafish strut crossed the room and the campaign hat he doffed had fluted a crease around his forehead.

"Deputy Goines," he said in a seedy baritone.

Right off, I identified his species—Goines had put in his twenty years on some city cop force, got pensioned off, and then landed this cushy job. He was stolid, pig-headed, and unimaginative. His hip-holstered 9 mil was a heavier model than mine, but mine was newer. All in all, he didn't inspire confidence. Old Man made my introduction.

"So you're the complainant reporting a theft?" Uninvited, Goines sat on the cane-bottom chair and spit-thumbed the pages to a pocket notebook. Old Man spotted over his shoulder. "Coming up your lane in the dark is an ordeal. I felt every bump," said Goines.

"Evidently my message got relayed wrong. This was no theft. Fill in the deputy, babe. Take copious notes, Goines. This one is weird," said Old Man.

"Tell me about it, Johnson."

I recapitulated my escapades. Throughout, Goines tapped his Bic pen against his buck teeth. Derision tweaked his lips as I summarized. Without a word, he stashed the Bic after the notebook and rebuttoned his shirt pocket. He'd recorded nothing. His pockmarked face (caused by an acid bath from an exploded car battery?) turned to regard Old Man.

"You've heard his yarn again. Plausible?" asked Goines.

"Every word. Pulling up here, I saw Frank's lantern glimmer down the way. When I reached him, he was unconscious," said Old Man.

"Mystifying." Goines tongue-clucked. "Absolutely mystifying."

I jerked up from my chair. "Goddamn it, deputy . . ."

Old Man hedged into my line of vision. "Feel the boy's knot, deputy."

Goines instead pushed out his interlaced fingers and the joints snapped. "I'm at the end of my tour." He yawned against the back of his wrist. "First off, it's way late and I'm only taking in every other word. We'll table this and at the change of watch tomorrow at five p.m., you show up at the station house and we'll hash through it again."

"That your final say?" I asked.

Nodding, Goines saw the bourbon bottle next to our shot glasses on the drainboard. "Uh-huh, I suspected as much. Corn liquor muddles memories. You better sober up. Tomorrow morning you might see things more clearly."

Goines tucked in his olive drab shirttail, then leaned a hammy palm on the 9 mil's butt. "Some free advice, Johnson. Duck if you see any more flying bedpans." A swagger marked his departure and we heard his rough laughter beyond the cabin door.

"Don't mind Goines. He's useless," said Old Man Maddox.

"It's okay," I said.

"Goines' daddy never amounted to more than a timber hick," said Old Man.

"Go see after your wife," I said.

"All right then, babe."

I downed four aspirin tablets and drifted off to a sunny field of broom sedge, one of my boyhood playgrounds.

I awoke Saturday dawn, after four hours sleep, to chattering teeth and blue lips. I ranged up, banked the stove coals, and tipped in some matchwood. Not soon enough, heat roiled off the oak. My bruised head still screamed in pain and I'd no zest for my usual three scrambled eggs, scrapple, and a cantaloupe half. Coffee, Sanka or caffeine, didn't entice me. So, I took a navy shower and shaved to reclaim some humanity.

Drying off on a souvenir beach towel, I felt a valve inside me close down. My alpine vacation had ended and I was back on the job as a professional investigator except this time I was working for myself. First things first. I ran a six-point inspection on the 9 mil. A check of the slide, grips, and frame showed no hairline cracks, more than I could say for my skull. Again the 9 mil went with me. We were, in fact, now inseparable. I went outdoors.

The heavy white frost I crunched over had left shredded coconut icing all across my yard. The grassy verge could stand a last mowing, but that was next spring's problem. Gray-blue smoke curling out of my chimney's rain cap reached my nose. Behind the chimney, a chicken hawk, its tail feathers blood red, sliced over the saddle. I groaned but not just from my headache.

My Prizm's front tires were flat.

I hurried over. The rear pair were slashed, too. My gas tank flap stuck out, its cap pitched. I dabbed the white grains on a thumb to my tongue. Yep, some fool had sugared my gas tank. I jerked out the 9 mil and slammed slugs into the chopping block until my ears whistled. Only then did I get a grip. Could a mechanic drop the gas tank and hose it out? Sure he could, but for what minor fortune?

I retraced my path downslope to where I'd eaten dirt last night. I drew on a pair of old hay gloves to preserve any latent prints. Charred rocket parts, including a tail section and struts by a chinquapin oak, lay strewn about me. A foot-long section of the drone's wingspan lay wedged in a hop tree. Were these molted chunks the drone's onboard computers? I spiraled out in my search grid and stepped on the sheared end of a propeller and the components of a gas turbine engine. I could relate to NASA combing the debris path the ill-starred Columbia Space Shuttle had scattered over six Southern states.

No IDs were inked on the Stinger parts. Everything looked defaced. My sap-happy pals had spirited off the Stinger flight motor case, the key piece of evidence I sought. A sober insight unclouded in me. It stood to reason the Stinger's shooters wanted to cover up their illicit act. By extension, that also made me a liability to them. I wanted to accuse myself of paranoia. Except I'd rubbed my palm over the motor case. Except I fingered a lump on my head. Except my woods was an ordnance proving ground. It wasn't paranoia, but still shivering, I took out the 9 mil and cycled in a fresh slug. Why all this edginess? I knew and feared the terrible damage Stingers inflicted.

Call it guilt but I felt responsible in a convoluted way.

I could dash off *An Idiot's Guide to Firing a Stinger Rocket* in my sleep. Anybody could become a Stinger gunner. You could tote the twenty-three pound Stinger inside a ski bag to take anywhere you pleased. Picture it: any U.S. jetliner on approach or departure was a fat goose for a Stinger. Take your pick of which airport. If it were me, I'd target one in the Midwest and throw a marrow-chilling fright into the country's heartland. Nobody in the U.S. was immune from terrorists.

The shooter might deploy, say, less than a mile away from the unlucky airport. He could be a chimney sweep on a roof. Or a college kid from his Hyundai's sunroof. Or a Sunday picnicker over his egg salad sandwich. The shooter balanced the bazooka-like Stinger launcher on his shoulder just as seen on the TV news. A crew of two was best, but one shooter could swing it okay. He'd load in a missile round, clutch the grip stock, and draw a bead on the ill-fated jetliner. Lead it, you see, like shooting clay out of the air. The electronics bleeped when the Stinger locked on the fat goose. The launch motor kicked the missile from the bazooka where the flight motor ignited and took over and speared the Stinger—swish!—to the vital spot. Boom!

The anonymous shooter gloated at the fireball and melted into the crowd, never seen or heard from again. Shoot and scoot, shit and git.

This nightmare wasn't a new one, but it knotted up my guts. I began the ascent back up the mountain to my cabin. The early sunrays hadn't pierced the orange pall. It was shaping up to be a gray, miserable Saturday, my first one like that in West Virginia.

CHAPTER THREE

_____

It was near eleven when Old Man arrived at the cabin, late because Jan's cold hadn't improved, though his had. We argued.

"It's just an old wives' tale," Old Man told me. The swizzle stick moved to the other corner of his mouth. "The sugar acts like a sediment and settles on the gas tank's bottom. The worst thing that can happen is your fuel filter and pickup sock get clogged up."

My fist bottom thumped on the Prizm's trunk. "Damn it, Old Man, the sugar dissolves in the gasoline. The motor's heat caramelizes the sugar that gunks up your spark plugs and pistons. Say hello to a new engine."

Old Man sucked in his cheeks. "Okay, try this experiment. Slosh a little gasoline into an old mayo jar. Dump in a half-cup of sugar, then shake it. Either the sugar will dissolve or it'll settle out. Then we'll see which of us is full of shit."

Old Man's acting all biggity egged me on. I unearthed a jelly jar slated for catching bacon drippings from underneath my kitchen sink. The sugar bag came from the pantry. I went out and mixed the ingredients on my car hood.

He unbuttoned his cuff to unveil a strap watch. "How long, babe? Three minutes?"

"Hell, make it five," I said.

Five minutes elapsed. I stirred the mixture with a dowel rod but sugar granules only swirled suspended in the gasoline. Six minutes later I got the same result. I pitched out the concoction by the tail pipe.

"At least it spares us from having to flush the gas tank," I said.

"Think again. Sugar gums up the fuel lines. I just wanted to show off," said Old Man.

"You're a dirty dog, too," I said.

Old Man brayed with laughter. Just then, I felt a pang of guilt about our goofing off like this. How many hours had we gone cutting oak and other boys' stuff while Jan had to stay home stuck in her wheelchair? However, Old Man had never brought up her disapproval and I kept quiet.

Dropping the Prizm's gas tank was a good diversion from last night. We worked like a NASCAR pit crew. While Old Man went inside the cabin to fetch my fire extinguisher, I used a ratchet jack to hoist each corner and fitted a heavy jack stand under it. Then I gripped the bumper and rocked the Prizm. Yep, it was up to stay.

I smoothed out a drop cloth, crawled underneath the Prizm, and found little room to detach the rubber hoses, electrical ground, and fuel line. Gasoline dribbled all over me and acorns poked me in the shoulders.

"This is more hassle than it's worth. A real mechanic owns the right tools, too. Hand me that pry bar and scrap lumber," I said.

"The genius you are, it'll be a breeze. Just don't go ape wild and wreck anything. Here's a shop rag," said Old Man.

"Thanks, Mister Goodwrench."

"Don't cut up, babe. I don't want to have to crawl under there and bitch slap you."

"Yeah, yeah."

I recited "lefty loosie, righty tighty" to unbolt the straps but still had the devil of a time. Bolts connecting the gas tank to the car frame required squirts of Liquid Wrench. Then the gas tank fell into my crotch. Cursing blue howls, I wormed for daylight where Old Man dragged out the gas tank, then me. I recovered in a few minutes.

Old Man stretched on a pair of blue rubber gloves. "If you see any puffs or sparks, you cut loose with that fire extinguisher. My skin isn't fireproof asbestos. It burns."

"Your every wish is my command," I said.

Old Man drained out the tainted gasoline (hell, it only ran a few dollars a gallon) behind a disused refrigerator also on my list to tow down into the deeper woods. The gas fumes made my sinuses tingle.

He sloshed in two liters of fizzy Coca-Cola and funneled in a clutchful of brass wood screws.

He shook the gas tank, moving like he was waltzing with a bear. Metallic screws rolled and dinged inside the tank and I laughed hard enough to bring tears to my eyes. He poured out the cleansing potion, then rinsed out the tank with fresh gasoline.

"Better than new. Strap that tank back on your car, babe, and snug down the bolts. If everything lines up right, you're back in business."

Finished with that, we headed off to see Sheriff Greenleaf. Buckled up inside the Valiant, we bumped over the chuckholes that I kept meaning to patch using a wheelbarrow of blackjack shale and a tamping bar. Yeah, I had a lot of big ideas. This tank trail we rode down was the only route on and off my mountain.

"Some dude has a hard-on for you, babe," said Old Man.

"You picked up on that all by yourself, huh?" Yellow dust leaking through the rusted-out floor pans made me cough.

Old Man fished out a pack of Marlboro Reds and gnawed at the tinfoil. "No more smokes? Oh, for screw's sake." He tossed the empty pack through the window vent. Two fingers, coppery as columns of Indian pennies, held a phantom cigarette. I half-expected him to thumb in the dashboard lighter and start puffing away. "That tire surgery is a blatant warning for you to stay mum on what you saw last night."

"The trouble is, I'm not sure what I saw," I said.

"We'll mosey down and sift through whatever wreckage is left," said Old Man.

"I already did. Nothing's there."

"A second pair of eyes can't hurt."

A clapboard chapel appeared in the windshield and I read a sign's curlicue letters in the style of a Coca-Cola legend: "The First Primitive Apostolic Church." I did a double take at something else. A lady at the top of an aluminum ladder stretched out to scrape a putty knife over the clapboards. Paint chips flew off. A red scrunchie caught her brunette hair but even in those loose bibs, she was an eyeful. Brushes, rollers, and paint cans lay piled at the foot of the ladder.

"She's Jan's preacher. And is reputed to be in search of soulful love," said Old Man.

"Everybody has a sad story."

"Some are sounding sadder by the minute. You need a wife," said Old Man.

"I'm a consecrated virgin."

"You need a wife," said Old Man.

"Been there, done that."

"I didn't know that about you, babe."

We withdrew into our respective shells. I enjoyed the bucolic scenery and reviewed how I'd ended up in West Virginia. Late in August, I'd surfed across a web site advertising real estate in By-God West Virginia, the next state over. Lung-pink clean air, frost-flavored persimmons, and buck fever beckoned Frank Johnson, mountain man wannabe. I had to leave my hometown of Pelham in Virginia. It'd changed. Some said it was for the better. Honeysuckle fencerows and mistletoe oaks had disappeared and good country manners had grown obsolete.

McMansions sprouted up in gated communities. CUVs, big box stores, and Starbucks were part of the new vista. Soccer fields replaced cow pastures. Loudoun County next door to us, once the nation's leader in family dairy farms, now had a pitiful two, the Collins and Messicks. Tinted-glass towers for office buildings proliferated and clogged the scenery. High tech firms competed for what little of the space remained.

But a more acute reason ran me out of Pelham. A distant cousin on my mother's side sat marooned on death row. Rod Bellwether, the ill-bred little shit I'd last known growing up, had turned into a killer. Or was he? I was still fuzzy on the details. Rod had called collect one evening in the middle of my Spaghetti-Os and Strohs dinner. He needed a favor. Sure, wasn't I handing out favors to everybody? Of course I did Rod the favor, but right now I did myself a bigger favor and blocked Cousin Rod out of my mind.

I found after moving to Scarab, West Virginia, I didn't have a clue about mountain living. Help arrived in an unlikely manner. A car horn tooted me out of bed at the ass-crack of dawn one morning. Grumbling oaths, I slitted the Venetian blind and peeked out at the lane. I had rare company. The man seated in a vintage Valiant saluted me, a forefinger slanting off his temple. So I went outdoors. His mottoed hat was from the Washington, D.C. "One In A Million" march and he chewed on a swizzle stick.

"Maddox, Old Man Maddox." A hand black as the core veins in anthracite coal shook mine. "I'm retired from government after thirty-seven years. CIA. My wife, Jan, and I live in the A-frame." He pointed behind us. "We're neighbors, babe."

"Frank Johnson," I said. My next comment, a little on the blunt side, slipped out. "Not many folks live here in these mountains."

"Yeah. The old folks die out and the kids move on for better prospects. Many enlist in the service. The local population only swells when it's time to hunt bear and deer."

"Looks like you get by pretty well."

Old Man showed his porcelain-veneered teeth. "Fact is, I'm one native who aims to live out my days on the home place. Family is all there is. I've learned that much in my life. I'm country as a biscuit but Jan is an urban cat. She was a real trooper last winter. Snow up to your ass and it didn't faze her. The roads stayed impassable until May. Our highway department doesn't run a plow up here much, but I don't bitch too loud. My property tax is unbeatable. On top of that, we're racking up 15% interest on our IRAs."

"The roads are socked in, you say, until May?"

Old Man shrugged. "It's even longer some winters."

"Longer?"

"But you've been busting your tail laying in firewood. Right, babe?"

"The last tenant left me a boxcar of pitch pine," I said.

Old Man cackled from his gut. "Stubbs, that crazy old coal miner? I love him but here's a word to the wise, babe. Pine is for suckers. You'd better rev up a chainsaw and cut some oak. Tow up some dead locust. It burns the hottest. Old timers claim a locust post left in a creek-branch will never rot. Aw, don't look so lost. Tell you what, I'll lend you a maul and re-edge my axe with a burrstone. My hydraulic splitter is on the fritz, but you've got a young, strong back."

I heeled up my palms. "Thanks but I run electric heat. My wood-stove is for ambiance."

"Ambiance, my nuts." Old Man grinned wider. "The first snow squall will knock out our electric power. The telephone quits, too. That woodstove is what heats you. I can't guess what hooey Stubbs fed you, babe, but that's the real deal."

That morning we forged an alliance. Old Man sauntered up my lane, a chainsaw in one hand and the other holding a new bourbon bottle. He was a born woodchuck but I didn't touch the chainsaw—its kick-back might chop off my head. Old Man sawed the scarf, then the back-cut. We stood well away and yelled, "Timber!". We sawed up a boxcar of wood but left a few dead oaks standing for Jan's pileated woodpeckers. I made a pretense of paying Old Man that first evening.

"Your money's no good here. I'll help you stock up, say, four cords. Come winter, you can repay me, babe. I'll hit you up for chess, poker, or whatever suits the time. Jan is a mah-jongg champ, but do you shoot any stick? I bought a heated table. It keeps the felt dry and lessens the friction on the cue balls."

"Like how? Fly over the snow?" I asked.

A pair of snowshoes materialized out of the Valiant's junk-crammed trunk. "Have cue stick—will travel," he laughed . . .

"Hey, babe!" Back to reality, I looked at Old Man alternating his eyes between the driveway and me. "I pointed out that we'll be in Scarab way before five o'clock to see Goines," he said. "Didn't you hear me?"

"Okay, park us by the station house. I'm speaking to their sheriff or emir or whoever is in charge," I said.

The Valiant's tires clunked off gravel toward the hardtop, where Old Man pinned the accelerator to the floor. Tires screeched and we rolled with a purpose. A lumber shed with a "Chew Mail Pouch Tobacco" advertisement painted on its flank came and went by us.

"Goines will bust a grape if you go over his head," said Old Man.

"My story goes on record. If Goines won't write it up, I'll find some-body who will."

"Just don't bring any heat with Goines."

"What other choice do I have?" I asked.

"Be cool about it. All I have on me is thirteen bucks and spare change. If they toss you in jail, I can't raise bail."

"Who's talking about jail? I'm going to see my sheriff is all," I said.

"Coal town sheriffs set themselves up as God. Ours is no damn different."

The state road banked up and away into a stiff grade making Old Man's biceps coil as he wrestled the wheel to hug the inside curve. My head throbbed. Better get used to it. I unscrewed the top of my aspirin bottle, shook out four tablets, and chewed them like gumdrops before swallowing.

"You can take aspirin with no water?"

"My innards are pig iron."

"Outta sight." Old Man's grin turned into a chuckle. "Bear in mind what we discussed. On second thought, I better go in with you and shove a cucumber in your yap if need be. You'll land in more hot water than any slick lawyer can save you from."

"Like Robert Gatlin," I said. "He practices in Pelham and on the odd occasion, I work for him."

"What do you do, fetch Mr. Gatlin's morning latté?" Old Man drove us down the shady flank of the final summit.

"No, never. Gatlin is a booze hound," I said.

"Man, I dig the cat already."

"Sure, sure. Everybody loves Gatlin. He's the underdog's best friend and plays it hard-assed to beat every DA he goes up against. His granddaddy was a Texas Ranger and his daddy welded seam joints up on the Alaskan Pipe Line. But not Robert. He left West Virginia and made his billions by dabbling in real estate and I don't know what-all."

Old Man glanced over at me. "Babe, you don't say much about Pelham. What gives?"

"I've nothing to say about it." I moved my eyes to the road's crown and concentrated them there. "But I'm not alone in my self-exile. A girl I know moved to Richmond. Dreema Atkins. She works at the state forensics lab."

"Don't you have any homeboys to pal around with?" asked Old Man.

"Well, besides Gatlin, there's Gerald Peyton." A snort flushed through my nose as I had a mental picture. "Gerald is a certified psycho. He's always up for action, the rougher the better. But I count him as a friend. You'd like him enough."

"Sounds like a good man to know in a jam," said Old Man.

Our destination rolled into view. Old Man's daddy had called it Butt Ugly, West Virginia, and he had it about right. Scarab wasn't a smashing lot to praise, seen either up on the mountain or down within its corporate limits. Three banners of steel rail ran as a backbone behind its stores and shacks. A yellow haze hung over the hamlet and the reek of hot roofing tar hung in the air. I empathized with Scarab's folks but not with Big Coal, who'd erected the slapdash infrastructure and bolted once the mined coal was no longer big enough.

We approached the Chartreuse Ironworks and I saw pony-tailed Native Americans shriek out warnings to the overhead crane operator. Frantic hands waved hard hats. I saw why. His boom jerked within inches of crashing into power lines and certain electrocution. The crane operator stopped a hairsbreadth away and all but had a coronary.

Five Kenworth tractors semi-circled the corral, their emerald green bodies, maroon fenders, flat-top sleepers, and chrome dual exhausts making for eye-candy. They gave jockeys all the sciatica they could handle. Any truck driver with saddle sores from hauling a load fourteen hours a day won my admiration. To my right, three mill workers grit-blasting something ferrous kicked up a dusty dervish. Elsewhere in the yard, welders in Darth Vader shields cropped an I-beam with oxyacetylene torches.

"It puts me in a Pittsburgh frame of mind," said Old Man.

"It makes me wanna belt out 'John Henry Was A Steel-driving Man'."

Old Man's thumb went down. "You sing, you hitchhike."

"Your loss, not mine," I said.

"I'll chance it. We'll finish up here right quick and get back to Jan."

"Yeah, I hope she feels better."

We passed an amber light blinking above a Bird Sanctuary road sign reporting Scarab's population as 983. Old Man turned into a bluestone lot and stopped at a mini mart.

They saw us first. Two tough corner boys blocking the mini mart's entryway. One wore a wallet on a safety chain. BAD MOTHERFUCKER emblazoned his T-shirt. They uncrossed old, black Doc Marten boots turning to see us. Skoal cans bulged in the hip pockets of their dirty, splotched jeans.

Old Man tossed a wry nod at their hanging post. "Check it out, babe. Your pussy-munching, drag-racing, and snuff-spitting redneck. And here we'd been led to believe they'd vanished by way of the pterodactyls."

I'd little chance of heading off this showdown. I looked over at Old Man. "Hey, we can buy your smokes at any gas station."

"Fancy that. Too late, though. My mind is set on buying them here."

As we climbed out of the Valiant, my sphincter puckered. Nearer to them, the smell of sweet pot and rancid body odor mingled.

T-shirt Tough hawked out a wad of puke-green phlegm. "Well, well, I'll be dipped. Look at this. A salt and pepper combo."

"Yep. Coon and cracker. Plumb pitiful." The second shorter tough stepped down and drew up within inches of my knotted jaw. "Fess up, cracker boy. You ever been dropped?"

Old Man lunged by my shoulder. I grabbed a hand to stop him but in a flash, he stuck it to them: a shotgun pistol. Their widening eyes fixed on the "O" at its muzzle. "I'll prune 'em off at the neck. Which one first, babe? Mutt or Jeff?"

"Show some leniency. Let 'em skate this time," I replied.

A second crawled past; the next one even slower. T-shirt Tough scraped a boot backing up. His hue, under the blackheads, was a match for a plate of giblets. "Come on. This spook is whacked enough to try it," he said to his cohort.

Old Man smiled. They retreated around the corner and lit out for the nearest piney woods.

I pointed. "Is that hog-leg straight out of the box?"

"Nope. It's a homemade special." Old Man put it back inside a bottomless pocket hiding a thigh rig. "The fools don't know how close they came to hell."

We filed inside the mini mart where the reek of Limburger cheese overlay Absorbine, Jr. Old Man asked the clerk for a carton of Marlboro Reds off the wire rack above the checkout counter. He paid the damages, then sacked his own purchases of garlic pickles and pork rinds on top of the smokes.

I ran my sweet tooth inventory: Atomic Fire Balls, Pay Days, Baby Ruths, Good and Plenty . . . my gaze touched a rack of T-shirts. Sizes: M, L, and XL. Colors: red, white, and blue. All bearing the slogan "The Blue Cheer! God Is A Lie!". A walking fish emblem encasing the word "DARWIN" separated the captions.

Old Man wandered back to join me. He flipped through the T-shirts on the hangers, his expression quizzical. "The Blue Cheer, eh?" He wagged his head. "Something hippy-dippy, my best guess."

The clerk, his arms folded over a pegboard chest, pretended to ogle out the glass front at a chrome slut pickup truck.

"Hey, slick. You know anything about the Blue Cheer?" I asked.

The clerk shrugged inside his dingy smock. "A sharp out-of-town fellow like you ain't ought to ask. And I ain't ought to spell it out for you," he replied.

I turned my irate eyes to Old Man. "You follow any of his lip?"

"Forget about him, babe. Let's roll out of here."

Heckling snickers tracked us out the mini mart door but we ignored it and rode into Scarab. The sheriff's station house was a brick cracker box capped by a flat asphalt roof under satellite dishes bolted to a radio tower. A V-8, fat fender cruiser topped by a roof light sat in Sheriff Greenleaf's reserved slot. "We Serve and We Protect"—a claim that was open to debate—underscored the five-star logo on the door. Old Man braked and reversed us into the next parking slot.

"To recap, tell your story but skip the conspiracy theories. Good, bad, or indifferent, this is a police matter," said Old Man.

"I've had my share of dealing with cops."

"Not ornery ones like these you haven't."

We strolled up the cinder-packed path. Perky red maple leaves eddied about our ankles. Bituminous coal dust coated every surface and sparkled where the sun hit it. Over a clipped quince hedge next door, I saw an elderly lady, rotund as she was tall, cleaning a hubcap with an orange tube sock. She nodded to acknowledge my wave. I counted scores of hubcaps arrayed on display racks built of 2x4s and creosote posts. She wasn't Scarab's mad aunt indulging her yen for chrome ornamentation. Rather, a hand-lettered sign explained: HUBCAP MADONNA KEEPS YOU ROLLING! Each of her wares bore a price tag on a string like old Minnie Pearl's store-bought hats.

Inside the station house, a wood railing corralled us in the waiting area. A crow-beaked girl, combing her mousy brown hair in a compact mirror, caught our reflection. She rotated in her chair, stored the mirror inside a straw bag, and turned down The Dixie Chicks on her radio.

"Gentlemen, how might I help you?"

"Sheriff Greenleaf is expecting us," said Old Man.

Six deputies, no-first-name Goines included, filled the department roster engraved on a brass shield hanging on the wall. Confusion clouded the girl's coarse features. "This, uh, is a bad time. What should I do? Sheriff Greenleaf goes to lunch in seven minutes." She fussed in the straw bag. "Switching from incandescent to fluorescent light has ruined my eyes. Here they are." She put on her gold-framed glasses. Her pencil eraser scuffed through pages in the appointment book. "Sheriff Greenleaf's afternoon calendar is packed, too." She slumped back in the chair, her hefty chest jutted inside the purple chenille sweater. I think she smiled, too.

"Why not right now? We'll only be a minute," I said.

"I'll try." The girl plucked up the phone receiver. "Who shall I say is here?"

"The Blue Cheer," I replied. Old Man's boot tapped my shin. I ignored him.

"Surely." The girl inquired in a diffident murmur, listened, and hung up. "Okay. Go straight back to the water cooler and through that alcove. Sheriff Greenleaf's office is the first door on your right."

Old Man grabbed me by the arm. "The Blue Cheer? Are you crazy?"

"It got us into the sheriff's office. "

"No more bullshit comedy. Are we straight, Frank?"

Sheriff Greenleaf's office had a mahogany desk, wall panels, hat rack, and credenza. He stood. One glance at Old Man, he frowned a little. Old Man and I traded askance looks. By the next beat, he pasted on his public servant cordiality, icy as his gray hair.

"Gentlemen." Sheriff Greenleaf's steel dentures outshone the Hubcap Madonna's wares. "What's this guff about the Blue Cheer?"

I subsided into an armchair with brass nail head trim and smiled, too. "You tell us, sheriff. We spotted their T-shirts in the mini mart. We inquired about them at the counter and the clerk almost foamed at the mouth. For shits and grins, I wondered how it might play in here."

Sheriff Greenleaf's burly neck and chin flushed red. "It plays to the tune of a jail cell."

Old Man cut in. "Mr. Johnson does have a legitimate reason to see you, Sheriff. Late last evening we talked to Deputy Goines. We wanted to follow up with you."

"Johnson? You're the one who saw the midair explosion? Yeah, Goines filled me in on that bit. He brought up how alcohol was instrumental, too. I take umbrage at my deputies' time being wasted on frivolous calls."

"Booze had no bearing in this. A missile hammered a drone over my place. Some fool at its crash site clocked me. And while I was out cold, the missile's motor case vanished," I said.

Sheriff Greenleaf arched a waspish eyebrow at Old Man. "You're Johnson's neighbor, the retired African-American bureaucrat? Can you visually corroborate any of his claims?"

Old Man grunted. "No, but then my A-frame is three miles off to the east."

"All right, so now I've twice heard your weird tale. Deputy Goines is on top of it."

"We don't want it dropped," I said.

Sheriff Greenleaf pooched his lips. "I have lunch with my boss, the mayor. Budgets are due. I said we'll look into it, Johnson. That's the best assurance I can offer you. Thanks for coming in."

Back at the front desk I glimpsed, through a boxed window, Sheriff Greenleaf sprinting out of a private exit. His cruiser roared to life and hooked a left at the second intersection, suggesting that they gave Scarab's budgets a hot priority. Hand mirror angled to tweeze her eyebrows, the girl, sweet as ever, saw us out with a set-face glare. I didn't hassle them about my vandalized Prizm or wait around to see Deputy Goines at five o'clock.

What was the use?

"Man, jawing with sheriffs works up an appetite," I said.

Old Man grinned over at me. "We'll stop off at our favorite mini mart."

We left Scarab lunching on stale Slim Jims Tabasco Style and Red Bull energy drinks bought at the mini mart. A young girl, a bit too heavy on the kohl and lipstick, had waited on us while speaking on the phone about doing High Vs and Touchdown Ts at her cheerleading practice. Later, while the Valiant lurched up Old Man's lane, I spotted three crows dive-bombing a red-tailed chicken hawk. I rolled down the window and heard its squawks. Swooping and yawping, it tried to elude the crows but they were relentless tormentors, striking it again and again.

"Jeez, look at it, will you? Jan didn't flip off the lights like I asked her," said Old Man. We cornered the driveway's last curve. "Some gals have this hang up about leaving lights on. Can you understand why, babe?"

"Because it's dark?"

"It's a waste of electricity. Makes me nuts," said Old Man.

His boot backed off the gas pedal as we slowed into the triangular patch of afternoon shadow cast by their A-frame. Old Man climbed out of the Valiant while the white duff of a milkweed pod floated by on the breeze. I grabbed a memory of my past visit to the A-frame and my intense conversation with Jan Maddox.

CHAPTER FOUR

My knuckle-raps had summoned a lady to the glazed front door. Jan Maddox smiled up at me. From a wheelchair. Trying to act sociable and recover my wits, I returned her smile. Long ashen-blonde hair, parted down the middle, curled at her shoulders. She wore a blue velvety skirt and a merino wool sweater. Her blue eyes warmed me and her age I put at about thirty, give or take a few years (but who bothered to count?). A hand-carved scrimshaw crucifix dangling from her throat should have tipped me off about her religious streak.

"Mr. Maddox has stormed off to Scarab. Raving about a new chainsaw. Ours works fine, but talk about obstinate. Old Man is all that and plenty more," said Jan.

"Johnson," I said. "Frank will do."

"Where are my civil manners? You'd think I was born in a zoo. Old Man told me he'd offered you the use of his axe. I'm Jan Maddox, his wife, by the way. Please, won't you come inside? Old Man fusses about your wood supply," said Jan.

I cracked a knowing grin. "We pretty near have that problem licked."

I passed into the foyer and kicked a milk can converted into an umbrella stand. Cut chrysanthemums scented the living room. A carnival glass vase held pussy willow boughs. Expensive black steel fireplace tools—a brush, a poker, a shovel, and a set of tongs—were stacked by the white brick hearth. I also saw, off to the side, Old Man's pool table with the heated felt.

Jan nodded me to an old overstuffed armchair. I still stood. She reversed her wheelchair in a dexterous arc. I didn't want to sit on the sofa slip-covered in brick chenille while wearing my dirty pants. She understood. Aluminum mini blinds directed sunlight to slant off her bare legs, knee to ankle. What the devil? I took a longer discreet look at her streamlined physique featuring not overly lush breasts and a trim waist.

Jan initiated the conversation. "Mr. Johnson . . ."

"Like I said, Frank, please."

"Likewise, Jan. You must wonder about this." Jan's hand patted the wheelchair's leatherette armrest. "Well. The doctors, even specialists, can't diagnose it."

"My mother had rheumatoid arthritis." The lie was easy to tell. I saw through the gingham curtains shadowy stick branches stir in a breeze. I wanted to get back to the woods.

"Old Man and you sure do pal around a lot," said Jan.

I shrugged a shoulder. "Just for cutting wood and whatnot. So, he's retired from the government?"

Tautness shrank Jan's eyes. "As am I. Well, I just resigned from the CIA but we signed confidentiality agreements and can't say too much more."

"Old Man has been a big help to me." I stopped. "But I should be getting back."

Jan shifted up in the wheelchair. "Frank, let me ask you out-and-out: are you a spiritual man?"

"Only when the bottle picks me up," I said.

A doleful frown and scratch-on lips anchored her face. "No-no, what I'm asking is have you accepted Jesus Christ as your Personal Redeemer?"

I dodged that by pitching her a more neutral topic. "Do you know how to get rid of house ants?" I asked. Jan didn't go for it, only upped the hard sale of her faith, a garden variety Pentecostal that I'd already tried out and quit. She said her church was a great comfort even before the strange malady left her a paraplegic. I didn't refute her. It just wasn't my church. My quips were carefree enough to verge on flip and the frosty silences between us lengthened. After excusing myself, I reminded myself why living alone was better for me.

"You're a spoke on my prayer wheel," Jan called after me.

"Dear God, strike me dead, please," I muttered, once out of ear-shot.

The A-frame's burning exterior lights now held my attention. Old Man's car door thumped shut after mine. We mounted four steps to a wraparound redwood deck also accessed by an aftermarket wheelchair ramp. Six angular windows were opaque in this shadow.

Did Old Man know how much I envied him? What a freaking cool place to live. The A-frame rode on a native rubble stone foundation. The roof lay sloped and the expansive glass walls let in loads of light. Old Man said he'd just mounted the three deluxe ceiling fans.

I passed the barbecue gas grill and noticed dime-sized red stains on the jute doormat. I did a double take. Bending, I touched the stains. Tacky. A chill leached into my heart. Was Jan inside? Old Man jabbed the door chimes. No response. Grabbing the knob, he twisted it. The door swung inward.

I put out my arm to stop Old Man. "Wait here a second." A burnt cork odor hosed over us. "Let me go in first."

"Uh sure, babe."

It was a nice kitchen. I moved into the foyer by the umbrella stand. My vision roved from the pool table to the Isotoner gloves left on the butcher block table. White crowns molding trimmed the spruce green walls and the custom-made cabinets were birch. A noise escaped from my throat. My heart plunged in my chest. Blood roared behind my ears.

"Ho, Jan." Old Man's holler chimed off the cathedral ceiling. "Jan? Honey! Jan? Jeez, that stink could bleach your eyebrows white. Phew. Who shit themselves?"

I saw Jan.

An instant later, Old Man knocked over a chair.

Jan swayed on the end of a rope centered over the kitchenette aisle. The green nylon noose had crushed her windpipe. The long rope swayed, tethered to a rafter. Jan's wheelchair sat collapsed against the sink. Sunrays washing through a skylight caressed her face—a blue-purple agony. All breath sucked out of me. My chest banded up tight.

"Mother of Christ—" Old Man choked.

Jan's puffy tongue protruded from her mouth. Red-veined, her eyes bulged. Her head, oddly askew, had been nearly severed at the rope's suspension point. The slick nylon savaged the skin high up her neck.

"No. No. No." I stopped chanting.

A 30,000-volt Taser stun gun on the countertop shrieked of torture. Blood. Blood on Jan. Blood pooled on the tiles. Blood spattered every damn which way. I felt light-headed. Jan's blue eyes had watched a monster usurp her life force in brutal dribs and drabs. His leering sadism was burned on her retina.

"Holy Jesus . . ." Old Man's oath trailed off.

"Fetch me a bed sheet. Do it! Go on!"

After a slow turn, Old Man disappeared. My 9 mil jacked straight out in my arms. I quartered the kitchen, praying to see the killer and empty a clip in him. No, we had exclusive claim to Satan's abattoir. I recouched the gun in my waistband. I scooted over a ladder-back chair, hiked up it, and pressed my fingertip to Jan's forehead. No pulse and her eyelids didn't flicker. Two signs she was dead. Rushing before Old Man returned, I hacked my Buck knife at the green nylon rope. She thudded into a heap on the floor. I cut the noose off her neck and pitched it into the wastebasket.

"Here." Old Man gave me a folded cotton sheet. Seeing his eyes were lumps of solder, I felt instant pity.

"Go wait on the deck for me," I said. "I got this!" He didn't move.

I snapped out the sheet and once covered, Jan's horror lost its potency. My mind focused on how best to minister to my friend. I picked up only static. "Come on," I told Old Man. "We'll go talk. How's that sound?" My fingers at Old Man's elbow were gentle but firm. He took mechanical steps. I docked him at a table bench on the deck and seized their cell phone left on the table.

A dispatcher took my emergency call. My rundown was terse. A deputy was en route, she told me. Remain on the line, sir. Do you need an ambulance? No ma'am. Are you alone? No ma'am. Do you know who murdered the young female victim? No ma'am. Hang with me, please, sir. Now again, are you the young female's husband?

No ma'am. Were there any eyewitnesses? No ma'am. Her fingertips tapped my responses into the computer. Are you in any danger? No ma'am. Do you have any estimate as to when this homicide occurred? No ma'am. Can you put on the victim's husband? I thumbed the cell phone's EXIT button.

Old Man, seated at the picnic table, studied his hands as if the horror had stained them like a dye pack. "I can't believe what I just saw," he said in a half-dead whisper.

"The sheriff is minutes away."

"The killer is gone," said Old Man in a monotone. "The undertaker and funeral come next. I've got to get to it."

"I couldn't agree with you more, but indoors is a crime scene," I said.

"I'm headed back inside. My wife needs me."

My hand put more pressure on his shoulder. "Old Man, don't go back in there. She'll be okay. Trust me. You do not want to go back in there. Sheriff Greenleaf will want to talk to you out here."

"Bourbon." It blurted out of him as a hollow croak.

"Sit tight. I'll go get it."

I went inside and found the hidden bourbon bottle wedged in the sink's gooseneck. I touched the stove. Cold. I wished I had a digital camera to record the murder scene.

Since Jan had a 'no alcohol' house rule, we sat on the deck and drank. We sipped in silence and I soon heard a cruiser bumping over the lane's cross-cuts. The deputy's response time had improved since last night. The Crown Victoria Police Interceptor, its blue-red light bar flashing without siren, prowled around the last bend and pulled up to park. Front doors fanned out wide. Old Man moaned. Two olive drab uniforms appeared, Smokey Bear hats bobbed up. The driver was none other than Deputy Goines. His sidekick, a bacon-fed, pale-faced rube, settled his piglet eyes on us. Old Man's forehead was perched on his raised thumbs.

Goines swaggered to the deck's bottom step. His thickset partner likewise threw his weight on one hip. The briefcase he set down held their homicide kit. Many police departments couldn't afford to buy tongue depressors but their homicide kit was an expensive lizard skin bag.

"Did you report a homicide?" Goines' tone was heavy on sarcasm. "First an explosion and now a corpse?"

My thumb directed his attention. "His spouse, Jan. She's back in the kitchen."

Goines shifted to look through the door glass. Cough, spit, sniffle. "You didn't muck around inside, did you?"

"Only to cut down Jan on the rope," I said.

"That's bush league, Johnson. Why would you do that? You know we videotape the crime scene." Goines paused. "The tipster is often the perpetrator. You got anything to get off your chest?"

I speculated how many teeth my first punch could slug out of his mouth. "Where are your crime scene weenies?"

Goines' partner spoke up. "Quit with the insults, sir. We're aware this is stressful. Just the same, we wouldn't like having to cuff you and haul you down to the shop. You'll address us as Deputy Goines and Deputy Swart."

"Sorry, Deputy Swart. Where are your crime scene folks?"

"*We'll* process the crime scene," said Swart, his tone more convivial. "Dr. Thomas is no more than a couple minutes behind us."

"The door is ajar," said Old Man.

"We'll be here a while. So stay out of our hair. And understand that this mess belongs to you once we've released the crime scene," said Goines.

"The door is ajar," repeated Old Man.

A gloved hand settled on Old Man's forearm. "Many condolences, Mr. Maddox," said Goines.

Old Man shook him off. "Do your thing and get the fuck off my property."

I trailed the two deputies into the kitchen. Swart set down the homicide kit on the pool table. "Christ, look at all the blood!" he said.

My fists balled up to let loose on him.

But a big-boned man in a beige lab coat over a pair of wrinkled chino pants and polo shirt bustled in through the deck door. His curt stride bespoke authority. Great. Another one to piss me off.

Goines glanced over. "Hi, Doc. The deceased is by the sink under the sheet."

Pointing a finger at the shredded rope dangling above us, the doc asked, "Who cut down the victim?"

"Him. You have to make allowances for Johnson. He has his head up his ass."

"You'd have left her strung up, eh, Goines? That doesn't make a lick of sense. Just make a note about it," said the doc.

"Doc Thomas, don't barge in here telling us how to do our jobs," said Goines.

"Shut up. Stand aside, deputy," said Dr. Thomas.

They roped off Ground Zero and rubber-banded lunch bags to Jan's wrists as death mitts to protect any evidence trapped under her fingernails. Dr. Thomas wrote something on them. Goines roughed out a sketch on grid paper and took various measurements. Swart shone a flashlight over the kitchen's hard, flat surfaces searching for any prints. None showed. When the time came, I witnessed their inventory of what was on Jan's person (a balled up Kleenex, a key ring, and a matchbook).

"Is your sketch finished?" asked Dr. Thomas. Goines said it was.

After incising an inch-long tract, Dr. Thomas registered Jan's liver temperature, took an ambient temperature reading, and studied the variance. I remembered that much from the crime investigative classes I'd had at MP school. "I'd say she died sometime before noon. No signs of a struggle except defensive cuts on her right palm. The killer's Taser stun gun paralyzed her. Does it belong to Mr. Maddox?"

My head shook.

"Bag and tag it. Goines, you're the searching officer. Everything will be given to you. And check the doormat. I believe blood drops spilled on it," said Dr. Thomas.

"No sign of forced entry," said Swart.

"Pinocchio could pick that door lock with his nose," I said.

Smiling, Dr. Thomas directed both deputies to load the sheeted

39

bundle on a stretcher. Old Man straddled the bench with his back to us and swayed to and fro, moaning. Ignoring him, the deputies ferried the gurney to the Lincoln morgue wagon. Its royal purple finish lent the moment a befitting somberness. Mid-go across the sloping yard, Goines' feet tangled. The fumbling stretcher bearers managed to balance their cargo and load it into the Lincoln.

Dr. Thomas, downcast head shaking, addressed me. "In the next day or so, you should pay a visit to Sheriff Greenleaf's office in Scarab. Get your statements down on paper."

The two vehicles backed around, crushing Old Man's turnip patch. Their withdrawal down the lane left me feeling angry and frustrated. Turning, I thought, what the hell? Old Man wasn't seated at the picnic table on the deck. I raced to the threshold and saw him in the kitchen.

"You keeping it together?" I asked him.

The bottle uncapped, Old Man dribbled bourbon, creating a circle on the kitchen tiles. "This is Grandmam Maddox's ritual. Will get Jan to heaven."

"You're too late. She's already cleared that turnstile," I said.

"Groovy. We'll send Jan flowers," said Old Man.

CHAPTER FIVE

"Let's snap to it before everybody and his uncle comes knocking," said Old Man.

"They'll just wanna help," I said.

Old Man grunted. "I don't need that sort of help."

"Maybe nobody will know about it for a while yet."

"When my cousin Betty finds out, she'll storm up here and try to take charge," said Old Man.

I had Old Man lead me through the A-frame's rooms but nothing struck him as out of order. Nothing was stolen. We ignored the yellow crime scene tape and for an hour or better scoured the kitchen. Vinegar-sopped handkerchiefs held over our noses cut down on the ungodly stink.

Old Man took out a 12-foot stepladder stowed in a crawlspace. I climbed up the stepladder and hacked my Buck knife again. I tossed the green nylon rope into the wastebasket with the other piece.

"Babe, where's the bourbon?" asked Old Man.

Seeing Old Man, distraught and shaky, cleaning up after his murdered wife impressed me and we did a respectable job. After we'd finished, I invited Old Man to come stay with me and finish cutting my fire wood.

"Thanks," he said. "Give me a second, babe, to throw together a bag."

Old Man's grooming kit could stock a barbershop. Magic Gold Shaving Powder, Mentos Shave Conditioner, Black Opal After Shave, Bump Fighter disposable razors, and a boar bristle brush. Shouldering the duffel bag with the Marine Corps bulldog, Old Man knocked Jan's photo off the bed table. He turned to stone staring down at the photo. His face then splintered into hurt. Tears seeped into his eyes. He grappled for the nearest bedpost and slumped forward on extended arms. His shoulders jerked and head sagged a little while his heart broke. Old Man cried the mute cry of men of his generation.

I faded to the redwood deck, giving him due space and privacy. I sat down on the steps. Jan's death had unglued me, too, but somebody would pay. Who was Jan's killer? And what was their motive? An obvious motive lurked right under my nose: their interracial marriage. Old Man had told me that as a mixed couple, even here at the dawn of the twenty-first century, they'd attracted hostile glares while out in public. Race prejudice would never disappear from some people's narrow minds. That wasn't all about the Maddoxes.

Being none of my business, I'd never asked Old Man about it, but Jan had to be thirty years younger than him. It'd never struck me as unusual until now. But I didn't trust my judgment since marriage, in my jaundiced view, was a turd of misery foisted upon mankind to perpetuate our species. Yeah, my acrimonious divorce had bred that lousy attitude.

"Ready to mount up?" Old Man asked me from the top step.

We piled out of the Valiant at my log redoubt and I offered Old Man the sofa by the woodstove. He was my guest, after all.

"It was a smart thing we laid in that firewood," he said. "Babe, I'm over here farting chalk dust. Do you have any Dirty Bird for a chaser?"

"Sorry. Got some cold cans of Iron City."

"I don't care for beer. I'll stick with hard liquor," said Old Man.

"Go easy, huh? Sheriff Greenstreet has a birddog nose."

"Greenleaf," said Old Man.

"I'm bad with names. Can I call him Dog Shit?" I said.

"Sheriff Greenleaf. Elected sheriff three times. But you're right. He's worthless as the Paris Peace Talks."

"What about that tour in Nam?" I asked. I thought talking about it would distract him, trading one misery for another.

Old Man collapsed on the sofa and spoke in a gruff tone. "I served from June '67 to July '68. It felt like an eternity taking orders from butter bar lieutenants and most of them deserved fragging. By some miracle, I gutted it out and rode The Freedom Bird back home to the States. I only carry one war wound. Nothing to win me a Purple Heart. Artillery fire screwed up my ears. The VA doctors diagnosed it as chronic tinnitus. Hardly a scratch compared to what many bloods got."

Fascinated by his story, I sat on a kitchen chair still holding the unopened can of cold beer.

Old Man swilled bourbon and wiped his lips. "That first noon, deplaning in Cam Ranh Bay, I was raring to go grab the bull by the balls. I had it dicked. Ha-ha! I did. Truth be told, no Cherry Boy had ever arrived in country redder than me. Only looking back now can I laugh about it."

"What happened next?" I prompted him.

"Well, they bussed us off to charm school where they taught us how to scout and kill Charlie. Then we marched through it all—rice paddies, banana groves, elephant grass. That hellhole was fucked up beyond belief. I'll never forget Sergeant Jackie Kent. He raved how Luke the Gook would storm California's beaches. Said we stood as democracy's last defense."

"Democracy's last defense," I repeated.

"Yep. Early one morning my main man, Lucas Tackett, a Georgia boy raised on pig shit and biscuits and later a Golden Gloves champ, stepped on a Claymore mine. Kaboom! They would've fitted Lucas for a new asshole if he had survived. Instead, the medic scraped up Lucas into a body bag and I wised up from that moment on.

"Those incoming rounds could kill me. I could bleed out riding in a medivac duster. Well, GIs were dropping like feathers spilling out of a split pillow. 'It ain't gonna be me,' I wrote my mom. 'I'm coming home standing up, not in a goddamn wheelchair or in a body bag flown to the central mortuary at Tan Son Nhut.'".

"America the beautiful. Nothing is as it seems," I said.

Old Man licked his lips. "Right on, babe. It don't mean nothing. That's how we joked about it. Say it again, my brother. It don't mean nothing. Right on." Old Man lifted a black power fist in parody, then dropped it.

I popped the top on the beer. Not a brilliant idea, my drinking again. Knocking around with Old Man lent a new urgency to my alcohol consumption. I came by it honestly from the Black Irish encoded in my DNA. My AA sponsor would pitch a duck fit. Except she lived in Virginia while I boozed here in West Virginia. I also knew alcohol might trigger an episode of depression but Old Man and I were operating under ever darkening storm clouds, so fuck it.

"Sorry I ran off at the mouth," said Old Man.

"I always like hearing your war stories." I ran a knuckle over my sweaty forehead. Took in a deep breath. Exhaled. "But now we have a killer on the loose. Let me lay this on you. Did either Jan or you piss off anyone? From your CIA days? Or somebody here in town?"

Unblinking, Old Man shook his head.

"Jan was religious." I paused. "Were you into it as much?"

"Jan kept her eyes on heavenly things and I loved her for that unshakeable faith in people's good. I kept my eyes on Jan," replied Old Man with elegance.

The day I'd shown up at the A-frame looking to borrow Old Man's axe, Jan Maddox had peddled her brand of salvation. While that wasn't a problem, at least to me, it might rub some different zealot the wrong way. "Did Jan attend a church?"

"Twice a week, Sunday morning and Wednesday night, I'd chauffeur Jan off our mountain to that church I pointed out to you. The First Primitive Apostolic Church is hard-shell Holy Rollers."

"You sat with Jan?"

"I ain't a sadist, babe. Somebody smart said, 'I don't believe in God because I don't believe in Mother Goose.' I like that saying. I caught an earful of their wails, screeches, and hollers waiting for Jan in the parking lot. Okay, maybe I got a cheap chuckle out of them. When Jan said her final amens, however, I went on my best behavior. I smartened up not to make waves. The couch makes for a cold bed. Why do you ask?"

"Jan once quoted me Scripture. You'd gone off to price chainsaws and I dropped by to pick up your axe."

Old Man bit a thumb knuckle. "Jan didn't get in your face, did she?"

"Not even close. Since I'm being so nosy, how did you two first hook up?"

Old Man smiled. "At our CIA jobs. I proposed to her at a Charley Pride concert. The scalper's tickets cleaned me out. But they were worth every cent. Charlie did an encore of 'Snakes Crawl At Night' and I popped the big question. Jan said yes and I was the world's happiest man." Old Man, shoulders sagging, stood up and trudged out my cabin door. I didn't follow him.

Rather than wait until morning, we went back to Scarab near sundown. When we traipsed in unannounced, Sheriff Greenleaf, crouched in the knees, was flossing his teeth at a wall mirror. His girl sentry had been too busy removing skirt lint with a sticky piece of Scotch tape to challenge us. Old Man claimed a chair with the brass nail head trim. I also sat in one.

"Pardon our intrusion," I said. My grin needled Sheriff Greenleaf a little.

He hurried to his throne behind the desktop's furniture-polish sheen. "I'm always available to serve our good citizenry." He belched into a fist. "My days are never done."

"Uh-huh," said Old Man.

"Please accept my condolences," said Sheriff Greenleaf to Old Man. "Jan was a—"

"Skip the bullshit," said Old Man. "When is the autopsy scheduled?"

Sheriff Greenleaf ran his necktie between two fingers. Warts studded his knuckles. "Look, can't we all agree that Jan Maddox died of strangulation?"

Old Man threw me a hard look, jasper eyes galled by rage.

"Every homicide merits an autopsy," I said in haste. "Who knows? Finding something could give us an edge here."

"My deputies leave no log unturned. But here's the thing. To do their jobs, they need some breathing room," said Sheriff Greenleaf.

"They've got ample breathing room," said Old Man.

"I'm just putting that out as a reminder," said Sheriff Greenleaf.

"Who is the coroner's boss?" asked Old Man.

Smugness showed on Sheriff Greenleaf's face. "Why, the mayor, of course. Dr. Thomas, however, has a dotted line of responsibility to me."

Old Man's elevating knees cracked. "Dotted lines never floated my boat. Water leaks in the cracks and the boat capsizes. We better go chat with the mayor."

"I'd be happy to clear up any confusion," said Sheriff Greenleaf.

I saw the dismay in Sheriff Greenleaf's face and winked at him. "Mr. Maddox will be in touch," I said.

We intercepted Dr. Thomas out on the street diagonal to a lit-up building. Green paint blistered off a sign. Its yellow letters read: THOMAS & SONS, FUNERAL HOME. Corpse disposal, I determined, ran in the Thomas family. A double-clasped handshake revealed Dr. Thomas' calluses and his pleasure to bump into us struck me as genuine.

"What's say we go grab a bite at Abe's?" he said.

Sidestepping me, Old Man obstructed the way. "Jan's lying on a fucking slab. You won't leave until she's been autopsied."

I chinned myself between them like an NHL referee umpiring a dispute. "Old Man is anxious to settle this, that's all."

"Damn straight I am. My wife was crucified and I'll make the murdering scum pay," said Old Man.

Dr. Thomas spoke with disarming sincerity. "Understandable. Try to see I'm processing your loved one as quickly as possible. Some irregularities have surfaced. Now I can tell Sheriff Greenleaf or . . ."

"You can tell us. All the more reason to go eat at Abe's," I said.

Old Man seemed intrigued. "Talk is good."

One block past Sheriff Greenleaf's office, we jaywalked across the street. Sundown, foreboding shadows now engulfing Scarab, drove the mercury below the freezing mark. I shivered in my CPO jacket and stamped my feet. Abe's was no five-diamond eatery, but under the forgiving streetlamps, it was a nice nook. I caught the door, no opening hours posted on it, and ushered in the two big men. An original Wurlitzer jukebox with Bakelite control knobs played all of the current popular country music stars. Now, a twangy crooner serenaded us.

Scooter tramps and Native Americans in brain buckets perched on a row of backless chrome stools. Longneck beers and onyx ashtrays decorated the shellacked bartop. My itchy eyes watered since the jalousie windows, open to emit cigar smoke, accomplished little. We grabbed the only empty booth under the Harley-Davidson logo in the window. A waitress, top-heavy and tired, distributed laminated menus. Baked ham and yam ran you $7.25. A T-bone steak (16 ounces pre-cooked) char-grilled cost $11.95. I went for the ham; Old Man chose the T-bone steak, medium rare, with a side order of boardwalk fries. Dr. Thomas treated us to a jumbo schooner of Michelob Amber Bock.

"Nothing showed up on that Taser stun gun. No prints, no smudges, no blood. Why?" asked Dr. Thomas.

"The killer probably wiped it down. Did you run a tox screen on Jan? I'm curious to know if any drugs were used," I said.

"The lab in Charleston is processing it," replied Dr. Thomas.

Old Man, forearms on the tabletop, leaned in. "Outside you alluded to an irregularity."

Dr. Thomas filled our frosty beer mugs. "Did your wife ever antagonize any individual?"

Old Man chucked a glance at me. "Are you two fools singing off the same hymnal? Jan was well liked, but you already knew that. What's going on here?"

I saw over the curved-top radio a mawkish watercolor of Jesus hovering over a big rig, His palms steering it on a straight, true course. We could do with a similar set of helping hands. Throat clearing, Dr. Thomas trembled through the shoulders. I felt a similar impulse.

"As you say, your wife was . . . savagely killed. So, our line of inquiry converges on just who would do such a thing. Tick off the possibilities with me." Dr. Thomas enumerated each on a finger. "One, a gang of crack heads zonked out of their ever-living. Two, a blood-crazed sociopathic killer. Three, a lover enraged by jealousy."

Old Man made an angry throat noise.

Dr. Thomas spoke faster. "But analyzing what I've seen of the corpse and crime scene, I'd say Mrs. Maddox's death falls under Number Four, a hate crime."

47

I set down the beer mug.

Deepening jagged lines contorted Old Man's face. "I knew it all along. Dare to be different and see what happens? Jan and I talked about the racism we might face after our marriage. But I didn't want to believe it could happen."

"Easy, Old Man. It's only one theory," I said.

"Theory, nuts. Some bigoted bastard couldn't stand it and killed my poor wife. I thought all that bad shit was in the past. Attitudes change. Laws change. Folks change. But that isn't what we face here now is it, babe? Nothing has really changed."

Old Man had a point. A geezer, using an electronic device for larynx cancer survivors, ordered another Black Label and dish of beer nuts. I shifted in my seat. My boondockers crunched peanut shells that patrons had discarded on the oiled pine floors.

"You're both on the right track." Dr. Thomas paused, then said in a somewhat dispirited voice, "Here come our meals."

The waitress mixed up setting down my plate with Old Man's, then switched them with apologies. I empathized. Double shift. Nickel and dime tips, if any. Wolf whistles. We picked at our food. But we drained the schooner of beer.

"Behold, gents." Dr. Thomas' flourishing fork waved around us to include the other patrons. "Beer, booze, broads, and billiards. Karaoke every Friday, five till nine. Mr. Maddox, you represent our token African-American in here. Does anyone complain? If so, they keep it under wraps. Political correctness demands it, but we know better. Racism thrives, only it's been driven underground. At least that's my humble opinion."

"You believe Jan's killer can blend in that well?" I said, not convinced.

Dr. Thomas gave a forlorn nod. "Like white on coconut, Frank."

"When will you autopsy my wife? I need to know," said Old Man.

"It won't be before Tuesday afternoon. My autopsy assistant should return home by then. Let's schedule it for late Tuesday to be on the safe side. Say five o'clock," said Dr. Thomas.

Old Man locked a truculent stare on Dr. Thomas. "I want to be there."

"I'm not so sure." Dr. Thomas paused. "Okay, but only if Frank agrees to be there with you." Both men looked expectantly at me.

I swallowed hard on a throat full of beer. "Absolutely. Count me in," I replied.

CHAPTER SIX

———

A flannel blanket was wrapped around me so that only my nose braved Sunday's pre-dawn chill in the chiaroscuro light. I heard rustling out front. The tread of feet. The gush of a faucet. The crackle and pop of the stove's fire box igniting. Then the metallic scrape of the coffeepot being shifted to the stove's front fender. Old Man was astir.

The ceiling fan worked its slow chop—I'd misplaced the remote again. My mind reeled back and forth. A drone had flown over my cabin and a Stinger rocket had pulverized it. Who put up the drone? Who tripped off the Stinger? Who sapped me over the head down in the hollow? Who stole the Stinger motor case? That green nylon rope, stretched from the A-frame's rafters, left my throat feeling tight. Nylon was too elastic. Wouldn't Jan, once hoisted up and dropped, have yo-yoed on its end like a bungee leaper off the New River Gorge Bridge? Last night at Abe's, after Old Man had left to use the john, Dr. Thomas told me that greased hemp rope was regulation for state executions. Hemp rope caused no recoil, no snags, and no friction.

"Was Jan's death quick and painless?" I asked in a strained voice.

"The rope detached her vagal nerve, thus inducing abrupt blackout. Her head"—Dr. Thomas' thumb and forefinger measured a sliver of light—"came this close to decapitation."

"Tonight just got loads darker," I said, a heavy curtain draping over my hope for an open-and-shut case.

Doctor Thomas had stared into the new pitcher of sudsy amber beer. "On days like today, I hate this profession."

The ceiling fan swirled back into focus.

"This motherfucker is definitely hot. Babe, are you going to waste all morning jagging off in the fart sack?"

"At least I didn't scald myself on the coffeepot. I keep ointment in the medicine cabinet," I said.

"I'll live, thanks. Eggs are on the griddle. Scrapple is browning. Hope you're hungry," said Old Man.

"Is a duck's ass watertight?"

"I never looked, to be perfectly honest."

I dragged myself up and felt my head start to ache. West Nile virus? Lyme disease? No, it was only brown-bottle flu and a blackjack for which there's no sure cure. My fingers drew out the nightstand drawer and under a shrinkwrap of flashlight batteries, I found a rosary that my mother had crafted from olive wood beads. I dug further and grabbed a rack of 9 mil cartridges near the back. I dressed and curried a comb through my bugtussle hair. The 9 mil was in the rig on the bedpost, not under my pillow. I checked the 9 mil's loads and joined Old Man out front.

"Grab the clean plates off the drainboard," said Old Man.

"You do dishes, too? Jeez. How about ironing shirts?"

When Old Man didn't react, I threw him a hasty glance. An oaten glaze matted his eyes. "Everything OK?" I asked him.

"Hay fever. Damn ragweed pollen," said Old Man.

Hay fever, bullshit. He'd been crying again. I cleared my throat after he looked off my stare and didn't comment.

"After breakfast, we'll stroll down to Trout Creek," said Old Man, scraping scrambled eggs into two melmac plates.

I forked in scrapple and chewed between my words. "It's been picked clean."

Old Man's forehead wrinkled. "Well, canvassing it again is worth the effort. By the way, something skipped my mind yesterday. Are you also a vet?" He lifted the coffeepot off the stove's fender. "Want some?"

"Smells good," I said. "Yeah, I was an MP at Fort Leavenworth for three years. We seldom stayed in Kansas but I didn't pull many heavy-duty details. I booked AWOLs turning themselves in at the post and wrote up the occasional speeding ticket. That sort of routine stuff took up my days. It was boring as hell so I ejected when my tour was up. Their scope has changed a lot in recent years."

"MPs are in Iraq," said Old Man.

"MPs ship out everywhere now, man. Iraq, Kosovo, Haiti, Bosnia, and Afghanistan. You could say they're a little overextended."

"Did that gig pave the way for your PI work?" asked Old Man.

"Yeah, it qualified me to apply for a PI license."

"Is there much else to getting one?"

I had to wonder about all his questions. "I took an Adult Ed course, aced an exam, and ponied up a small fee for the license. I have to complete CEUs at a community college to keep it current."

"Is your PI ticket still in effect?"

"It expires on December 31st." I yawned into my hand. "Why?"

"My life is in the shitter. I tossed and turned all night. Got up. Paced the floor. Surprised you didn't hear me. And, no, the couch is fine for sleeping on. This was about Jan, justice, and a sheriff with no balls. I thought long and hard and, just before sunup, I came up with a solution. You're a cop and a private one just puts icing on the cake. I'd like to hire you to help me catch Jan's killer."

The coffee cup was midway to my lips. I returned it to the saucer. "A slight hitch. My PI license carries no weight here. Virginia has no reciprocity agreement with this state. West Virginia statutes also stipulate that I register with the state cops as a PI. The damn application costs $150 and I need to bribe five character witnesses. Isn't that a laugh? I can't get one, except maybe for you. For thirty bucks more, I can carry a brass PI badge. Also, I'd mull this over, Old Man. Surveillance will eat up hours and drain your IRA savings. And the results will be spotty at best."

"Fair enough. But I can't sit on my thumbs. How much do you charge?"

"For you, a buck twenty-eight and a can of cashews. Old Man, if I can help, spot me a token dollar and that'll bridge our contract," I said.

Old Man unclipped one dead first president. "Let's get started."

I tucked his banknote in my wallet. "Listen you, finish eating your eggs first."

A little later, I saw that last night's frost had been heavy again as we schlepped around the cabin to regard my Prizm, still flat on its sliced tires. Thankfully, Old Man's Valiant had warded off any vandalism. He strode down to the big boulders ahead of us. Trout Creek jingled over mossy, black rocks at the base of my mountain.

"I tripped over you about here," said Old Man.

"I sorted the debris into piles. Gone now. Somebody swiped it," I said.

"H'm." Old Man toed up a rock slab. "The Coleman lantern, as I recall, sat here. But you're right. I don't see any metal pieces."

"So, it's all hocus pocus. And that fireball I saw in the sky? We'll write it off as a hallucination."

"Quit putting yourself down. It's for sure shit real. Same as my wife's murder."

"Okay, help me run the most likely scenario. Back up here in the sticks, a low rent crew launches the target drone to fly over the mountain," I said.

Old Man took up the ball. "The shooter trips the Stinger rocket. It zips off. Whammo, a solid hit. But wait, there's trouble. You saw it, so they panic. They're desperate to cover their tracks."

"When I mosey down here in the dark, they slug me on the head," I said.

"Then they spirit off the motor case. You wake up with a lump and a migraine and I take you up the mountainside."

"And now I find out who they were and repay them."

"My thoughts exactly. Let's get started on it." Tackling the ascent, Old Man huffed ahead of me and spoke over his shoulder. "Yesterday at the mini mart, I almost blew the heads off two racists."

I nodded. "Then they skied out for the tall timber."

His voice gruffer, Old Man asked a stunning question. "Now just where do you think they headed?"

I paused, wondering if he was thinking what I was thinking. "Well, I know a short while later we found Jan dead," I said.

"If Jan's murder was a hate crime like Dr. Thomas says, we know who had plenty of hate in them," said Old Man.

"I did notice stains on their jeans. It could've been blood. Maybe they'd already been to your A-frame. Maybe they washed in the creek. Maybe that's a bunch of maybes. You know them?" I asked.

"I've seen them hanging around town. Let's go see if we can find them," said Old Man.

The morning Andes dropped by my cabin on his return trip to Racine University, he nicked me for a favor. Since North Carolina was too far for him to make weekend trips home, would I mind keeping an eye on the fire tower while he was away? Being the Generous Gus that I am, I agreed. That's the excuse Old Man and I used now to stop by en route to Scarab. Climbing up the fire tower for a bird's eye view of the mountains was the real reason.

The jeep trail up to the fire tower ran underneath a snaggle of colorful leafy wahoo and musclewood trees. We negotiated the rutty trail. I saw, just below a basalt outcropping, a swatch of ground that wild turkey toms had clawed up. They were feeding on locust seed pods, fattening themselves up just in time for autumn hunting season.

Old Man grabbed a lower gear and we rumbled across the split-log bridge.

Andes had intrigued me from the start. Somehow or other, he'd wangled this fire watcher's job. If I had to hazard a guess, I'd say the job was the result of family wire pulling at the state house in Charleston. I'd overheard in Abe's one night that his dad served as a federal judge, probably a political hack appointee. Any salary was undoubtedly miniscule but Andes enjoyed a blissful solitude for five months during the high fire danger.

Yet I had a feeling Andes was a volunteer. Weren't fire towers obsolete? I'd read that aerial surveillance and Doppler radar now pinpointed forest blazes. Prop planes and choppers did the heavy lifting these days, dumping lake water from 660-gallon Bambi buckets. Choppers also dropped hundreds of those new ping-pong gizmos that ignited on the ground and touched off backfires to counteract the main blazes.

The Monday morning after settling into my cabin, I had driven over at Andes' telephone invitation. His perch sat atop a square, four-legged pillar of rusty angle iron. Steel plates reinforced the bolted connections while a trio of copper lightning rods lined the hipped tarpaper roof. I grabbed hold of the ladder's bottom rung and scuttled up the next thirty. I counted every one of those suckers. I tapped on the trapdoor in the platform floor. Never once did I hazard a look down. My host, all smiles, hoisted me through the hatchway.

"Greetings neighbor," said Andes.

Winded, I gave him some free advice. "I'd start budgeting to install an elevator."

"It's a piece of cake. For me, at least. This, though, should reward your efforts."

His sweeping hand indicated glass panels in the aluminum sashes surrounding us. The diorama, for some screwy reason, reminded me of Lee Harvey Oswald eating his liverwurst sandwich in the Dallas Book Depository. I took in the mountain greenery but also kept an eye on Andes.

He had craggy brows and a high forehead. His thin lips produced expressive tweaks. A silvery blot showed on his dirt-brown hair. He offered me a look through a pair of binoculars. Waving off his offer, I stepped over the geological maps that had blown to the floor and took a seat in a canvas chair. A cell phone caught my attention until I saw the Red Hat Linux screensaver on a laptop.

"When I'm not catching a few rays or scouting for smoke columns, I like to bang out a little fiction. I write crime novels," said Andes.

"No kidding."

To me, Andes looked like a shady character in some crime novel. His ready laugh, though, sounded like a regular guy's. "Right now I'm editing the first in a series. *Bringing the Heat*, I've called it. Racine University's writing program had better accept it for my MFA thesis. Then I'll publish it."

"I'll look for it at the bookstore." I pointed out of the window. "You can see Old Man's place."

"Yours, too." Andes scratched his goatee.

I noted how from this angle one of his eyes appeared blue and the other black. A glass eye? I had enough civil breeding not to ask him about it.

"You also own a jim dandy cabin." Andes' eyes lifted over my shoulder. I gazed behind me. The level of detail I saw of my place, such as the dry-stacked retaining wall I'd recently built, took me by surprise and left me with a vague sense of unease.

That same unease returned as Old Man and I now parked by the fire tower. Gazing up was enough to turn my knees into gel. The rungs of the steel ladder, slick from the morning frost, invited disaster, beginning with an attack of vertigo. But before I tackled the scary climb, something scrawled on the concrete footing distracted me. A crude, large fish on crocodile legs swallowing one word: DARWIN was chalked in blue.

Two gunshots popped from the distant woods. Ducking, Old Man knocked us both flat to the ground. "Lay tight, babe. Look. Down beyond those pines . . . see that dude hauling balls?"

At some twenty yards, a gangly man in a scarlet hunter's cap turned tail and scampered off. Old Man sprang up, broke into a run, and cut into the laurel thickets.

Right behind him, I churned my legs trying to stay in the chase. I stomped on rotten logs and slewed over leaf-hidden rocks. Old Man drew out his shotgun pistol and aimed on the run. Boom! Red Cap's jackrabbit start spared him an ass peppered with birdshot. Fear sent him sprinting and we conceded ground. We pulled up short where the ridge adjoined the next one. Red Cap had fled into a dark hollow ripe for dry-gulching us.

We trudged back uphill, Old Man toting the shotgun pistol at half-cock. Our footfall was soft on the pipsissewa ivy and pine duff. We climbed further, broke out of the woods into sunlight, and saw the fire tower. We made it back to where we'd started, leaning our rumps against the Valiant, and caught our breaths.

"Trespassers are rare up here," said Old Man.

I shook my head. "According to Andes, lost hunters aren't uncommon."

"Now ain't that some shit." Old Man pointed around us with his shotgun pistol. "The mountains on both sides of us are posted property. The Federal government owns this land."

CHAPTER SEVEN

———

We rode to Scarab, listening to the music playing on Old Man's in-dash CD player. We shared a taste for bluegrass music. His thumbs tapped the steering wheel, keeping tune with The Osborne Brothers. Bobby and Sonny ripped through 'Rocky Top,' the state song of Tennessee.

We nipped from a pint of sipping whiskey that Old Man had stashed away in the glove compartment. After joking around a little, he told me about his outrageous Uncle Nimrod. "Bagging a whitetail buck with a high power rifle and a scope? Fag's stuff, in Uncle Nimrod's book. Real mountain men indulge in the ultimate extreme sport. Bare-knuckle snake wrestling."

"You're shitting me."

"Better believe it. Come the autumn's first cold snap, Uncle Nimrod heads up to a limestone bluff so secret even I don't know its location. And then he frisks through the rocks, and doesn't let up until he finds a harem of the toxic serpents."

"Copperheads? Rattlesnakes?"

"Please, don't be interrupting me, babe. Anyway, Uncle Nimrod wades into the serpents like at a riverside baptismal pool. Irate snakes rattle their gourds. Slicing and dicing, they attack him from all angles. But with mongoose reflexes, Uncle Nimrod evades them. Now dig this part, babe. He does all this butt-naked."

I snorted in disbelief. "Shit." Bobby and Sonny launched into some silliness about the cuckoo being a pretty bird.

"Better believe it, babe. And Uncle Nimrod doesn't pack any anti-venom, either. Well sir, this war wages on and naturally they tire out, and then it's—"

"Brilliant. Kill all the snakes. So, the rats will overrun us," I said.

"—then it's garbage time. He plucks each snake behind its heat sensors. That's the trick, babe, if you ever encounter the need to handle a snake. Uncle Nimrod whips it over his head and there's one less rattle-snake."

For a beat, Old Man didn't speak. When he did, it was a snarl. "I see righting Jan's murder the same way. A duel to the death, if need be."

"It's premature to think like that," I said.

"Sure. We'll just pretend nobody shot at us by the fire tower."

Talk trailed off. I concentrated on listening to the great tunes to lighten the load. How could any man hit such a high note? Bobby and Sonny sure pulled it off on 'Up This Hill And Down,' 'Tennessee Hound Dog,' and 'Big Spike Hammer'.

About 11 a.m., we dipped out of the hills into Scarab. An amber pall hung over its rooftops and steeples, trapped by the domino mountains, that threatened to cave in and crush everything below them. The sun burned, a garnet wafer in the overcast sky. Further down the line, we passed by the smoke-choked Chartreuse Ironworks. I couldn't help but wonder how much more wheezing the damn town could take before it screamed out for an oxygen tent.

"Let me off here. I want to buy one of those Blue Cheer T-shirts," I said.

Old Man dropped me at the mini mart and headed on to Scarab, anxious for an update from Dr. Thomas. We'd then go ask around town about the two toughs.

A Ford pickup, its side mirrors cracked and baby-moon hubcaps dented, sat by the propane recharge station. I saw a scoped rifle mounted on the cab's gun racks. I patted the 9 mil under my CPO jacket and shoved open the glass door. In the time it took me to reach the rear of the mini mart, my vision adjusted to the dimness. Huh? I looked again but saw no Blue Cheer T-shirts.

A draft from the forced air heater made the empty hangers tinkle. Goose bumps paraded down my back and, circling the aisles, I saw nothing of the T-shirts. The same punk-ass clerk finished sacking a Colt .45 tallboy for a gaunt man leaking a trail from his sawdusty bibs.

"A deck of Mule Briars, too, son." He illegally paid for the cigarettes with food stamps and departed.

"Are the T-shirts sold out?" I asked the clerk once we were alone. "Or were they ripped off?"

"We never sold any T-shirts here," said the clerk.

"They were red, white, blue and bore the name, 'The Blue Cheer', " I said.

"Weren't they, like, an acid rock band from way back when?"

My annoyance hiked up a notch. "Yesterday afternoon, two fellows were slouching by your doorway. Do you know who they were?"

The clerk's pupils shrank into dots. "Hey, I worked here all yesterday but you're a stranger to me."

Further tail-chasing here was futile. Ten would get you twenty, yesterday was a blur to his chemical-altered mind. I burrowed into my upturned collar, tramped out of the mini mart, and started on foot down the highway for Scarab. What was a scarab? The *Funk & Wagnall* dictionary in my cabin loft defined it as a beetle-god the Ancient Egyptians had worshipped. Talk about your misnamed town. I spat on a rusty harmonica. I punished my lungs by breathing in the hot stink by the apple cannery. Twisted shit went down in dirty, little towns and I had a good mind to leave this one. Except I had a stake here, ownership of my mountain cabin.

A siren's single blurt from behind made me almost shit my pants. I saw through the cruiser's grimy windshield Deputy Goines sneering behind a pair of locked handcuffs dangling off the rearview mirror. Black wall tires nosed off the asphalt's yellow line and the red-blue roof bar light blinked. Anger welled up in me as Goines stretched out, cool in his wool blues and Ray Bans. He folded his forearms to lean on the roof. "You're in violation, bud."

"I don't follow you, deputy."

"Hitchhiking is prohibited inside town limits."

"Do you see my thumb stuck out? I'm walking. Or is that against the law, too?"

"Are you disrespecting me?"

"No more than you're hassling me."

"You and me"—Goines' hammy finger jabbed at me and then at himself—"had better go iron this out at my station house." As I waffled, he moved around the cruiser and knocked me off balance. Then he pulled my hands behind me, palms out and thumbs up in the prescribed way, and slapped the handcuffs to my wrists. He kneed me into the backseat cage and beaned my head on the doorframe. It smarted, too.

Decisions, decisions. I could ache on this cold, hard concrete or I could ache on the cold, hard bunk. Either place, my cranium still throbbed. I wondered if maybe somebody could X-ray my skull and cement shut its cracks. My vision wobbled down my dungarees, over my boots, and into the vertical steel bars. It was a bummer because my 'Get Out Of Jail Free' card had expired. One cell down, a fellow shrieked in hysteria how his cell-front bars were "curling into snakes".

We'd taken a little ride in Goines' squad car, "Vicky," his special Crown Victoria police pursuit package. He drove and I squirmed. We tromped through a rear door at the station house. An old Crimedog McGruff decal on the window 'took a bite out of crime'. Goines then took a bite out of me.

It's a cliché out of every police B-flick: the interrogation stall. Goines added one quirk. His stall was semi-dark, no drill-bit of light boring into my eyes. He unclipped the radio mike off his shoulder and, grinning, shucked down to a wife-beater T-shirt. My first and last question was, "Am I free to go, officer?"

"Going over my head was a stupid move." Goines finished securing me.

Thunk! The first smack hit the spike of my nose. Thunk, thunk came the swats on my head. Why didn't I holler? Well, I couldn't. The duty belt anchored a glove now wedged between my teeth. Thunk! My lights snapped off.

When I came to, my shoulder rig was empty. Two teeth were loose. Coughing, I vomited blood and my immobile left arm registered nothing. My thinking grew a little goofy. While Goines laid a licking on me, didn't a tiny green gremlin videotape it all through an electric receptacle? Yeah, boy, if a citizen with a video cam rescued Rodney King, well by damn, a tiny green gremlin would rescue me. I'd sue Goines for police brutality. Sue, hell, I was going to—

The steel door squeaked on unoiled hinges.

My jail cell neighbor yapped, "Snakes! Everywhere! How do I defend myself? Answer me, goddamnit."

"Get bent," a man's voice in the hall replied.

Shoes scuffed on concrete. I cricked my head to the right and saw beige cinderblock. Wrong direction, stupid. Voices, male, came from six o'clock. Two men, tones low and stringent, conversed as shoes swung into my worm's eye view. One pair was black dress leather, the laces double-tied. The second set, larger, was nicked-up Tony Lama boots.

"Balls, sheriff. Frank looks as if he's been pulled backward through a knothole." Old Man Maddox, knees crinking, crouched inches away from me. "Can you hear me, babe?"

"M'm." Sheriff Greenleaf jiggled coins in his pockets. Or maybe he had a maraca for a dick. "After Johnson head-butted Deputy Goines, it took due force to subdue him. Isn't that how the arrest ticket reads, Deputy Braintree?"

"Sheriff Greenleaf tells it straight," said a third pair of shoes. Also black dress leather.

"Head-butted, my nuts. You're all lying," said Old Man.

"Careful." Sheriff Greenleaf did his best black scowl. From where I lay, it looked convincing. "I've got plenty more empty jail cells."

"Stick it, sheriff. You should be out looking for that guy who was shooting at us," said Old Man.

"Just a few boys a little wild with buck fever. Nothing as alarming as this," said Sheriff Greenleaf.

My jaws unhinged and a word wiggled free. "Lawyer?"

"Mr. Gatlin is in the wind," said Old Man.

Sheriff Greenleaf tapped a toe on the concrete floor. "Well, bottom line, it's my deputy's word against the prisoner's."

"The merits of your arrest ain't my bag. Mr. Gatlin will thrash that out," said Old Man.

Sheriff Greenleaf raked fingers through hair thinning at the temples. "Deputy Braintree, escort our prisoner to the booking room. Mr. Maddox, go park yourself in the bullpen."

Old Man, at his full, impressive height, said, "Wherever Frank goes, I go. Until Gatlin gets here, I'll play his lawyer."

Sheriff Greenleaf objected. "But Johnson hasn't invoked his right to counsel."

My lips trembled. "Old Man is my lawyer."

"Nope, you aren't pulling that bullshit in here," said Sheriff Greenleaf.

"A reporter has pestered me about the lackadaisical investigation of Jan's murder. Imagine handling the negative press while a major league lawyer chews on your butt. All that and your re-election is just days away," said Old Man.

As Sheriff Greenleaf's jaws tensed, a blue vein in his forehead pulsed. "Don't try to buffalo me."

Old Man rummaged in his shirt pocket. "Where's that reporter's beeper number?"

"All right. Go with Johnson until his legal counsel arrives. But only until then. Deputy Braintree, stick to both of them."

"Much obliged," said Old Man.

Braintree and a temporary deputy escorted me down corridors smelling of wet pasteboard. Two overweight uniforms chewed the fat by a Mr. Coffee. Thumbs hitched in duty belts, they were amused to get a load of me in a 4-piece restraint. They sat me down on a wood bench and hooked my cuffs through the bolt. The deputy watched me while Old Man watched him. Deputy Braintree cozied up to the desk sergeant and my paperwork was processed in record time.

A concrete blonde girl in espadrilles and low-rider jeans plunked down beside me on the wood bench. She dabbed an ice pack to a shiner and nosebleed. I gathered that her bastard husband, laid off from the tractor parts store, had drunk himself into a mean self-pity and through no fault of her own she'd wandered into it. The deputies, skeet-shooting pals of her husband, had written it off as another marital misunderstanding. Old Man patted her on the knee and she responded with the thinnest smile.

Sheriff Greenleaf blustered over to us. His spanking new Glock bounced in a black basket weave holster. He recited from a standard card and nailed the Miranda without a glitch, then said, "Mr. Johnson, you've been formally charged with assaulting a deputy. We'll blow off the original charge of hitchhiking inside town limits. You're detained in custody of the Sheriff's Office, Fordham County, West Virginia. Have you been made sufficiently aware of your legal rights? Do you comprehend the serious nature of these criminal charges?"

My head wagged and nobody had to tell me because I imagined myself looking straight out of the bargain basement. An icy ache needled each temple.

Deputy Braintree's shoe-taps clinked over to us. "Follow me, Mr. Johnson."

"Do you need an arm to lean on, babe?"

My head wagged no. It lied.

Deputies herded me out a door and down a breezeway into a mildewy alcove to the shakedown desk behind panels of one-way bulletproof glass. They undid the penal jewelry and patted me down. They photographed me and the computer cranked out an ID bracelet. I was surprised how detainees no longer held up the information placard for the mug shot camera. They managed after much discussion to fingerprint me on a Wang computer "mainlined" into the FBI's database. A deputy inventoried my street clothes. Another one collected my personal possessions and sealed them in a manila envelope.

Hanging off Braintree's shoulder, Old Man oversaw it all. "Whoa, deputy, not so fast. Add up the cash in Mr. Johnson's wallet again. Count out loud, too. Go on and do it . . . no bellyaching . . . forty-four dollars, twenty-eight cents? Solid. Now, initial and date the voucher. I better countersign it, too. I reckon a Xerox of it would be groovy, too. No back sass, now. You heard your boss. I'm the lawyer."

The damn orange jumpsuit didn't fit me. Stretching and wincing, I managed to get into it, much to my audience's amusement. My feet were shod in Jesus sneakers. That accomplished, we scuffled back and Deputy Braintree put me in the same jail cell and left us alone.

Old Man rustled up a 5-gallon bucket that he overturned and sat on. I undid the bedroll. A ditty bag contained a disposable Bic razor, toothbrush and toothpaste, stick deodorant, and generic shampoo. My cell looked all of 6'x6'.

"Don't get too comfy. You ain't going to be here long," said Old Man.

"Famous last words."

"What's up with this beating? Did you call Goines' mama a good cock grind or something?" said Old Man.

"Don't I wish I had."

"They're using trumped up charges, huh?" said Old Man.

"Without question."

"Goines is a punk-ass." Old Man spat. "Well, I ain't budging from this spot until you leave here."

"What's Gatlin's ETA?" I asked.

Old Man uncuffed a sleeve to check his strap watch. "A couple of hours, at least."

Two hours in this hellhole? Christ, I thought. The commode didn't flush, accounting for the reek. I went over and splashed cold water from the tap into my face. "What did Dr. Thomas say on Jan?"

Fingernails scratched Old Man's head as the swizzle stick in his mouth drooped. "He harps about it being a hate crime. But who? And why? Lots of unknowns." A heavy sigh. "It's too much, babe."

"You got more than enough gas in your tank."

Old Man's eyebrows tilted at me in a funny way. We carried each other. "Fucking A, more than enough, babe. Look, can you cough up enough dough to make the bail?"

"Don't worry about that. Gatlin is a billionaire," I said.

CHAPTER EIGHT

A rude hand jostled my shoulder. With a start, I goggled up at Deputy Braintree. "Your hot-shit lawyer has put in an appearance. Mount up."

"Old Man?" I said.

"I got your six, babe. Let's rendezvous with Mr. Gatlin."

An eye slit was my keyhole to the world and ankle restraints forced me to move as though slopping through wet concrete. I entered the break room and first saw Robert Gatlin's broad beam squeezed over each side of a chair. Old Man dropped two other chairs off the table to the floor.

"Hello, Franklin. Goodness sakes, just look at you," said Gatlin

"He ain't in shape for much talking," said Old Man.

Chins undulating, Gatlin's tone coarsened as his eyes centered into glowering beads. "Sometimes the police even in my native West Virginia overlook the little fact that we have a Constitution granting citizens civil rights."

Gatlin wore his signature suit, a three-piece brushed brown corduroy. He patronized Big & Tall Men's Warehouse not because he enjoyed slumming so much as he was frugal. A skinflint, really. Since I'd last seen him, he'd cultivated a Vincent Price mustache above that muletrader smile. On occasion, I'd done his heavy lifting that ran the gamut from babysitting his star witnesses to investigating his brilliant leads. Gatlin motioned with his fingers.

"Mr. Maddox, will you please take our deputy colleagues over for a cup of coffee? Thank you, sir." I watched Old Man drape a firm arm around each deputy and forcibly escort them across the break room. He enjoyed it. They didn't.

"I will be brief, Franklin. At 9 a.m. tomorrow, you will stand before

Circuit Court Judge Rickover for arraignment. I have already filed my motion to represent you and the court has admitted me *pro hac vice*. You'll have to endure one additional night in prison."

"And then what?"

"I will make my eloquent argument to have you released on bail. The Prosecutor will object that you are a flight risk but his objection will be to no avail because he does not know that Rickover and I are old colleagues. You will be freed on a $50,000 bail that I shall post. But in the meantime, you go and convalesce. A doctor will be by to minister to you directly. Mr. Maddox will escort Doc Edwards and me to our overnight accommodations. Doc, bless his heart, chauffeured me here from Pelham."

"And what about Goines?"

"Judge Rickover has discussed that matter with Sheriff Greenleaf. Deputy Goines will cease his personal abuse of the prisoners. How you choose to deal with him later is your own affair."

My reaction was cynical. How much weight did a judge's orders carry in the dead of night down in a hellhole like this? "I'll know what to do about Goines later," I said. My thoughts on cynicism continued. "Are you working on Rod Bellwether's case?"

"Rod and I have been in contact. At the moment, his situation is a little precarious. For the immediate future, though, we should concentrate our resources on securing your release from this prison."

"All right then," I said.

"By the way, Gerald Peyton asked me to relay a message to you."

Hearing Gerald Peyton's name jolted my memory. Months earlier, Gerald had had a big hand in my collision course with a crew of Neo-Nazis. They'd set up headquarters in a mountain redoubt further north in the West Virginia panhandle. They took casualties. Then the fight flared up again in my hometown. They took a lot more casualties. Their Grimmest Reaper had been Gerald Peyton.

"Gerald said you should call him unless both your goddamn arms are broken and your jaw is wired shut."

"Message received. Just don't tell Gerald about my arrest. We don't want him charging up here," I said.

When Old Man and Gatlin left, the deputies escorted me back to my jail cell. Prone on the bunk, I thought about my cousin, Rod Bellwether. I went so far as to feel a pang of sympathy for Rod since my relocation to Scarab had been to evade my guilt for not helping him escape death row.

Later, the dour Deputy Braintree served our Sunday dinner trays. Canned carrots, moldy Wonder Bread, pork rind, and a half-pint of curdled milk. No marmalade on zwieback. I cleaned my plate.

A hiss came through our adjoining wall. "Hey, you there, new fish. You chilling straight up?"

"Straight up," I said.

"You eat your pork rind?"

"I did."

"What were you collared for?"

"Talking garbage to Deputy Goines."

"What a bitch. Goines was being groomed for lieutenant with the State boys until he was sacked for screwing a hooker in exchange for a walk."

"How did you end up in here?" I asked him.

"Last winter I near froze to death camped in a shack on the New River. I dropped thirty pounds. Never again, I swore. Three hots and a cot are what I score inside here and if I crack a little loony to land it, well, that's nobody's business but my own. The most I have to do is pick up after myself every day. Where did you get busted?"

"Near the mini mart. I'd gone inside to buy their T-shirt . . . "

"The Blue Cheer? You can't be one of them!"

A hot wire burned me across the shoulders. "You know about the Blue Cheer?"

"Just a bunch of rumors. A secret crew, they hook up to . . ."

The clanging steel door echoed off the concrete and steel. I felt a cold draft blow through my cell. Deputy Braintree clacked his baton between my neighbor's cell bars. "Yo-ho, this is your lucky day. You get reassigned. By direct orders of Sheriff Greenleaf. Shake a leg," he said to my neighbor.

"Where am I going?"

"Up front. Transpack your gear. Don't make me order a cell extraction."

"Hello, Mr. Johnson," said a different voice.

I saw, through the slit in my swollen eyes, Dr. Thomas standing outside my cell. "Hey, Braintree, undo this cell door," he said over his shoulder.

"How about showing me a little civility?" said Deputy Braintree.

"Yeah, yeah. Just put me inside here." Dr. Thomas' T-shirt motto read "Ginsengers: Beware of Poachers!" I couldn't recollect if ginseng or marijuana was the bigger cash crop here. I sat up on my bunk, groaning. The others filed back through the hall's steel door.

"Hey doc, holler when you want out," said Deputy Braintree, before it closed behind him.

"I got word about you in Abe's. It left me wondering what these people are thinking," said Dr. Thomas.

"Are you Gatlin's doctor?" I'd been expecting Doc Edwards to come by. But then he was a veterinarian.

"Is that so bad?" A brown plastic bottle and dressing appeared from Dr. Thomas' lizard skin satchel. He wetted a gauze pad with peroxide. "Goines sure did ride rough herd on you. We'd better get your head X-rayed in Elkins."

"I'm fine. At least my eyeballs have stopped spinning." I gritted my teeth as he dabbed my head.

"That Goines. Someday somebody's gonna break his balls."

"That's a fact," I said.

As Dr. Thomas bandaged my skull, I judged his medical skills surpassed those of your average mortician or even veterinarian, but I couldn't argue with the bill so I kept my mouth shut.

Dr. Thomas zipped up the satchel. "We'll spring you first thing tomorrow."

"Is your postmortem ready?" I asked.

"For Jan Maddox? Uh, I'm prepping for it." Dr. Thomas smoothed down the adhesive tape dressing on my head. He spoke just above a whisper. "Jan was a trophy kill. I didn't tell Old Man but the perpetrators enjoyed it. They're animals."

"Was Jan still alive when the killer used the rope?" I asked, feeling rage heat inside me.

"Two facts indicate that she was," said Dr. Thomas. "One, the pretechial hemorrhaging evidenced underneath her eyelids. And two, that black-blue contusion on the strangulation line. The preliminary scan of her body uncovered no puncture wounds. The defensive cuts on her right palm tell us she didn't go too gently into the night. Her autopsy will show more."

"Is it still Tuesday at five o'clock?"

"If my autopsy assistant returns from out of town in time, yes. She's a smart, young lady. Goes to college in Bluefield."

"Make me a copy of Jan's autopsy report." I swallowed only dry air, no spit. "Old Man, you see, is now my client."

Dr. Thomas gave me an okay nod. "How are you now?"

"A whole sight better than Jan Maddox," I replied.

CHAPTER NINE

Scarab's 19th century courthouse was a maize-yellow stucco. Hourly, a moon-faced clock, visible from the gentrified square below, played the recording of a tolled bell. Nine peals rippled out on this Monday morning. Flyers tacked by color-coded pushpins curled in the breeze. Gatlin and I bustled up the stairs. Old Man and the Brylcreem deputy duo of Swart and Braintree followed in our wake. Unlike on *Law & Order* where Wardrobe clad the defendant in a Brooks Brothers suit, my daywear to court was the chic orange jumpsuit.

Gatlin primed me with last-minute pointers. "You're to respond as 'Yes, Your Honor' and 'No, Your Honor.' Are you listening to me, Franklin? I'm your advocate so defer all queries to me. And take your cues from me. Here's the first. Look repentant and deferential."

My head pounded. "Isn't this one in the bag?" I asked, trying to fit Old Man's brown fedora on top of my gauze turban.

Beet-faced from his exertion, Gatlin looked at me. "Who said?"

The courtroom smelled of mothballs and age-old varnish. A mountaineer wearing an olive drab shirt buttoned clear to his corded neck, and a young girl in a cornflower blue sack dress, sat whispering on the rearmost bench. Gatlin and I claimed our ladder-back chairs and pulled up to the defense counsel table.

"Quaint digs," I told Gatlin.

"Repentant and deferential, Franklin."

Gentlemen in formal livery peered down their beaky noses at us from larger-than-life portraits mounted on the wall. Prosecutor Irving, who bore a resemblance to those dead coal squires, tried to dismiss Gatlin with an imperious look. Gatlin stared down his adversary until he blinked. First blood to us.

"Silence . . . all rise," said the bailiff.

Judge Rickover, angular and stoop-shouldered in frayed black robes, shuffled in from a private portal. We stood until the bailiff commanded us to sit. The judge gaveled us into session on People v. Johnson (No. 4-02-0625) after which my alleged infractions were read into the public record.

Prosecutor Irving sipped ice water before commencing his stilted speech. "Due to the nature of the egregious offenses with which the defendant is charged, the People contend that bail is out of the question."

"Oh?" Judge Rickover yanked at his black sleeve where a loose thread distracted him.

"The physical assault upon any representative of the sheriff's office is unconscionable, to say the least. Precedents establish any criminal committing such an offense should never see sunlight before going to trial. Moreover, the People deem Mr. Johnson to be a flight risk. Indeed, as we can ascertain from his rough countenance here this morning, he is a man of brutish, unpredictable impulses."

Gatlin's chair grated backward as he too arose, the tiger opals on his three fingers tugging down the brushed brown vest. "Your Honor, I would respectfully submit that Mr. Johnson has no criminal history, currently establishes his residence as a homeowner here in Fordham County, and even holds a valid Private Investigator license in the Commonwealth of Virginia. In addition, he has community ties to Scarab."

Hulking near, Old Man jabbed me on the shoulder. "Almost home free, babe," he said.

Judge Rickover snipped the loose thread with a pair of small scissors. "Community ties?" he said.

Old Man plucked the swizzle stick from his mouth and bolted to his feet. "If it pleases the court, that would be me, Allen Poe Maddox. I stand here this morning as a character witness in Mr. Johnson's behalf."

"Duly noted, Mr. Maddox. Please seat yourself," said Judge Rickover.

Inspecting his thumbnail, Prosecutor Irving smirked. "Since defense counsel has thrown open the door on the defendant's profession, I will point out that one year ago he went to trial for a double homicide . . ."

"And was subsequently acquitted by a jury of his peers," said Gatlin.

"Nonetheless there was evidence enough to effect an arrest," said Prosecutor Irving.

"That evidence was shown to be manufactured. Only the final outcome is relevant here. Mr. Johnson was found not guilty," said Gatlin.

Prosecutor Irving almost knocked over the glass of ice water at his elbow. Papers rustled as he consulted them. "Need I remind the court that the two slain victims were sworn law enforcement officers?"

"That, in and of itself, does not ennoble them a god status. Unfortunately, a few police officers are corrupt and venal," said Gatlin.

"If I may complete my thought—"

Judge Rickover gave Prosecutor Irving a nod. "Proceed but be brief."

"In summation we all can agree, then, that Mr. Johnson is a cop killer. I repeat, a cop killer. Dare we sanction such an execrable psychopath to walk our peaceful town streets? Of course not! The defendant's request for bail is denied. He has no right to bond out. End of discussion."

"Mister Prosecutor, you don't rule here. I do. Has defense counsel anything further?"

"Yes, Your Honor, I do. Those so-called law enforcement officers had proven Neo-Nazi affiliations. Good-bye and good riddance, I say. And so the jurors, all prudent men and women, stated by their not guilty verdict. A verdict, I hasten to add, returned after less than one hour in deliberation," said Gatlin.

"What? Good riddance? Why, that's shocking. My god, Your Honor. Just because they were of a particular political persuasion, no matter how repellant, doesn't condemn them to death by Mr. Johnson's vigilante justice."

Gatlin's eyes whisked over to Prosecutor Irving. "The jury rightly saw this vigilante justice as an act of justified self-defense. Do you dare now impugn their integrity?"

Somebody, the mountaineer I suspected, clapped his hands.

Judge Rickover rapped his silver-banded gavel. "Gentleman, enough caviling. I've had opportunity to study defense counsel's thought-provoking brief. I observe the arresting officer is Deputy Goines who I don't see in my courtroom. That speaks volumes, doesn't it? I affix bail at fifty thousand dollars. Mr. Johnson, do you come with counsel prepared to post bail?"

"Yes, Your Honor, I do."

"Very well. Bail will be cash or property with title in West Virginia paid to Office of the Clerk of the Circuit Court. Trial date is set for November 12th. Court is adjourned."

Prosecutor Irving, turning, this time did tip over his glass of ice water and it spilled down his front. "Your Honor, the People request that the defendant wear an electronic monitoring bracelet as a condition of his bail."

"Denied," said Judge Rickover.

"Your Honor, you don't grasp the severity of . . ."

"I ruled on that motion already. It is still denied. Court is adjourned."

The bailiff stepped up. "All rise."

We piled out of the courthouse and October's crisp, smoky air rejuvenated me. Joy streamed through my veins. I was a free man. Old Man pumped Gatlin's hand. "You kicked ass, Counselor."

"My humble thanks for your good words, sir. It was really nothing. But I must return to Middleburg to emcee a Walkathon for Breast Cancer. Doc Edwards is waiting and, Franklin, you're now on a short leash. Caution becomes your watchword."

"All right then," I said.

"I for one hope your return to Pelham is imminent. At any rate, you should store my home and office numbers on the Palm Pilot I gave you for Christmas," said Gatlin.

My move to West Virginia had suffered casualties. "I'm here for the time being," I said.

"Very well then. Please stay in close communication with me," said Gatlin. Doc Edwards, in the Cadillac, pulled to the curbside and Gatlin climbed in. I made a mental note to phone Gerald Peyton as I watched the Cadillac disappear down the road out of Scarab and into the hazy hills.

Two deputies squired me, minus the hated shackles, over two blocks to their station house. Once there, I shed the chic orange jumpsuit and signed a property receipt before hustling into my street clothes. They smelled of roach spray. I tore off the hated ID bracelet. A cashier's check was cut to cover my $44.28. I preferred cash. They didn't care. The manila envelope of my pocket wares came from lockup and my shoulder rig was returned empty.

"Mr. Johnson came strapping a rod. A Kel-Tec niner," said Old Man.

The manila envelope sailed into the In-Basket. "His concealed carry permit is invalid here. I'm keeping that niner until such time as he's ready to leave my town and state," said Sheriff Greenleaf.

"Unbelievable. And to think I voted for you in the last election. I'll know better at the one coming up," said Old Man.

"Look, I'm doing my job the best way I know how. Maybe I'll be out of a job come next election. But until then, I'm the top dog here. What I say goes, like it or not."

Old Man took a different tack. "Has any headway been made on my wife's murder?" he asked.

"Three full-time deputies are canvassing the county. Progress reports are being made as needed," replied Sheriff Greenleaf.

"Have you bothered to pick up your phone and call Dr. Thomas?"

"We keep in contact, yes."

"My wife's postmortem is tomorrow at five."

Sheriff Greenleaf's face reddened. "Impossible. Our budget won't allow for an autopsy."

Old Man grunted. "Sheriff, I'd love to see things from your point of view, but I can't get my head that far up my ass."

"We'll, uh, be leaving now. Come on, Old Man. Time to go, hear me?" I said.

"I see the stay in my pokey wised you up, Johnson. Better keep your nose white-hanky clean," said Sheriff Greenleaf.

"You bet," I said.

Sheriff Greenleaf snorted. "You'll be back."

"Up thine," said Old Man.

The Valiant waited for us under two metal flagpoles in the parking area, a gust clacking their steel grommets. I didn't spot Goines' cruiser. Old Man and I flopped down inside and buckled up.

"Uncle Nimrod dropped some names on me before breakfast. Those two punk-asses at the mini mart are Dot Christmas and Woody Sears. He's seen them up in the hills collecting pine duff to sell. I know you just dodged a bullet, but what say we go see them about Jan's murder?" asked Old Man.

"I like the idea," I replied. "A lot."

"Solid. You'll find a pair of sunshades in the glove compartment. Also a .44 Charter Arms Bulldog."

After opening the glove compartment, I sniffed Hoppes #9 solvent, a cherished cologne from my gunsmithing days. The 5-shot .44's skinny rubber grips felt good in my fist. The 2½-inch stainless steel barrel with its bead-blasted texture imparted a peachy balance at a light 19 ounces. I thumb-cocked its bobbed hammer, fingered its filed combat trigger, and dry-fired once. "Sweet." A leather holster put the mighty mouse on my right hip.

"I bought 200-grain load. Hollow points," said Old Man.

"Big game bullets. Sweeter, still."

"That Lee-Enfield stripper clip holds five rounds for extra ammo. The rim diameter for a .303 is the same as it is for a .44," said Old Man.

"Man, you're Santa Claus with a tan."

Old Man chuckled. "Firing that hardware won't rip out your arm at the socket either."

"I hope the need never arises."

"Hey babe, Mr. Gatlin couldn't say enough about your extreme sports back in Pelham. You're too modest. He told me how those Neo-Nazis teed off on you. Said you went berserk and killed two deputies in cahoots with them before busting up their gang."

"It was all bullshit." Hearing again about this former case depressed me since I'd done my damnedest to forget about it. Now I'd been reminded about it twice in the same morning.

"My CIA service had red-meat days like that," said Old Man.

"Yeah?"

"I can't disclose more," said Old Man. Seeing his drum-taut face spurred me to visualize CIA-sponsored hit squads in Panama or Columbia. It was safer to track along our other conversational thread.

"Like every lawyer I've ever known, Gatlin has a big mouth. Should we eat lunch now?" I said.

Old Man parked us under the Golden Arches across the street from the glazier shop. Inside, I chowed down on a Big Mac with fries and a Diet Coke.

"Not hungry?" I asked him.

"My liquid fortification is under the console out in the car. Besides, what you're eating is a far cry from the ghetto burger I like." Old Man lifted a doleful glance beyond me into the lobby. "Look at what the polecat just coughed up."

Two deputies, holstered .357s on their pudgy hips, strutted up bow-legged to the counter. "Lunch is on the house," we overheard the clerk tell them. "Like always, deputies."

"I pay for mine to subsidize theirs," said Old Man.

"Chill out," I said.

Balancing their food trays, the deputies neared our table. "Morning, gentlemen," said the lead one. I recognized him as Swart who'd made the A-frame call.

"Why ain't you out nabbing killers instead of in here stuffing your fool faces?" said Old Man.

"Department policy gives us a thirty-minute lunch," said Swart.

The portly corporal broke in. "We're man hunting our entire juris-diction. Sheriff Greenleaf will keep you posted."

"Aw, go suck on your milkshakes," said Old Man.

"My appetite's gone. I'm done here," I said.

Back in the car, Old Man mashed the accelerator to the floor and the Valiant roared up the roadwork slab. The swelling had gone down enough to see out both of my eyes. My loose teeth had tightened in their sockets. My sunshades tinged everything a surreal green. Even so, I much preferred this scenery over yesterday's vertical and horizontal iron bars. The bourbon bottle alternated between us.

"The Blue Cheer. What we read off those damn T-shirts and at the fire tower. The phrase repeats like a mantra inside my head," I said.

"My memory's hazy but I'm sure blue cheer was first a damn laundry detergent. Then a rock band from Frisco cribbed the name. After that, it identified a mind-busting LSD. We also called it purple haze, cherry top, or blue moon. Man, wartime Saigon was awash in acid. Those were spacey days. Swallow a sugar cube, trip out on Iron Butterfly and Jimi," said Old Man.

"Did you ever dump acid?" I asked.

"Excuse me?"

"You know, take LSD, blue cheer?"

Crimped lips exhaling air, Old Man nodded. "You mean *drop* acid. Sure, I tinkered with it, babe. All of us sailed away on hallucinatory trips."

"Do you get flashbacks?" I asked.

"No, none. But LSD makes deformed babies."

I debated if that was why Old Man had forsaken fatherhood or if there was a more complex reason. Like a black man living in a white man's town. He made a right turn, skidded in the loose gravel, then stabilized the tires. We flushed a covey of ring-neck pheasants from the fencerow and soon a shotgun house came into view. A young girl—wrought tall like a lighthouse—teed off, smacking an orange golf ball into a stand of persimmon. Tiger Woods dreams? Hell, why not? The girl glared at us as we went around the washboard bend rippling her road.

Old Man gunned the gas.

CHAPTER TEN

The state motto for West Virginia's fifty-five counties is "mountaineers are always free." Their living on inaccessible roads like this one showed me why that was true. Switchbacks took us up a limestone ridge and, once topside, the road narrowed to a rabbit path. Tree branches slapped the Valiant's rocker panels and it was all Old Man, sweat on his temples, could do to straddle the ruts. We pressed on.

"Grab a hold of your shoulder harness, babe," he said as we rumbled by a root-bound escarpment. Kicked-up rocks and sticks thumped the floor pan and skid plate. Russet foliage blocked out sunlight and entering a cold zone stirred a sliver of fright in me. Old Man cranked his window handle just as a whack smashed out the rear window glass.

"What the hell was that?" he asked.

I turned my head. "A deadfall limb."

The lane petered out at a crazy-quilt meadow stitched by blue asters, orange poppies, and yellow daisies. Old Man scanned east to west. "Look out for a shanty. Dot and Woody are often seen scooping up pine duff behind it," he said.

My hand was a compass needle. "Swerve right. See it?"

A pearly haze kept the sun from shining on the small cabin's worn chestnut planks and tin hip roof. Smoke curling from a rubble-stone chimney harked back to the hardscrabble 1930s, a time capsule dug up and left here for us to find. Old Man stopped the Valiant. "We'll mellow here for a bit, babe, if you don't object," he said. I didn't.

Squawking guinea hens and Domineckers flounced over the crushed oyster shells. They drew our eyes over to what I believe the hill people dub "a granny woman". Gravel-blind, she plucked a handloom like an adroit harpist. Her seeing fingers tucked the rug's ravelings and passed along a wood shuttle the size of a boxtop. Her quicksilver hair was twined into an oblong knot and an ecru shawl covered her bony shoulders. Her nod beckoned us to approach. Our car doors popped free and we stretched out. We walked two abreast through the boogie lice sticking to our pants legs before we joined a pathway.

"She's creakier than grandpa's buckskin rubber. I bet granny witches could do devil worship up here," said Old Man.

"Do you see any broomsticks? Any pointy black hats?"

"Uncle Nimrod tricked us," said Old Man.

"C'mon, hey. Will you relax?"

We walked the rest of the way to the cabin in silence.

"I felt you as soon as you topped the cliff," said the granny woman, her unprepossessing smile putting me at ease. "I'm Hattie McGraw." She offered Old Man a liver-spotted hand to shake. "You're a colored fellow?"

"Nothing could be truer. Old Man Maddox, ma'am. That there is Frank Johnson."

"Hello, gentlemen. Light and hitch. Do tell, Frank, are you white? Younger than Mr. Maddox?" asked Hattie.

"You're right on both scores." My turn at astonishment came. Her hand felt tough as crocus cloth. In contrast, mine must've felt slack to her as we shook.

Hattie settled into a pillow-bottomed chair. A toadstone charm hung on a rawhide string about her wrinkled neck. "Frank, you're Irish, too. The trace of a brogue underlies your speech. The Irish drove our steam engines, dug our coal, and tended our new ground. You weren't yet born back then."

"My daddy's kin raise a little burley tobacco. Coal is their mainstay, though," I said.

Hattie's girlish laugh stirred. "Coal, it seems, is king everywhere, but why trek up here? Pish! Those mountain roads are almost straight up and down. It was a fool's errand, I can just bet you."

"We're after two men. Dot Christmas and Woody Sears," said Old Man.

Hattie turned cagey. "I ain't tight with sheriffs. Deputies, either."

"We've got nothing to do with them. We want to talk to Dot and Woody is all," said Old Man.

Hattie hoisted her sinewy shoulders. "I can just bet they've no business with you."

"Well, I'm making them *my* business," said Old Man.

"Oh, are you? I'd steer clear of those Klan boys if you want to see another sunrise," said Hattie.

"Klan?" I felt my heart kick over.

"Surely. Dot and Woody's people once kept a Klan cemetery on Bremo's Promontory over in Curtis County," said Hattie.

"Do you know if they belong to another secret group? Something like the Klan?" I asked, now suspicious.

"That I can't say," replied Hattie.

"Does the name the Blue Cheer mean anything to you?" I asked.

Old Man also made the connection. "This racist cult calls themselves the Blue Cheer."

"A man I saw in town told me as much," I said.

"Don't know. But you'd better leave Dot and Woody to Sheriff Greenleaf. Satan never made a more hateful pair," said Hattie.

"This we mean to iron out for ourselves. Somebody in town said they come up here to bag up pine mulch," said Old Man.

"Gathering pine twinkles is a side job." Hattie doubled a finger joint to rub the white orb in her eye socket. "That path through the yellow thicket turkey-tails out to spruce pines by the slate dumps. Do you smell their smoke?"

That accounted for the rotten egg odor.

"Or try at their day jobs. Last I heard, it was the ironworks," said Hattie.

"Ma'am, we need to leave. Obliged for your help." Old Man tramped toward the Valiant and matching his stride, I fell in behind him.

"Let Sheriff Greenleaf handle them," Hattie hollered after us.

Old Man cut a doughnut. The Valiant's tires whined like cheater slicks as they sought traction and off we went, backsliding down Hattie's mountain. The red-haired girl still honing her golf stroke gave us a hard look. Old Man mentioned there wasn't a golf course within 150 miles.

Twice my crown dented the roof's headliner, but Old Man didn't slack off his speed. At the state road, the turning Valiant's rear end bounced onto the paving. I nudged around the rearview mirror relieved to see that our gas tank hadn't reamed off. We pointed toward Scarab.

The Chartreuse Ironworks outside of Scarab had clanged into its afternoon grind. Old Man had burned off his first fury as we drew into its red gravel lot. A gantry crane jogged an I-beam girder onto an idling eighteen-wheeler's lowboy trailer. A smaller auxiliary crane, its steel load a swaying pendulum straining both chain hoist and hook, looked ready to snap off. An air horn yawped over the sheds and outbuildings including the Director of Engineering Office, a green and white trailer. Old Man parked us there and on a no-knock raid, we barged inside the trailer.

A short, disheveled man squinted up at us. He wore a narrow, red necktie and starchy white shirt. Blueprints fell off a draftsman table where a handbook opened at a page of numerical charts made him look busy. Displeasure wrinkled his acne-scarred face. "John Wingo. May I help you?"

"Dot Christmas and Woody Sears—"

"—are they on the yard?" Old Man finished my question.

"They clocked out early today." Wingo's colorless eyes turned shrewd.

"We need a word with them," I said.

"Oh, now I know who you are. Mr. Maddox who lives up near the old fire tower. I heard what happened. I feel bad for your loss," said Wingo.

Old Man counterfeited a smile. "Thanks. Where do they live?"

Wingo came around the draftsman table. "Neither Dot or Woody had anything to do with your tragedy. I can vouch for them. Seeing this might help ease your minds."

After crossing the red gravel lot, Wingo ushered us into a long sheet-metal building where meager light fell on a steel girder. "Let me tell you about us. We handle structural steel doing bridge rehab and these days, it's a niche market. Our goal is simple. To produce a high quality, low man-hour product."

Old Man growled.

"Please bear with me. Once a girder is painted and inspected, we need to deliver it to our client's construction site. That's where Mr. Christmas and Mr. Sears come in. They're our oversize hauling experts."

Wingo led us past a crane operator who bellowed over the uproar of throttling diesel engines. Wingo nodded and waved. We went behind the sheet-metal building. A tall man wearing wraparound sunshades power-washed a Kenworth T800 tractor gray-caked with road grime. Four other trucks awaited the same treatment.

"We hitch up two of these Kenworths to act as one colossal hauling engine. 1050 horsepower, 24 axles, 86 tires, and 36 gears. Pretty impressive statistics?" Wingo gave me a smug smile.

"It's some might, for real," I said.

Old Man sounded impatience, louder and lower in his chest.

"Hold on, I'm almost finished. Usually my two scheduled drivers leave near dawn and creep thirty miles an hour till they arrive on site," said Wingo.

Old Man glared at him. "I'm guessing our boys hauled steel on Saturday."

Wingo scratched his scalp through graying hair. "Yes sir and transporting that steel took them six hours driving nonstop."

"That's a lie. We saw them in town." Hulking his shoulders, Old Man stepped up to intimidate the smaller Wingo. "So unless you're alibi-ing for them, give me directions to where they live."

"All right, maybe I mixed up the days. Anyway, go back toward town and a mile or so before the posted limits, look for a long driveway that winds into the trees."

"At the milking machine on the mailbox post?" asked Old Man.

"Mr. Sears' sense of humor is a little weird," said Wingo.

Making for the Valiant, Old Man called back over his shoulder to Wingo, "Thank you, man. I owe you a beer."

Old Man one-handed the steering wheel and jacked his elbow out the car window. After flipping down the sun visor, he plucked a lace valentine card from a metal clip. "Jan dabbled in poetry, babe. I kind of like this one." He put the valentine on the dashboard. I read aloud:

Vietnam War Memorial Triolet
—*for Old Man Maddox, mi amor*

On rainy afternoons it's hard to tell
where The Wall stops and clouds begin.
There's a darkness no sun can dispel.
On rainy afternoons it's hard to tell.
Count 58,183 names for a grave spell
of the question: Did anyone really win?
On rainy afternoons it's hard to tell
where The Wall stops and clouds begin.

I nodded. "Hell, I like it. Did you talk to Jan about over there?"

"Nope, I never did, babe, but Jan and I fended for each other." A bourbon bottle appeared from under his car seat. "We scrapped. Marriage is fraught with a little strife, see, but did I ever cheat on Jan? Never did. Never wanted to." Bourbon hammered down his throat. "I saw a lot of gore in Vietnam." A longer bourbon swallow followed. "But nothing I saw over there tops what I saw at my A-frame."

"Don't think about it," I said.

Again, Old Man swigged. Then he said, "The Good Lord better explain it because I for shit sure can't." He gave me a grim-crazed scowl.

I posed no response—I had none—and my reserve may have offended Old Man as a reluctance or disdain to get my hands dirty. My hope was it didn't. Through a darkening vision, murder glimmered uppermost in my mind. Murder and motive. Dot Christmas and Woody Sears had motive. Racial hatred.

"Action is the anecdote to despair," I muttered.

Old Man looked at me. "Proverbs?"

"Joan Baez."

"Ms. Baez was a wise lady."

At the milking machine on the post, Old Man turned left into the packed clay lane. Shotgun shrapnel had peppered the milking machine. NO TRESPASSING! signs were nailed to trees and posts along the fence. Little dust billowed from our tires. Good, because stealth and speed were our chief assets. Old Man's thumb arched over his shoulder.

"Hand me what's under that seat, babe."

I swept away the pieces of window glass, looked under the seat, and found his Remington 20 shotgun pistol. I put it in his lap, and took out my .44. Hedgerow cedars gave way to harsh white sunlight and there it was, the tenant house we sought. The house was two stories, shingled in gray, and sat in the back of a thistle-choked field. Rust striated its tin roof. The bookend brick chimneys crumbled at the top.

We rode on, the driveway hugging the fencerow. I felt edgy.

Closer up, I saw a dismantled Kawasaki, its parts strewn about like in a high school auto shop. A toolbox lay under its handlebars. Chrome socket wrenches and a breaker bar glinted on the banana seat. The house's screen door swung on its last rusty hinge below four windows.

I palmed the .44. "Did we scare off the good ole boys?"

Old Man one-handed the Remington 20. "No sir, the snipers are upstairs."

"They won't let us play through."

"Yeah, but here's an opportunity to excel." Old Man stomped the brakes and muscled the steering wheel. The masterful Valiant lurched, its tires sizzling over the turf. Looping in a Batmobile 180, we touched down parallel to a paling fence and leaped out, guns drawn. We hunched behind the trunk.

"I'll dash in and draw fire," Old Man whispered.

"I'm right behind you."

Old Man surged through the fence's gateless gap and I executed my own zigzag charge to make their muzzles flame. Blunt reverberations stunned my ears and I realized their long barrel shotguns could be bad news for us. Old Man and I fell flat. Two dozen steel pellets clawed the turf and mud too close for comfort.

Two pump shotguns, high and tight, chambered fresh rounds, an unmistakable noise—*click-clank, click-clank*—that petrified hearts and gelled knees. Or at least it did mine. Old Man, belly-crawling, tucked in the skimpy cover behind the Kawasaki. Boom-boom-boom! His shotgun burst strafed each window. Their return volley dinged the Kawasaki's chrome and sprockets. Elbows digging and hips scuttling, I paddled up to Old Man.

"How do you see it?" I asked, gasping for air.

"Fall down five times, get up six."

"How about getting our asses shot off?" I asked.

"We've already got that down cold."

"They're hunkered behind those windows. We'll storm inside the house and flush 'em out," I said.

"Just like Tidy Bowl."

I crouched like a sprinter poised in his blocks and yelled, "Cover me."

I saw, from the corner of my eye, Old Man brace a forearm on the down-bow to the banana seat. The staccato of 20-gauge shells fed from his clip parried the skittish snipers off their high perches. I vaulted up to the porch, put an arm to the door, and shoved it.

Inside, I cleared out all quadrants, the .44 extended over chicken buckets, 40-ounce malt liquor bottles, and pizza boxes. Terrified, a dark bird flapped by me, shit spattering all under it. Twisting, my boot heel slipped and my body tumbled against the sheet rock. I righted myself, somehow, without shooting off my thumb.

One of the loud-mouthed snipers taunted me.

I dove sharp right a split second before he discharged a round into the spot I'd just occupied. My brown fedora sailed under a hobbyhorse and my tailbone hit the flooring as Old Man stomped through the threshold. I jerked the .44 up. Its slug axed out a chunk of balcony. My ringing ears pricked at hearing a windowpane squeak, an exchange of words, and a stampede clattering over the tin roof. I flew up cluttered steps to the open dormer just in time to see Woody Sears jump off the roof's end.

"They've lit out around back," I said to Old Man.

He turned around and plunged toward the porch. An engine spluttered, then revved up. "Son of a bitch!" Old Man, me right behind him, came on the double.

It couldn't be true, but it was. Their van blitzed from the nearby barn. Their rebel yell drowned out the getaway motor. The van's side door cracked and a shotgun barrel vented out. "Duck!" I said. The extreme angle of fire and the van's acceleration, not swift thinking, saved our bacon. Their shotgun blast mutilated a porch post.

"Hound 'em to the road. Wipe 'em out!" said Old Man.

I stiff-armed him in the chest. "Let them go."

The fight in Old Man boiled too hot while mine was cooler, but not by much. He shoved me back in the chest. I stumbled a step. As he knifed inside me to clip my jutting chin, my head bucked up and conked him in the nose. Old Man let out a surprised yelp and backpedaled. Two fingers dabbed at the blood over his upper lip.

"Let them book," I said again.

"Where's the car?" Bewildered, Old Man left the porch, car keys rattling in his fingers. Rocketed in a flying column, I wrestled both his ankles, and his knees faltered. "Let me go, dang it." Old Man hefted me up by the shirtfront to see eye-to-eye with him. "You done farting around here?"

My right hand jarred his chin and I wrenched free. "Listen." I breathed hard and put up my hands. "Whacking them sends us to Bitterroot Prison. Leave that for them, not us."

"They're mine alone to deal with."

"It'll score you worlds of grief."

"Babe, don't oppose me." Old Man, his large chest flexing in and out, massaged his chin. Seconds later, his fanatical ire cooled to rational thought as his fists relaxed. "Okay, maybe you do talk sense. Let's shake down this place."

Before you knew it, we unearthed our treasure on the porch under a rat-gnawed army poncho. I picked up the motor case, part number XYX-2309QQ. Old Man then rotated it in his shiny palms. "So this is a Stinger. More souped-up than the Redeyes I remember firing. The right weapon in a tight spot." He lifted his intense gaze from the Stinger. "Let's see what else they've squirreled away here."

Flashlights on, we cased the upstairs. Nothing. We scrabbled down to the basement and then out to the barn. Both places, nothing. I wrapped the Stinger motor case in the poncho, saying, "We'll crate up this puppy and express mail it to Dreema."

"Who?"

"Dreema Adkins. My Richmond pal at the forensics lab. She'll run the science and report back to us."

"Why, babe? It's only a fired rocket."

"It's evidence. Dreema will know what to do with it," I said.

"Is her helping you on the up and up?"

"Dreema does it after hours sort of as a courtesy to me."

Old Man one-eyed his bleeding knuckles. "Was Jan killed to cover up the Stinger firing?"

"Very possibly. It's all got to be tied back to the Blue Cheer," I said.

CHAPTER ELEVEN

———

We returned to my cabin. The adrenaline jolt had worn off and my guts ached. The plain brown envelope in my mailbox at the foot of my lane may as well have been a letter bomb. Its big news exploded off the page. My cousin Rod Bellwether had run down my mail address. I recognized the same stylized block printing.

Based on a possible reexamination of the physical evidence (a DNA analysis that Rod had paid for out of his own pocket), Richmond was mulling over his petition for a retrial, and he wanted to know if I wouldn't resume my investigation on his behalf. A carbon copy had been routed to Robert Gatlin, my lawyer. I sat back on the sofa and let my mind backslide.

Bitterroot State Prison was Virginia's flagship super max, a 1200-cot correctional institution, the modern equivalent of Devil's Island. Our balls-on-crime Governor, George Allen, claimed that voters had mandated its funding by his election. At Level 6, it rated as the most severe by our Commonwealth's Institutional Assignment Criteria and for good reason, too. All hard-case one-percenters, what the officialese called "single or multiple life-sentenced prisoners," went there. They amounted to squid shit—no inmate could sink lower and only Hell came next. You turned into an animal behind those eggshell-white walls. You had miniature portals to the natural outside light. Steel doors featured holes cut for bean chutes and cuff slots.

As it was, I had already journeyed to Bitterroot Prison. Things all started two months before—and I relived this now with profound regret—when the telephone rang as my frankfurters came to a boil. I still lived at my trailer in Pelham at the time and I'd tuned in to *The Antiques Road Show*, that week broadcasted from Memphis, Tennessee, home to Sun Records ("We record anything—anywhere—anytime.").

The buggy stammer I heard on the line belonged to "Rod Bellwether, FBI No. 48743ZZ, VA Inmate No. XXX3577." I fumbled for words. "What's up, Rod?"

"I'm dangling by a cunt hair, Frank. In two months, they'll belt me to a gurney and pump cyanide into my veins."

"Sorry to hear that, Rod, but I haven't talked to you in—what has it been, now?—twenty-odd years."

"Listen up. I almost shanked a Bama to get this phone. Don't hang up on me. I swear on my skin I didn't kill my wife. I loved Kathy. I'm pleading for your help, Frank."

"My help? *Me*? You're a laugh. My credit cards are maxed out. I eat Chef-Boy-Ar-Dee out of a can and cut my own hair. My best pal is a flea-bitten, one-eyed tomcat. What does that tell you?"

"That's nothing. Come walk in my bo-bos, cousin. Do cockroaches crawl in your mouth while you sleep? Do you live in a shit-lined cage? Do you hear the cornholed pretty boys shriek the night away? I do. Every stinking day."

A cogent memory grabbed me. "Didn't you flunk a polygraph? It was in the papers."

"Naw man, the polygraphs were rigged. Both times. Besides, they're inadmissible," said Rod.

"H'm."

"I know you do legwork for that righteous shyster, Gatlin. I saw him on TV. He traffics in long shots and his ballsy style suits me."

I already knew the answer but I was on an unavoidable collision course with stupid, so I asked the question. "What can Gatlin do for you?"

"Not Gatlin—you. Find Kathy's killer. Then Gatlin can win my appeal. You want me to get the needle when my own cousin, the PI, could've helped but didn't?"

"My conscience ain't at issue," I said through clamped teeth. He had me by the short hairs. "Okay, fine. Pencil me in, tomorrow, twelve noon. But I ain't promising you dick."

Bitterroot Prison was located in Mantis, Virginia, the county seat to Bainbridge County, deep in the Blue Ridge Mountains. If remoteness was to deter escape, the prison was well placed atop a strip-mined mountain. Its architecture plagiarized Alcatraz's, was my first thought when confronting its numbing, gray façade.

Mecca towers presided over all and the electrified death wire—they typically packed 5100 volts—scared the piss out of me. Next was a no-man's zone and then a second barrier of high tech razor wire euphemistically called "Prickly Sentry Barbed Tape" even bolt-cutters couldn't sever. Its two-inch razor tufts chewed up any would-be escapees. Rescuers had to saw them out of the razor wire like from inside a VW crushed under a Peterbilt.

The instant I cleared the gate, the rain-bloated clouds let loose. A deluge sent me streaking to the Admittance area. Why did I come here? Why? I shook hard enough to rattle my ribs. Metal detector wands combed me and rottweilers sniffed my crotch. Bull guards patted me down.

"Carrying any narcotics? Maybe in a condom?" asked the bull guard.

"No, sir. May I have my copy of the visitation rules?"

"Don't sweat it. I'll steer you clear of any trouble. You brought books. Who for?"

"My cousin, Rodney Bellwether."

"Waste of time. Bellwether can't read," said the bull guard.

"Can't all be born geniuses," I said.

We threaded our way through Ad Seg to a warren of visitation booths. "X Row" for death row was printed over the booth equipped with a red telephone. A bull guard seated me there. Blue trim encased the Plexiglas separator. Inhaling recycled air, I noted four gun ports above me and visualized a firing squad. Electric locks clicked. Steel banged against steel. A door clicked open.

To look at, Rod was a Billy Bad Ass. Razor-cut sideburns, a wispy goatee, a bulldog tattoo on his forearm. He wore blue that matched the needle studded in his bluish tongue. He laughed at my jitters. Two bandy-legged bull guards accessorized with twelve gauges lorded over us. Some other bull guard had sneaked a Maxi-Pad to the seat of one's britches as a joke. Rod jiggled his leg shackles. A hand wearing an I.D.

bracelet was left unencumbered. He tapped the Plexiglas separator, pointed at me and then at the red telephone receiver. His was off the hook.

Rod's Southern drawl poured into my ear. "You slink around like a fucking whipped hound."

"Hiya, Rod. This joint depresses the shit out of me. I checked in some reading material up front. Charles Williams' *Dead Calm* and all his sea stories. A couple bricks of cigarettes. Marlboro Reds. You smoke, eh?"

"Like a burning tire dump. I may or may not get them, depending on The Man's mood. Fucking law books might do me better. Say, is your bumhole plug intact?" said Rod.

"Bumhole plug, nuts. Doc Edwards, the vet, sewed up my ass." Rod laughed. "Heady thinking." The chitchat ended. "Did you bring me any fucking good news?"

I tore off contact with his half-dead eyes. "Rod, I'm less than an exemplary citizen . . ."

"Excuse me all to hell, but priests I don't need. I need you to nail the cockeyed motherfucker who killed my wife."

"What about your DNA appeal?"

"Inconclusive, they said. Seventeen thousand cases go into forensics DNA and mine has to tank. No white bunnies are left in the magician's black top hat. No chance to live out my days here." Blood rushed from Rod's pasty face. He teared up. I felt sick. "I loved Kathy. Believe me. I swear to God and with all my life and I ain't scamming you."

"M'm. What happened, Rod?" I asked him.

Rod sniffed. "That Sunday morning I went fishing. Drank a little and read the comics. When I got back home, Kathy had been butchered."

"You've no idea who did it?" I asked.

"Shit, no. But go snoop around. Start in that bumfuck town where we lived. Somebody there is getting away with murder."

"Last Thursday, your daddy gave me a holler," I said.

"And?"

91

"And he asked me to look into your situation."

"And?"

I swallowed hard. "And I agreed."

"So, get off the fucking stick and go do me some good," said Rod.

"I packed the Stinger in this." The cardboard box Old Man held once contained a shoddy tinsel Christmas tree. He handed me the brown fedora.

"First, let me go phone the lab," I said.

Dreema Adkins had fled our native town of Pelham that had shriveled to obscurity alongside Interstate 81. She earned a National Merit scholarship and graduated from Virginia Tech *magna cum laude* in Criminal Justice.

"Why, Frank Johnson," said Dreema with characteristic exuberance, even here on a late Monday afternoon. "How is your tomcat?"

"Mr. Gatlin's taking care of him right now."

"Say it ain't so. You didn't move into a condominium?"

"Nope, I moved to West Virginny. Bought me a mountain cabin," I said.

"I see. Well Frank, what's on your mind?" asked Dreema.

I told her. Dreema said she was swamped but she'd try her best. She acted as if my request was nothing strange, like lots of folks kept Stingers as mantelpieces. "Same as before, the whole shooting match, pardon the pun?" she asked.

"Please. I'll just owe you."

Dreema laughed in that erotic manner some ladies have over the telephone. The sensation was a hot tongue curled inside your ear. "You don't know how much, Frankie boy. Yet. Richmond is pretty all lit up at Christmas. Keep your calendar clear."

Less sure of myself, I thanked Dreema.

Old Man took a break from studying his next strategy on the shot glass chess set and lifted his inquiring eyes.

"Let's roll," I said.

The Valiant ferrying us downslope scared an oriole's electric-orange tear into the hemlocks. I thumbed 20-gauge shells into Old Man's clip, then tapped it to align them. I used the .44's ejector rod to pop out the expended brass and loaded in new ammo. Before seating each round, I checked for bulged casings and flawed noses. I flicked a sub-par bullet out the window. You didn't scrimp when it came to self-defense ammo. My preferred cylinder load alternated ball and hollow rounds, which guaranteed better penetration to rip through vital organs. I looked for the oriole but it was gone.

Old Man, on the main road, shifted through the 3-on-a-tree and punched the gas pedal. "This is a tits machine, babe."

"Amazing it's still road-worthy. I'd no idea."

"I love 'em. Barracudas, too. Mopar rules."

The speedometer on the classy instrument cluster clocked seventy-eight. The slab's surface vibrated through the torsion bar suspension. At The First Primitive Apostolic Church, a fresh coat of white paint now gleamed on its clapboard siding. Its steeple was a vertical rectangle of glass and right before my eyes, the red neon crucifix inside flickered on.

"About Jan's lady preacher, did you mention a name?" I asked.

Old Man put on a cunning smile. "Zelma Roe. She's single and in search of love, too. Did I say that already?"

"Yeah, you keep pushing it at me."

"I met her only the once. Jan invited her over for dinner, oh, near the summer's end. Miss Roe is a foxy lady. You'd like her," said Old Man.

"Maybe I should look into it." Something occurred to me. "It's late. The post office will be closed."

"The postmistress is my cousin, Betty. She'll take us right on. Any ideas on how we come at Dot Christmas and Woody Sears? Obviously, we can't shoot it out with them."

"We need to convince Sheriff Greenleaf that they weren't driving that truck Saturday morning. I expect any experienced trucker can haul a wide load," I said.

Old Man flipped on the headlamps. A road sign advised us about an antler alley. "You mean other truckers could've stood in for them?"

"Not just any truckers but ones sharing their particular hatreds," I said. "That way the substitutes keep their mouths shut. After all, Dot and Woody were out correcting a crass injustice. It's a slick alibi—"

"—until I beat a confession out of them," said Old Man.

The post office, in harmony with Scarab's squatty cinderblock architecture, appeared uninhabited. Old Man braked by a fire hydrant and we hopped out. We cupped our palms and peered through the dirty sheet glass. A weak light and a low radio prompted Old Man to bang on the door until an attractive lady with her hair in a French roll opened up. Old Man smiled at her.

"Did you bring me mail, Al?" asked Betty through the crack. Old Man bent from the waist and she kissed his cheek. "I'm terribly sorry about Jan."

Old Man fed through our boxed-up Stinger, his voice husky. "Don't worry. Something will be done about it. Meantime, can you stick this aboard tomorrow's UPS?"

"Never a problem. Who's this, dear?"

"Meet Frank Johnson. I'm helping him out."

Betty smiled. "Frank looks as if he can take care of himself."

"That's debatable," said Old Man.

CHAPTER TWELVE

At a long, strange Monday's end, Old Man and I assumed our usual booth under the Harley-Davidson logo at Abe's. The same chalkboard lunch specials had jumped by fifty cents. The same frazzled waitress in the paisley sweater memorized our orders. Mine copied Old Man's: strip steak medium rare with coleslaw and onion rings on the side.

My eyes went to the TV flickering behind the bar. A stud in denim cutoffs and a salon tan was vamping for the camera. The twilit beach under him was pink lava. His castaway cohorts were going hungry—Stud had sabotaged their stew with starfish and kelp. They hadn't cobbled it together yet but he was 'the mole'. A close-up showed Stud's white, even pearlies.

A barfly in sluggish contempt peered at his sudsy mug bottom. The barkeep chewing on a panatela in his dentures aimed the remote to flip on the NASCAR channel. Mark Martin—in the Viagra/Pfizer Ford—edged the lead Mopar in a wily slingshot stunt. Watching NASCAR was an elixir. The barfly jacked up his head. His unshaven jaws slackened in awe.

"Did you find Mr. Sears and Mr. Christmas?" John Wingo, the Chartreuse Ironworks Director of Engineering with a beer in one hand, stalled at our booth. Half in the bag and still humorless.

My eyes worked him over. "We did. Strangest thing, though. They were lying in ambush for us. I didn't tip them off."

Old Man removed the swizzle stick all chewed up. "I didn't either. Who's left?"

Our glares caught Wingo in a crossfire. "Mr. Sears and Mr. Christmas are cussed about folks showing up unannounced. Sorry if I didn't tell you but you have to telephone ahead."

Groaning upright, Old Man pushed away Wingo. "Why don't you just move on?"

"Isn't this a public place?" said Wingo staring down at the beer he'd spilled on the floor.

"You give it a bad smell."

Wingo flexed his stance as his arms fell limber to his sides. His body English sharpened and his nasty words sounded off. "You know what? You sure are sassy for an old, gray nigger."

One second Wingo was vertical and the next he was horizontal. I may've seen the shotgun pistol slink under Old Man's coat. A stool toppled to the floor. The throwdown attracted a few lukewarm appraisals from the bar patrons. Balancing a food tray, our waitress, in mock concern, asked Wingo, "Did you slip on a mountain oyster, sir?"

"Wet spot. We'll rush him to a doctor," said Old Man.

"Please do. He stiffs me all the time," said the waitress.

Over-tipping her, I asked, "Can you brown bag our dinners?"

"Least I could do," replied the waitress.

Wingo stood up, shook off our hands, and put a napkin to his bloody nose. The barfly saw us escort Wingo outdoors to the sidewalk. The night lights just outside of Abe's door threw down a greenish incandescence on the Valiant's roof. My stomach churned, either for our brown-bagged dinners or in fear of Old Man taking Wingo apart limb by limb.

"I was out of line back in the bar. A little liquor—and, oops—my gums outpace my brain. You understand?" Wingo's hand rode up to shake ours. "No ill will, eh?"

"Wrong." Old Man's right uppercut clubbed Wingo's chin. He made a sickening whelp as he fell.

"Don't kill him," I said.

Old Man's glasses steamed up into blank discs as he gaped down at Wingo shaking his dazed head. "I ain't yet whittled him down to size."

"W-w-what do you want?" asked Wingo.

"Hear that, babe? The man now asks what this old, gray nigger wants before he really breaks bad."

I crouched at Wingo's ear. "We want the names of the men who drove that steel Saturday when Old Man's wife was killed."

"Don't say Dot and Woody because we know that's bullshit," said Old Man.

Wingo leaned his shaky forearms on the Valiant's hood for support and we gave him a few more moments. "They sub-hire drivers," he said at last.

"Names, Jack," said Old Man.

"I don't know. Dot and Woody always arrange it. Maybe Goines could tell you, but he's gone off, too."

"Why would Goines know? Where did he go?" asked Old Man.

"Goines is friends with Dot and Woody. And every October he hunts elk in Montana," replied Wingo.

"In the middle of my wife's homicide investigation?" said Old Man.

"That's all I know," said Wingo.

"Get the hell out of here. Go on," I told Wingo.

Wingo folded into an Olds and we watched his red taillights dissolve into the dark hills. I unwound the gauze turban from my head, then sidearmed it and the brown fedora into a trash receptacle.

"Fabulous. Another damn dead end," said Old Man.

CHAPTER THIRTEEN

———

Climbing out of Old Man's Valiant after we'd crested my little mountain, I felt a hot needle skewering my tender short ribs. I let that joy pass through me and formed a mental picture of Sheriff Greenleaf in his cruiser with its blackout grill, waiting and watching. I'd made a monkey out of Sheriff Greenleaf. As promised, he'd hold that rat cage in his jail for my next, more permanent stay. I hailed from a tank town and knew what it meant when the sheriff had a bone up his ass about you. No doubt about it, I'd shot to the top of Sheriff Greenleaf's shit list.

Old Man followed me to the cabin. I clacked my key in the door and, of course, the telephone rang. We went inside and I grabbed it up to hear Robert Gatlin's greeting. My toenails curled at hearing the grate of his too-effusive voice.

"Franklin, late this afternoon the warden at Bitterroot Prison contacted me," said Gatlin.

Old Man reclined into an armchair.

"So?" I asked.

"So they had a prison breakout. Rod Bellwether, your cousin, went over the back wall," said Gatlin.

"Shit." My gut reaction was Rod had gone mad.

"Their visitation logs indicate you saw Rod a little less than two months ago. They are very interested in speaking to you," said Gatlin.

"Yeah, from inside a damn jail cell," I said.

"I put them off by pointing out that you spent that morning in Scarab's court with me," said Gatlin.

I fought off an impending aneurysm. "This is bad."

"Very," said Gatlin. "My counsel? Pre-emptive strike. If you start driving now, you'll be at Bitterroot Prison tomorrow morning. Plead your case by saying you had nothing to do with Rod's ridiculous stunt and say nothing else. Be sincere. They'll listen."

"And suppose they don't?" I asked.

"Then, as I intimated to the warden, you will engage your high octane counsel," replied Gatlin. "Me."

I racked the phone and brooded. Half a million parolees feud and fuck in the Lower Forty-Eight while 7000 prison escapees also move amongst us free, law-abiding citizens. Reassuring statistics, huh? My cousin Rod Bellwether had now incremented that number to 7001. A desperate man resorted to desperate actions. How he'd managed to break out of a citadel like Bitterroot Prison baffled me. One prison inmate, an ATF agent once told me, had sandwiched himself into an old, fat mattress to be trucked out of the gate with the rubbish. Rod had at least that much imagination.

No sooner had we gotten back to my cabin than we turned around and headed back down the mountain. Old Man grumbled a lot en route to Scarab. We made ready for the trip. He stopped at the mini mart to top off his tank, check his fluids, pump air into three tires, and squeegee the bug brains off his windshields. Next he loped inside to purchase a quart of 10W30 SAE oil and DOT 3 brake fluid. To repair the rear window—busted out by the falling tree limb while we traveled up Hattie's mountain—we duct taped on a patch of clear plastic. I scrounged up my map and connected the roads from here to Bitterroot State Prison.

We flipped a nickel for it and Old Man took the helm first. Cruising by, we watched the lobster shift at the Chartreuse Ironworks chug at full bore. Exterior lights girded on lofty steel poles beamed down a midday brightness on a steel girder. Native American hardhats scurried about trying to belt it to a flatbed. Old Man glanced at Old Glory flapping aloft the microwave tower and sucked between his teeth as if in disgust.

We summitted the first mountain above ragtag Scarab and the night turned pitch dark. Our dash southeast on Route Six humped over the Allegheny Mountains dividing Virginia from West Virginia, one monolithic state before the War of Northern Aggression.

A damn good sport to make this trip with me, Old Man asked, "Are you and Rod friends?"

I was in brain fade from the advanced hour and abundant anxiety. "No. He's marginal kin on my mama's side. Both my folks died in a car pileup when I was a kid. This drunk CPO T-boned them. His blood alcohol was .27 with .09 the legal max. Christ, I wonder how he still drew breath. I was seven. But my memory is like it went down this morning. Anyway, I thought that all my relatives were dead. But that wasn't the case."

"Why is Rod on death row?" asked Old Man

"For shanking his old lady. Police lifted a fingerprint partial off the murder weapon, a Gerber knife. It matched Rod's. That was enough evidence to convince a jury."

"Does Rod have a brother? The same fingerprints, you know, can be inherited between siblings," said Old Man.

"No brother and there's a slim chance Rod didn't do it. I never met his wife Kathy and hadn't seen Rod since I was in elementary school. One evening, out of the blue, the telephone rings. It's Rod. 'Gee, hiya Frank,' he says. 'What's up with me? Oh I'm just scheduled for a lethal injection in two months. Can't you do something for me, cousin?' Now I ask you, who am I? Mister Clutch?"

Old Man's tone grew grave. "He's your only family, Frank."

I didn't curb my churlish temper. "Rod whipped the guilt trip on me but I'm not my brother's keeper. He's eked a slime trail to every rehab clinic and psych unit in the state."

Old Man made a sardonic grunt as we flew by the umpteenth sign warning of rock slides. "How much further?"

"Two hundred twenty miles, more or less. Better plan on driving for five hours. Right along dawn, we'll see the mountain lockup in all its raging glory," I replied.

"Bitterroot. That's a snazzy name. For a rat poison. What are we in for?"

I heard real worry gird Old Man's query. "Big and ugly. Sits on a peak. Max security prison. Rod is—I mean, was—doing hard time."

"What, no butterfly collecting? No badminton?" said Old Man.

"Funny man. I went only the once and it gave me ulcers. No weight yards. No GED classes. No recreation outside the cellblocks to play spades and dominoes. Inmates toe the line and do their time. Death row is nothing new in this state. I read where Virginia executed the first criminal in the nation. A poor settler by the name of Daniell Frank back in the day of Pocahontas and Captain John Smith. It occurs to me that Virginia hasn't come too far in its penal system."

"What did Daniell Frank do that was so reprehensible?" asked Old Man.

"He stole a cow." Frowning, I paused. "Check out the rearview mirror. See that pair of headlights?"

"Yep . . . I see 'em, babe . . . are they tailing us?"

"Never mind. They're signaling a left turn. Man, I'm hyped up."

"You're just playing it smart. Just staying alive. Reminds me of Nam. I mean there I was popping smoke at those damn zipper heads, not bucking for any big medals or promotions, see? Just staying alive. Survival of the fittest, yeah, a Darwinian trip. If a gook's bayonet ever slit my scalp, the medic would diaper the gash with gauze. Then we'd break station to go torch some more thatch-roofed hootches. But we had our jazz playing on AFVN radio."

"You listened to jazz in Vietnam?" I asked.

"Damn straight, we did. Basie, Ellington, Wes 'Big Thumb' Montgomery—"

"Hey, I remember my parents had a few Montgomery records," I said.

"—Oscar Peterson. And Jimmy Smith, too. The call letters were K-L-I-K and it broadcast from the base camp in Lai Khe." Old Man broke off and thrust up the bourbon bottle for a chug-a-lug. He wiped his mouth. His jaws clamped, joint knotting and unknotting.

"Besides listening to jazz, what else happened?" I asked.

"It rained. God, did it pour, babe. Gully-washers that could've capsized Noah on The Ark. Mud—red laterite, it was called—up to your cojones. The filth was rampant. Dogs and roosters and hogs wallowed in the alleys. Mama sans wore those black PJs and toted baskets balanced on idiot sticks. They'd squat and piss in the middle of oxcart paths. We'd pop the jungle cobras with our M-16s. It made for a great sport. Kids in those Uncle Ho sandals plugged fingers in their ears whenever the bombs fell and, man, did they ever rain down. 'When you fini Vietnam, GI?' they'd say. 'Any day now,' I'd tell them."

Old Man fell hushed.

"Go on," I said.

Old Man let his chin slump to his chest. The storytelling had deflated him. Then he laid his shiny eyes on me. A chill traveled up my spinal cord to my skull.

"I got a load of that rock star on FM radio played all the time. You know, the one drowned out by the ten-ton brother on the sax?"

"Springsteen? Bruce Springsteen?" I said.

"That'd be him. What a phony. One hundred percent bullshit. Khe Sahn. How'd Bruce know about it? How? Did he ever serve there? I doubt if he ever served a beer in Saigon."

"The lyric, if I recall it correctly, goes that he had a buddy or a brother at Khe Sahn."

"No matter, babe. It's still crap."

To switch topics, I said, "This road goes on forever."

Old Man laughed. "This won't take long. We'll go in quiet as the sun comes up, do what needs doing, and ease back out."

"Sounds like a plan." Something different bugged me. "Say, did Jan have any relatives?"

"No immediate family. Her folks died in a motel fire at Colonial Beach." Old Man pondered a bit. "We met at work. Jan still walked back in those days. The goddamn wheelchair came later. You know, thinking back on it now, skin color never caused me any trouble growing up in Scarab. Maybe that was because all men came up from the coal mines covered in black dust."

"Dr. Thomas puts Jan's murder as a hate crime," I said.

"Yeah well, hate cuts both ways. Mine now is for the Blue Cheer. I'll start my own hate cult to hate theirs," said Old Man.

I said nothing and soon took over the driving. Our talk had brought Old Man a little peace.

We invaded the outskirts of Mantis, Virginia, and Tuesday's orange sun bloodied the east horizon. We pushed on to the prison and Bitter-root's gray bulwark soon loomed up. Razor wire unfurled like a Slinky toy. I couldn't for the life of me visualize any prisoner scaling such a fence here. Maybe, and a big maybe at that, if the prisoner had a major death wish the possibility could exist.

Just where, I also ventured to wonder, would a graveyard sit on such a rockpile? All the hard-cases sent to Bitterroot aged and died like on a raisin ranch. The woodwork shop probably built coffins from locally milled pine planks. When a dead detainee left a vacancy, the bull guards shitcanned any personal effects. A trustee swabbed out the cell. Within a day, a new fish took up residence.

Old Man deposited my .44 in a fake heat vent. His Remington 20 vanished under the rear bench seat. If the bull guards shook down the Valiant, even if half-hearted, we were sunk.

"This is no white-collar country club, babe."

"Right. Like we agreed, Old Man, we're nothing here but nice and conciliatory. Our replies are 'yes sir,' 'no sir,' and the always safe, 'I don't know, sir'."

Old Man, discarding the swizzle stick he'd chewed in half, scoffed. "Hey, welcome to my life, babe."

At the central gate, two knot-jawed bull guards in navy blue uniforms flagged us down, their hand motions unhurried. They resembled a couple of knuckleheaded bouncers at a skanky strip club. I worked the window's handle and put on my best deferential face.

"We're here to see Warden Breeden," I said.

The bull guard's hard eyes, a snap-brim Stetson shading them, sized me up. "Who da' fuck is 'we'?"

"I'm Frank Johnson and he's Allen Maddox." Our drivers' licenses with photo I.D. corroborated my claims.

"You're kin to that snotty puke who busted out, ain't you?" A wolfish jaw jutted open to show gold inlays. "A sheep-fucking prick like you should roll up here wearing chains."

"The last time I voted, I was a free citizen," I said without adding the "sir" part. Things were already pretty fucked up for using any formalities.

The second bull guard lifted a walkie-talkie off his utility belt to announce us. The gregarious one crooked a finger at me. "I don't know you from dirt, but you're Bellwether's cousin. All the same crap. You'd be smart to shed that smart aleck attitude."

Fuck you, jack, my brain said, but I kept my trap shut.

"Heed my words, Johnson," added the bull guard.

The second bull guard hollered. "Wave them through. The warden has okayed it."

Old Man cuffed the column shift into first gear and tapped the gas. We poked into a satellite parking lot. The idling Blue Bird bus took us to the Admittance area. I was relieved to see through a sooty window that the bull guards weren't tearing apart the Valiant in search of contraband like our hidden weapons. So far, so good, I thought.

The registration process was methodical. Bull guards patted down our upper bodies and herded us through a metal detector. Old Man aced it like a pro. In contrast, my stiff body resisted every prod and command. Warden Breeden's penthouse wasn't an insufferable jaunt. In fact, we never left the Admin building. Three beer-gutted bull guards squeezed in with us. The nickel-plated elevator hummed up to Floor 3. The corridor we entered had sterile beige carpet and tall walls paneled in honey maple. A citrusy furniture polish conjured up an image of Martha Stewart, the ex-con. The sappy "Theme from Summer Place" playing on the Muzak was irksome enough to give me hives.

The thin girl wasn't a morning person. Her surly glare raked over us as she murmured into the telephone. She batted her lids at our door. We entered and behind an executive desk, I swear on my eyes, sat Saddam Hussein's body double, only he had more cheek warts. A finger pointed to stuffed chairs. We sat.

"Mr. Johnson?" he said over the desktop. "Warden Breeden."

My deadpan expression tried not to show boredom.

His nostrils widening, Warden Breeden gave Old Man the up-and-down. "You I don't need, so go grab some bench and have a Krispy Kreme or a mug of coffee because we might be here for a while."

We waited, and waited until Old Man withdrew. Warden Breeden seethed. "Johnson, your cornholed cousin has ruin't my perfect retention record and I am fucking disgruntled."

"Understandable." My sincerity was anything but heartfelt.

Warden Breeden opened a red ledger, fingered some papers, and tapped the ends straight. "You're a private license detective. Interesting. That must require some brains."

"Do you need a PI with a Mensa IQ? Or does it give you a hard prick baiting me?" I asked.

Warden Breeden's brutish glare riveted on me. "My K-9 Corp swept the outer fence perimeter. They got no scent hits so I ordered them to work the adjoining property, and guess what? Again, nothing, so I must conclude Bellwether didn't high-jump it over my fence. Well sir, I factor in other considerations. Like visitors. And Bellwether had one who I'm talking to now. My shift commander played me the tape of your conversation. Bellwether hired you to find his wife's killer."

"Hey, wait a second." The blinders exploded from my narrowing eyes. A peppy heartbeat sloughed off my lethargy, too. "We discussed some things in the broadest scope. No deal was brokered. No contract signed. No money ever exchanged hands."

"Bullshit. You consummated a deal in every sense of the word and it's on tape. I got you," said Warden Breeden.

"I don't know anything about Rod's getaway."

"Yeah? Well, I'm making you my whipping boy until this matter clears up. I keep super predators inside here and the last thing I want is to encourage their lying awake at night scheming up escape plans."

I shrugged. "Your director of prisons retired recently and got his gold watch. Maybe the inmates think the thumbscrews are loosening a bit."

"No thumbscrews ever loosen at Bitterroot," said Warden Breeden flat out. "My guards once threatened a sick-out and I sacked the whole bunch because there's a big labor pool here begging me for work."

"Rod's not dense." My hand made a circular motion around us. "That prickly wire can snag a man like a blowfly in a spider's web. Rod would stow away in the bowels of a garbage truck. Or shinny down a remote drainpipe. Or worm his way through ventilation ducts. He sure wouldn't try to scale a damn razor blade fence."

"How's it you know so much about what Rod would do?" asked Warden Breeden.

"I'm talking off the top of my head, strictly hypothetical," I replied.

Warden Breeden braced his salon-tanned hands on the green blotter. A braided gold chain necklace fell out of his open collar. "First, we compact our garbage three times before it ships out the gate. Second, this is what comes next for you. Since you purport to be Sam Spade, Johnson, bravo. Here's the seminal case of your illustrious career—go nab your client and cousin, Rod Bellwether."

"That's coercion," I said.

"That's why I'm letting you leave. Elsewise, I'm using this tape recording to issue a warrant for your arrest. It'll eventually get thrown out of court, no doubt, but in the interim you'll sweat a big hurt somewhere because I'm on a first name basis with every warden in Virginia. The sheriff in Mantis will keep an eye on you, too. Cool, huh?"

"Cool," I said stuffing the rage boiling on my insides. But I had to play along with Breeden if I was to stay out of a jail cell. Then I remembered something about Rod never sat too clear in my mind. "What was Rod's alibi for his wife's murder?"

Warden Breeden snorted out a breath and sneered. "Bellwether testified that he went off catfishing with a trotline to read the Sunday comics and sip Irish Rose Whiskey. Getting on a daytime drunk while his old lady bled out and died. Your cousin is a standup guy. A mealy-mouth liar, too. You got twenty-four hours, Johnson, or you get a butt-buddy and I know just the one, too. A former Sumo wrestler who's been in solitary for six months."

"Back off, warden. I'm gone," I said.

Later schlepping out of the Admin building behind Old Man to board the Blue Bird bus, I saw a poster advertising a law firm's services to new parolees.

LUKE & WARM, LLC
  Attorneys At Law
  •Bankruptcy
  •Divorce

- Custody
- Car/Accidents
- DWI/Criminal
- Immigration
- Wills
- Passports

Luke & Warm couldn't begin to measure up to Lawyer Robert Gatlin, the unorthodox champion of underdogs and now underachieving PIs.

CHAPTER FOURTEEN

I rousted Rod's father from a deep sleep. "H-h-huh? Franklin? Is that you, Frank Johnson? Hell, it ain't even six o'clock . . . where are my bifocals . . . uh, what's this on Rod you say? But first, where in the 'H' are you?"

"At some skeevy motel," I replied.

"You've visited Bitterroot?"

"I had a conversation with Warden Breeden himself a quarter of an hour ago."

"Fine. I advised Rod to stay cool, but he couldn't do it," said Mr. Bellwether.

"Given his options, you can't fault him too much."

"Don't I know it. Aw, double nuts. Rod wins an appeal, then screws it up by pulling this stunt."

"In his place, I'd have done the same thing."

"Yeah, yeah . . . the state cops have come and gone. . . careful what you blab . . . I think this phone is bugged . . . they tossed the same idiotic questions at me, stuff which I'd no answers for."

"Their fighting blood is up," I said.

"It's as if they hoped I told Rod to go for it. Yeah, me, the master-mind of his escape. Seventy-six years old and rooted to a wheelchair."

"Are any of Rod's cronies local?" I asked, not caring about the phone tap.

Shrewdness honed a cautious edge to Mr. Bellwether's counter-question. "Why your interest in my son, Franklin? Did the authorities put you on a string?"

"Sort of."

"Either you nail Rod or they nail you? Is that their dirty deal?"

"Yeah, except now I say fuck 'em."

"Good." Mr. Bellwether's yawn incited my own yawn. "That's some prison, ain't it? Out in the wildest ass-end of nowhere. I heard the cons say the wind gusts up there all night long."

"Mr. Bellwether, I'm nodding out. If anything breaks, you'll know it first."

I gave Old Man the receiver and he cradled it. "The poor guy's tied in knots over this," said Old Man.

"His wiretapped phone makes a lot of talking risky," I replied.

"Well, he got the gist."

Man, I must've run out of brains doing this. That's all I could think. Old Man put on a new TV crime drama and turned down the volume. A computer zipped through a database recording billions of thugs' fingerprints. Lady detectives with blockbuster breasts and sculpted asses were wonderstruck when a fingerprint match glittered on ithe monitor. Their big break was pure Hollywood hokum.

"We'll grab some sleep. Then catch this with a fresh set of eyes," I said.

"We'll catch hepatitis sleeping here. One detail bugs me. The most brilliant college-educated engineers designed Bitterroot to be escape-proof but in a matter of a few months, your country boy cousin figures a way out," said Old Man.

"Your point being?" The electric lamp winked out. Flat on the double bed, I sagged to its midpoint like settling into a shipboard hammock.

"Is Rod a ghost who walks through brick walls? Are you awake, babe?"

"Shush up. I gotta sleep," I said.

I saw a big stopwatch ticking away the twenty-four hours before the sheriff in Mantis threw out his dragnet to grab me. A not-too-pretty picture next formed of Warden Breeden and his sadistic Sumo wrestler. I drifted off to sleep hearing muffled man-sobs, although I didn't recall the sound until weeks later.

Old Man hollered. I snapped awake. Boom! Scrambling, I windmilled off the bed. I wrenched sock feet from the sheets, floundered behind the mattress, and fell to the floor. Moans preceded the *click-clank* of pumped big-gauge shotguns. My hand went up and I groped under the pillows, but my fingers grasped at nothing. My breaths sucked in, out hard.

"Polish him off."

"Got it. You go whack the nigger-lover."

"Here's my insurance round." Boom! Old Man didn't shriek. Was he dead? That scared me. Who were they? Breeden's bull guards? Rogue deputies? Rod's enemies? The Blue Cheer? The .44's grips filled my fingers on my next grope under the pillows. It was hammer time, now or never.

I bolted up from behind the bed and leveled the .44 down on a burly torso. Head shots were low percentage but one in the chest was a show-stopper. My finger pinched the trigger. The .44 flamed, its report lost in the chaos. Wide right. I ducked down.

"Skip looking in the crapper."

"Huh?"

"The nigger-lover just sank behind the bed."

I jerked up, my arms poled straight out. They threw up shotguns but not fast enough. I streamed two shots right, turned left, and clipped off two more rounds. Both bullet pairs hit in fatal strikes.

My wad expended, the .44 clicked on spent brass. Collapsing, a dying shooter's shotgun blast gouged out the ceiling plaster. Shock waves scattered. Frozen solid, I waited until the plaster dust settled a little. My ears whistled. My heartbeats hammered at my ribs. The damn telephone rang and, tilting the lamp shade, I yanked its plug from the wall jack.

"Christ!"

My hand clapped over my mouth. I dashed to the crapper and retched up half-digested booze. I came out. "Old Man? Do you hear me?" He sat slumped against the white rattan headboard. Dead as lead. One shotgun blast shredded his skull, another his abdomen. Blood graffitied the bleached white linen. He looked from the nose up like Chinese Takeout. The Remington 20, unfired, lay under his legs while his mangled swizzle stick and glasses lay on the nightstand. Bulling through the door, the shooters had gotten the drop on us and two shots had blown out Old Man's bulb before my bullets blew out theirs.

I stepped over the corpses and pitched into the queasy shakes. I knelt to check for pulses but both were dead as dolphins in a tuna net. Tears seared my eyes and streamed down my cheek stubble. Blowback cordite strangled my chokes and the new grief tasted bitter. A police siren began in the dark distance.

"Hey! What's all that ruckus?" the innkeeper blurted over. "I sicced the gun-cops on you. Hear me? You can't come barging in here busting up my place . . ."

I nudged Old Man's hip with as much tenderness as time allotted. I fished out a key ring (the Valiant's was well-worn brass), then fanned the wallets off our rude visitors. They'd get by okay—admittance to Hell was free. Should I stick by Old Man? What for? Sheer panic heaved up in my chest. I forced myself to calm down. Think, think. One thing stood out. I didn't stand a chance once I got bounced around the Mantis sheriff's interrogation cell. Sure, that was it. I'd make out a whole lot better freelancing on my own. Shriller police whistles spurred me to act.

I tucked the .44 in the top of my pants, snatched up the shotgun pistol with my bag, and plunged out the door. The Valiant backfired twice and kicked to life. I rolled away from our end unit. I glimpsed through a chink in the office's curtains the heavyset innkeeper loading a shotgun as his matronly wife yelled into the phone.

Curbside, I cocked an ear. Sirens howled on my right, the same direction I elected to turn. My headlights came up a second before the cruiser's red wig-wag lights vaunted into eyeshot. I was only another Tuesday morning commuter off early to work when the second and third responding units wailed by me in red blurs.

CHAPTER FIFTEEN

A hand-printed NO DUMPING sign was posted at a glutted landfill where I pulled off in the Valiant to steal a moment. My car's glare-proof mirrors remained clear and the fuel gauge's needle grazed the half-tank mark. Despite the busted rear window, the Valiant was in pretty good shape. The same couldn't be said about me. My forehead sank to rest on the steering wheel. Even with my eyes open, nightmarish images seethed: Jan Maddox twisting on a rope end; Old Man writhing in gore; Stinger rockets arcing by me.

My teeth clacked from a violent shudder as I wiped my sweaty forehead. Old Man still rode with me. His cigarettes and strawberry Afro Sheen filled the car with his smells. As if in tribute to Old Man, Charley Pride's 'Kiss An Angel Good Morning' struck up on the radio. I sat awhile, listening. Next up, a bluegrass standard by Red Smiley, Don Reno, and the Tennessee Cut-Ups with Reno's crisp banjo riffs and Smiley's mellow whiskey vocals.

I fell into a heavy, hard funk. Here I had moved to a strange mountain and Old Man had befriended me. Then I lost that irreplaceable friend through my own ineptness. For penance, I was left with my sorry, no-account self to carry on the fight. Why hadn't we taken the necessary precautions and stood guard? Too tired to think straight?

The Del McCoury Band, taking the microphone, did the old Flatt & Scruggs anthem, 'Rolling In My Sweet Baby's Arms'. However, it let me down because no music could bring me up. I dinked out the .44's cartridge empties, seated their brass replacements, and slid the gun over the dashboard. Hugging myself, I swayed back and forth, my shoulders bouncing off the seat's back. Oh Lord, I was in this shit too deep, way too deep. The window now down, the balsamic scented air infused me with hope.

First things first, I coached myself. The intruders. Neither rang a bell with me. I'd derived no satisfaction in killing them either. Some higher-up had sent them but who was he? Cold rage said go bang on some doors. Bust them down.

Two fronts meant two wars, one in Scarab and the newest here in Mantis, Virginia. The conversation about home I'd had with Old Man coming over the mountains reminded me of friends who'd walk through fire with you. Who did I know like that? Who'd help me? My fists pounded the dashboard. I knew.

Old Man's cell phone was in the glove compartment. I raised a signal and jabbed in Gerald Peyton's home number from memory. I ticked off six rings. Disappointed, I was set to cancel the signal but a gruff snarl stopped me.

"Gerald Peyton, Bounty Hunter Extraordinaire."

To which, I said my name.

"Frank! What's up?"

"I've got a little predicament." I gave him the short version, omitting Old Man's fatality only because my emotions were still raw over it.

"A little predicament? More like your nuts are in the garbage disposal. Again. Unreal." I could detect excitement heating Gerald's words. "Where is this fucking Mantis? Never mind, I'll map quest it. Chet's upstate bulldozing a goddamn golf course. That's his loss, not mine. You sit tight, bud. I'll buzz down in a few hours. Whatever you do, don't start it without me."

"Thanks, Gerald. Once you hit town, look for a foreign car dealership on the main drag across from an auto repair shop. I'll be hanging loose in the new cars."

"Communication understood. Later."

I felt better. I plundered my pockets for a piece of rock candy and the wallets fell out. Just who had I dispatched to Satan's doorstep? I peeled out thirteen dollars from the slender billfold stitched together from pigskin. A West Virginia driver's license gave the unlikely alias of Alfred Doe. Glossies of a beaming blonde right proud of her shaved beaver spilled from an inner compartment.

Having a fancier feel (ostrich or morocco leather?), the second wallet gave up three $100 bills and a gold toothpick. This stud didn't pack nudies, only an unused Trojan Latex Condom and three Viagra vitamins. His driver's license supplied the name Wolfgang Doe.

How about that? Tuesday morning in Mantis, Virginia, I'd offed the infamous Doe brothers for $313 and a few rubbers. Wait, what was this? My thumbs traced walking fish logos stamped into the leather on the rear flap's corner to both wallets. The same logo had appeared on the T-shirts at the mini mart and scrawled on the fire tower. The Blue Cheer. Twice was a coincidence. Thrice was an enigma and I hated enigmas.

By now the Mantis deputies had cordoned off the motel room, tying up yellow crime scene tape. In short order, the extracted murder slugs would match Old Man's registered .44. The trick was not to do time for killing two low rents. Old Man wouldn't approve. So, I had to ditch the .44 and the wallets.

I drove up a dirt road branching left. Slim and bumpy, it skirted a disused power plant shaded by elms. I neared a two-room shanty tarpapered in fake bricks where underneath a mulberry tree, a shapely girl with lank, palomino yellow hair sat in a slat-back chair. An older lady clad in a much-patched brown sack dress worked a pair of scissors and a shank of yellow hair fell to the leaves.

I pulled over and hand-motioned through the car window. Both pigeon-toed ladies came over to the passenger side.

"Any old mines hereabouts?" I asked them.

Her twang almost an Emerald Isle brogue, the girl asked, "Why, are you a forty-niner?"

"Huh?"

The older lady elaborated. "You looking for gold?"

"No. I'm looking for old coal mines, not gold," I said.

"You've lost a coal mine?" asked the girl.

"No."

"Keep on straight the way you are. I expect you'll drive across what you're after," said the older lady.

"Thanks, ma'am."

The objective, as my overheated brain saw it, was to worm my way far back up in the sticks. I passed by the remnants of a pear orchard and a stone fence but I knew kids would play in those places. Moving on, I prowled through a stand of American hornbeams. Timbering and strip-mining vehicles had carved these ruts decades ago and sure enough my sight soon alighted on an old coal tipple and donkey engine where I stopped. Landmarks included a silo for storing mined coal, a sand house for abrading steel tracks that the trolleys made hot and slick, and a machine shop for mechanical fix-its.

The mine's portal yawned nearby. A nameless creek was an ulcer oozing a yellow-red-blue slurry. OSHA and EPA would never bring their pollution crusades this far. Nowadays Big Coal didn't mine the ground but decapitated mountaintops to scoop out their precious ore. "Shoot and shove," they called it but outraged environmentalists called it "rape." Waste products left behind created the slurry I now saw.

I hopped out of the Valiant, hiked a short piece, and scared up a rabbit. I saw WARNING and NO TRESPASSING signs posted. Coal companies sometimes bulldozed up earth to block the mine's mouth and discourage curious kids. Companies preserved enough of a crack for the bull bats and whippoorwills to fly in and out. Wire mesh and barred gates also capped a mine's entry, but this one featured none of those impediments.

I stepped over a bunch of coal hods and looked inside. The long wall roofing bolts securing the timbers appeared sturdy enough. Beautiful. My flashlight still lay in the glove compartment. Undaunted, I prowled into the mine's dank murk. Phew. A bedpan stink hit me. I endured it as best I could and my boots crunched on the rubble between the wood ties.

Darkness swarmed in on me. I dared not close my eyes or I'd disappear forever. My ears stepped up their play. One more pace and I stopped when a few pebbles I'd kicked fell down a shaft. They plinked into a liquid. It sounded deep. I tossed in the .44 and wallets and with arms outstretched hurried back to safe daylight and the Valiant.

The shotgun pistol beneath the Valiant's rear bench seat was in as good as any concealment. A glass flask was also stuck fast under the coil springs. Old Man had kept a rainy day reserve. Whiffs from its unscrewed cap wanted to seduce me, but I resisted. My interest wandered to a box of 20-gauge shells. I fidgeted with the shotgun pistol's clip and knob until a new shell poked into its breech, then I got out. I aimed at a dangling pinecone. I thumbed off the tang-mounted safety and pressed the trigger. Boom! The recoil almost clobbered me in the head and, worse, I overshot my target. Several trials obtaining the same dismal results proved to me that this weapon in my hands was a catastrophe.

I wheeled the Valiant around and retraced my route out to the paved road warming in the morning. By drifting into Mantis from this side, I circumvented the murder scene at the motel. Old Man had poked into its lobby to register us and the innkeeper hadn't seen the Valiant or me last night, but why taunt the Fates by going that way?

I occluded myself in the overcrowded car sales lot and kept my sightlines to the highway unimpeded. I browsed to kill time until Gerald arrived. Sticker shock was like waking up to hostile shotguns fired under your nose. Rainbow color banners flapped around me. I admired the new sporty compacts. One model got an extra nod of approval because it ran a hybrid motor using electric and gasoline power. The bigger models turned me off.

Just that instant, stuck here checking out all of these new cars pissed me off. My best friend by now lay on a morgue slab and here I was comparison shopping. Balling my hands into shaking fists, I saw Old Man's blasted-up body bleeding out in that hole-in-the-wall motel room. My heart pounded icy-cold fear through me. Warden Breeden and the Mantis sheriff had their tentacles out to snare me. But I couldn't take flight until Gerald had my back. My head tipped in the direction of the road.

The salesman's shoulders hunched in his blue parka. "Are you in the market?"

My wave was as curt as my voice. "You'd be wasting your time following me. The way I like to work is kick the tires and make up my own mind. Given enough time, I'll take a shine to one of these beauties. Do you have a business card?"

"Fair enough, sir." The salesman smiled while a hand darted inside the parka.

I glanced at the card he slapped into my palm. "Can you give me, say, twenty minutes, Mr. Vogel?"

"You betcha," he said. "And it's Chuck. I have everything on this lot, starting with just your basic key and heater. Now that model your hand rests on is very popular. There's the misconception its engine bogs down on hills. Nothing could be further from the truth. I zip mine up and down Hawksbill Peak daily with plenty of pep. Did you bring me something in trade?"

"Not with me. The wife dropped me off and went shopping for a new sewing machine," I lied.

"Well, take all the time you need. If you get cold out here, pop on inside. The coffee's fresh perked and there's doughnuts, too. I've got tons of literature. We'll go test drive one and turn some folks' heads, won't we?"

"Bet on it, Chuck."

Winking, Chuck fired imaginary pistols at me as I ambled to the front row. The highway thrummed. Working stiffs were off to regular jobs with regular hours for steady pay. I envied them while nosing the Valiant between two boxy minivans, and climbed out. I went around and studied a few more window stickers. Meantime, the dealership sprang to life. "Chuck Vogel," was paged over the PA system. A bald mechanic humped up the bay doors, a trouble ticket pinched in his teeth. 8:36 a.m. and Gerald was still on the march.

Seen out the corner of my eye, I then locked on a deputy in her tan-and-white cruiser. But her speed held steady. I ducked and rapped on a front grille while Chuck's gaze from inside the showroom followed my every move. Why I'd picked this vantage point was now a puzzle to me. I forced myself to read what each new car sticker said, my lips moving to pronounce each word.

By and by, a patriotic red, white, and blue Mack Bulldog hit its air brakes: *pfffssst*. Its right directional blinked. Yellow letters on the purple door read: "Buddy Row's Transport." The Mack rolled to a stop where a passenger debarked. He high-fived the gear-jammer, hollering "Thanks, Buddy!" over the idling diesel engine. I felt a pang of new hope.

Gerald Peyton stumbled a step or two as if on cramped leg muscles. His dusky profile held gold granny glasses that shielded molten blue eyes. He carried himself with a cocky self-assurance some who didn't know him found off-putting and even arrogant. Kinky hair fell in Jheri curls down his moose neck and at six feet six, he broke the scales at 300-plus pounds. Watching him, I made an insightful comparison. Where Old Man was reflective and meticulous, Gerald seemed more impulsive and reactive.

Arms closing in, Gerald bearhugged me. "What's buzzin' cuzzin'?"

I wheezed after he released me—no ribs or sternum cracked. "Where's your car?" I asked.

"In the shop. I hitched a ride at the truck stop and now I'm here." Gerald stuck on a grin. "Let's rock. Any fucking Hum-Vees on this car lot we can hotwire?"

CHAPTER SIXTEEN

After I outlined for Gerald all the events from Friday night until now, he asked, "All the prison warden has on you is this tape of your visit with Rod?"

I went right at Route Six, a hilly stroll from the outskirts of Mantis, Virginia, to Scarab and pinned the gas to the floor. "Warden Breeden told me to find Rod. Or else. That threat made inside the prison scared me. That's why I took off from the motel."

"How's that?" asked Gerald.

"The Mantis sheriff is buddy-buddy with Warden Breeden. Both want a piece of me," I replied.

"Gatlin is the legal wiz, but I'd say this warden is blowing smoke." Gerald undid the red tab on the cellophane wrap for a pack of cigarettes. "The tape is illegal and inadmissible, for starters. Any objection if I poison my lungs?"

"Only if I can bum a cigarette, too. Yeah, a threatening call from Gatlin might pry the warden and sheriff off my butt. But Rod is on his own. He's probably beating it for Toronto or Tijuana. Canada is the smarter bet. It's closer."

"Sure. Rod's a big boy who can take care of himself." We both lit up. Gerald took a puff and flicked cigarette ash into an empty beer can. "Be straight up with me, Frank. What made you decide to leave Pelham?"

I had a prefabricated reason. "Because I retired. Private detectives today have it tough. Ex-MPs and retired cops jump into the game every day. Competition is cutthroat. Even Gatlin throwing me some business couldn't keep me solvent."

"PIs now are mostly computer geeks," said Gerald.

"They can be. For me, though, this one case took the cake."

A pleased smile came to Gerald's face. He liked hearing offbeat, off-color stories. "Lay it on me," he said.

"One Monday morning this bubba comes moping into the office with a sad face that would make you cry for your mama. His old lady had bagged her job, packed her Samsonite, and skipped off with a tire salesman. What he needed, Bubba said, was the goods on her promiscuity to sue for a divorce."

"Teed off, was he?" said Gerald.

"Big time. As a rule, I pass on these peeping tom cases. But being stone broke, I couldn't be too picky. This case struck me as solid, low risk. Besides, Bubba's tale of woe got to me."

Gerald broke in. "His story sounds fishy."

"Something did smell bad. That's why I gave it some further thought. Why else might Bubba like to know his wife's whereabouts? I played it safe, contacted an ER nurse I knew and, yep, Bubba had twice sent in his wife for a fractured jaw and concussion. In view of that, I refunded his deposit and voided our contract."

"Duty can get dirty. The same is true for a bail bond enforcer but you know how the bills pile up. You can't just up and quit," said Gerald.

"Hell, I should've stuck by our motel room with Old Man. I feel like a real shit for leaving him," I said.

"You did good, Frank. Let the local cops run the crime scene. Physical evidence will speak for itself. Later, with Gatlin, you can plead self-defense and say your life was in imminent danger or some shit. Your arrest now will only spur the cops' rush to judgment. Your story will jibe with what their investigation turns up."

"Old Man deserves to be buried next to Jan," I said next.

"When the M.E. releases his body, we'll be there on his behalf to accept it. For the time being, we keep our shit tight in Scarab," said Gerald.

"You figure those shooters for pros?" I asked.

Gerald would know. His résumé showed seven years as a fugitive recovery agent and a talented one at that. The last time I checked his tote board, he had nailed over two hundred skip captures. Grueling. More than 33,000 fools post bond every year in the United States, only to fail to show on their court date. A bench warrant is issued for their arrest and the chase is on. History isn't on their side. Specialists tracing back to Wyatt Earp, Bat Masterson, and Doc Holliday fix this problem. If I went on the lam, I'd drop fast into a vast sea of anonymous, average faces, say, in Detroit or Albany. Most skips, however, predictably flee to California and Florida for sun, surf, broads, and booze. Dream on, because big trouble always stalks them.

Gerald spoke. "They tracked you from Scarab to Mantis. Since you didn't make them, I'd say both were cunning and experienced. A tail job on a rural highway at night isn't easy. Headlights can warn your quarry even if you use tricks like varying your road speeds. Who knew your destination?"

I blanched. "No one else that I know of, but the wallets I lifted off our two attackers had the Blue Cheer's symbol stamped on them."

"What the fuck is a Blue Cheer?" asked Gerald.

"Like I told you, the slogan was on those T-shirts sold at the mini mart. A late 1960s psychedelic rock band in Haight-Ashbury adopted the name from a strain of LSD. In this case, I believe it's a secret hate cult headquartered somewhere around Scarab."

Gerald, staring at the roadway, asked, "Do you finger them as the Maddoxes' killers?"

"Very likely."

Gerald extinguished the cigarette butt and flipped it out the wing vent. "Mr. Gatlin came to West Virginia to bond you out of jail. What was up with that shit?" He stroked his lips with a Chapstick tube.

"A deputy, Goines by name, jailed me without cause." I gestured to my head. "This black and blue came from his headache stick."

"Do any decent folks live in this Podunk?" asked Gerald.

"At least one does. Dr. Thomas, the town's undertaker." A red-tailed hawk hulked on a telephone wire. Any road pizza became its gourmet dinner. Even birds of prey were too lazy to hunt down vermin anymore. They just waited for cars like our Valiant to run over their meals. "Listen, since Chet is out of touch working construction, if we need reinforcements, who can we tap? Who's left? Bertie?"

Bertie was Gerald's girlfriend.

"No. She's at a damn Texas Rangers barbecue with her dad in Dallas. It's just you and me but we got it together."

For an interval, I felt all at sea, then said, "Dr. Thomas is expecting Old Man and me to be at Jan's autopsy at five o'clock."

Gerald rummaged through his duffel bag before a Browning 9 mil flopped into my lap. "Here, stick this in your belt, Frank. If anybody gives you more shit, use it. Stay safe. Now, let's set our stories straight about Old Man, then it's on to the morgue."

The mid-afternoon sun gleamed on THOMAS & SONS, FUNERAL HOME written in yellow letters on a green sign. Gerald, his eyes sweeping to and fro, had curled up a lip at the Chartreuse Ironworks and the village of Scarab thrilled him about as much, too. Sheriff Greenleaf's reelection campaign posters had appeared overnight on telephone poles, trash receptacles, and stucco pillars. Patriotic red, white, and blue ribbons were tied around trees and the Hubcap Madonna's display racks. Pedestrians—a petite mother pushing a baby stroller and two old men telling lies in the shade—never saw me drive by in Old Man's Valiant. I breathed easier. Maybe the news of what happened to us in Mantis hadn't reached here yet.

"Where is our righteous sheriff's office?" asked Gerald.

"Down the block. My place is over a few ridges," I said.

Gerald brandished Old Man's rainy day bottle and tipped it at me.

"Not unless you also partake," I said.

"Let it roll." Gerald took the eye-opener, not his first of the day. I did likewise. Thus fortified, we ambled from the Valiant to the morgue. A girl sat Buddha-like on a cedar bench beside a terra-cotta urn ablaze with gold zinnias. Her Converses were a mismatched blue and red and a Merit smoldered between her fingers. Jumbo hospital scrubs fell loose from her arms and legs in comical folds. Her stare bypassed me to eye-fuck Gerald. Like many of the ladies, she couldn't help but be smitten.

"You here for the Maddox autopsy?" she asked us.

Gerald ran his fingers through his ringlets. "Don't say we're too late."

"Don't sweat it. Doc Thomas is unloading the autoclave. If you hurry on in, he'll fix you up. I'm Eva, by the way. You've proper ID, I hope? This isn't open to the public."

My PI license and Gerald's bail enforcer license satisfied Eva. Despite her tight-ass caution, I liked her instantly.

"A couple more puffs and I'll be in, too. Secondhand smoke doesn't bother our clientele, but Doc carps about it. The damn radon in that basement will be the death of us first. Well, well. Make welcome for our sheriff." Following Eva's glance, I couldn't imagine more unwelcome company.

A cruiser double-parked beside a Pontiac Firebird displaying "Just Married!" soaped on its rear windshield. No doubt the newlyweds weren't off anywhere soon. Sheriff Greenleaf's glare collided with ours. He climbed from his cruiser and primped at a side mirror adjusting his sidearm and dress hat's tilt. Black Oxfords brought him over to us through the sultry October late afternoon.

"Johnson, why are you here?" asked Sheriff Greenleaf.

"Got to be somewhere."

"Where's Old Man?"

I coughed on the hot bile flushing into my throat. "He stayed behind. Sheriff, say hello to Gerald Peyton, a hunting pal."

Spitting, Sheriff Greenleaf notched his nuts. "Watch that you don't get your pecker shot to shit. What's your line, Peyton?"

"I'm a water witch," replied Gerald.

"Sure you are." Sheriff Greenleaf sniffed. "You've also been drinking."

"Mouthwash," said Gerald.

"Ha-ha. Are you kindergartners ready for fun and games?" Sheriff Greenleaf's smirk slid from Gerald to me, back to Gerald. Eva, embarrassed, gave a small laugh.

Gerald grinned. "The dead don't bite too bad."

"You said a mouthful. Let's go do it," said Sheriff Greenleaf.

Recycled air immersed us clomping down the steps into the state-of-the-art morgue no doubt funded by Dr. Thomas' family money. He also probably bought the homicide kit made of lizard skin the deputies had brought to the A-frame the day Jan had died. Eva steered us down a catacomb passage into a changing room where my nostrils flared at the stench.

"That odor, gentlemen, is tissue preservative, astringent, and mortal flesh undergoing decay. You better get used to it," said Eva.

"I'll be gol-danged. Who all bought ringside tickets, Eva?" Dr. Thomas, in a floppy green gown, waddled up to us. His iron-gray hair was tousled, his hazel eyes bleary. He clapped a hand in mine. He bade Gerald welcome but didn't acknowledge Sheriff Greenleaf's slight nod.

"Where's Old Man?" asked Dr. Thomas.

"We left him with some army buddies. He's still pretty ripped up inside," I replied, finessing this lie better than the first time.

"Poor guy." Dr. Thomas undid a metal locker. "You better stretch into these bibs."

"It can get gory," said Sheriff Greenleaf as if we didn't already know.

"Here, take procedural notes." Dr. Thomas shoved a yellow legal pad into Sheriff Greenleaf's paunch. "5:10 PM. Five attendees. Eva, yourself, and me. Frank Johnson and Gerald Peyton are guest-witnesses."

"Guests? Authorized by whom?" asked Sheriff Greenleaf.

"By me," said Dr. Thomas.

I put on the bibs over my street clothes and Dr. Thomas led me aside by the elbow. "This isn't pretty, Frank . . . have you ever field dressed a buck or a bear maybe? . . . yeah, good, I reckoned as much . . . uh, the same deal with Gerald? . . . right-oh, then you'll do okay."

"Do I keep an eye on Eva?" I asked, for lack of anything more intelligent to say.

"Believe it or not, the dolls are less squeamish than the guys down here," said Dr. Thomas.

The glass-walled suite only just accommodated us. Dr. Thomas and Eva fitted on plastic aprons and facial splash shields as an ampoule of wintergreen oil circulated. I dibbed on a bandito mustache and handed the ampoule to Gerald. He abstained as did Sheriff Greenleaf. It was a hell of a time to get into a pissing contest but I kept silent.

Eva thumb-tapped a thermometer at the cadaver cooler's handle. "Thirty-eight degrees Fahrenheit," she reported. Numb, I thought. Just like me. She dragged the blue polyethylene body bag out by its side handles off the cooler's storage shelf onto the cart, reminding me of how a LPN moves a hospital patient in bed. Eva handled herself as a capable, bright autopsy assistant who kept all the balls in the air.

Our package on the cart then drew alongside the autopsy table. Eva toe-locked the casters and again moved the body bag that she unzipped down the center. The earthly remains of Jan Maddox emerged from the grungy bed sheets.

"Ugh! Yech!" Recoiling, Sheriff Greenleaf, forearms raised, toppled into the autoclave.

"Too much for you, is it?" asked Gerald.

Sheriff Greenleaf, eyes slitting, bridled. "Hands off me, Peyton."

"Bed sheets from the crime scene are contaminated by that environment. In this case, however, I understand and commend Frank's act of mercy for Old Man," said Dr. Thomas.

"Well, sir, I don't. Johnson, by butting in, you interfered with a homicide investigation. I could bust you for hindering prosecution," said Sheriff Greenleaf.

Dr. Thomas switched on the autopsy saw, its blade cutting at a fierce speed. "If that should ever come to pass, sheriff, I'll lop off all your fingers. Maybe more."

Eva giggled under her plastic shield.

Sheriff Greenleaf's lips pressed into a gash. "Quit your clowning and get on with it. I'm way past due back at the office. Phew. Where's that damn wintergreen? Doesn't OSHA require respirators in here?"

"A naked nose helps me diagnose. I guess I'm immune to discomfiting odors," said Dr. Thomas.

"You can eject any time, sheriff," said Gerald.

Sheriff Greenleaf glared at him. "Maybe I'll make you eject right now."

"You're welcome to try," said Gerald.

"Fair warning. Watch yourself, Peyton," said Sheriff Greenleaf.

The epoxy sealed floor had two drains. My armpits leaked cold, nervous sweat. Lists and charts on white-tiled walls gave out gruesome statistics. I gawked at a sponge bowl under a spigot for washing off human organs and gory tools. A ficus plant withered in a clay pot under a wall clock running five minutes fast.

Dr. Thomas snapped on a second pair of gloves. "Some son of a bitch did you a hard, tough knock, darling. But who was it? Now, talk to me."

Running tap water gurgled like in guppy tanks at a pet store. My curious glance saw the bottom steel tray flushing whatever drained down from the autopsy table. Wiping her brow with a sleeve, Eva read off the ankle tag, "Jan Maddox is the deceased's name. J-A-N. M-A-D-D-O-X." She dug into Jan's drawstring shoulder bag. "The ID is confirmed by the deceased's driver's license."

"Yep, I'm with you," said Sheriff Greenleaf, after a cough.

"Subject exhibits normal lividity throughout except for more maroon below the knees which is typical for hanging victims." Dr. Thomas put a stethoscope on Jan's temple and fitted in his ear bits. "No cardiac activity," he said. Only Sheriff Greenleaf reacted by laughing. Doctor Thomas taped the body's length and announced, "Sixty inches on the button."

A bread knife, serrated forceps, pruning shears, scalpels, and what I took to be retractors lay on a cork-topped table. All the instruments gleamed. A Hagedorn needle with an oversized eye, pack thread, and fiber fill were for the final stitch job closing up the corpse. Eva straightened the shiny instruments. Dr. Thomas peeled away the first fold of bed linen to unveil Jan's nudity, a puffy, green inertness. Gerald pivoted Sheriff Greenleaf around on his heels.

"Eva requests some privacy," he said.

Sheriff Greenleaf glowered at Gerald, a bright truculence beading his eyes. "I've had a bellyful of your shit. Touch me again and I'll deck you."

"Touch him," I sidemouthed to Gerald. "I dare you."

"Patience, grasshopper," said Gerald.

When we revolved back around, white hospital towels covered Jan's top and bottom sex. Humming, Eva snipped rubber bands securing the paper bags to Jan's wrists and ankles. Sheriff Greenleaf consulted a shaky wrist, scribbled down the hour to extend his timeline of autopsy events. Dr. Thomas muttered into the handheld recorder.

"Eva, go fetch me a rape kit, please." Dr. Thomas climbed up on a stool and leaned over to focus his 35mm camera.

"Say cheese," said Sheriff Greenleaf. Nobody laughed.

"No vaginal tearing. No visible evidence of sexual assault," Dr. Thomas spoke into his handheld recorder. "Gerald, please help Eva."

"No problem." They rotated the corpse. Bolder bruises and wounds on Jan's upper legs showed more barbaric abuse.

"Odd . . . what's this?" puzzled Dr. Thomas. He withdrew a glass vial lodged inside of Jan's semi-cloaked buttocks. He unsealed and tweezed out a scrolled-up slip of green paper. We huddled over his shoulders. "The Blue Cheer," he read aloud.

My heart took flight. "The Blue Cheer," Gerald and I said together.

"Treat that as physical evidence. I'll voucher it," said Sheriff Green-leaf.

Dr. Thomas laid it aside, ignored Sheriff Greenleaf, and rapped the scalpel's butt on the steel table. "Gentlemen, dissection commences. Last call for queasy stomachs to vacate." Eva mock-tooted a Harpo's bulb horn.

Sheriff Greenleaf, forehead veins bridging up, growled his words. "Get on with it."

Wielding a scalpel, Eva pierced the skin and a pitiful small animal noise escaped from Sheriff Greenleaf's mouth. She sliced a precise arc from the left shoulder to end just millimeters shy of the right one.

"Eva could do this procedure asleep," said Dr. Thomas.

Brackish blood leached up along the incision. Eva cut at the semi-circle's base downward over the sternum with a left curvature to detour at the navel and complete the Y-incision. Sheriff Greenleaf coughed. Eva screwed on a new blade, twirled the scalpel to puncture Jan's chin, and sliced parallel to the windpipe down from the chin and throat to chest.

"We'll examine Jan's strangulation point," said Dr. Thomas by way of explanation.

"Chaw of chewing tobacco?" Gerald asked Sheriff Greenleaf. "A plug of Red Man might settle your nerves."

Eva pinched up the bottom corner near the navel and dragged up a fibroid flap of flesh to reveal pink tissue and yellowish fat. Too engrossed, I neglected to watch Sheriff Greenleaf. He swooned and collapsed at our feet.

Gerald squinted down in disbelief. "You got any ammonia salts, Doc? Boy, he sure showed his backside."

Dr. Thomas gazed over. "We can't halt in mid-procedure. Just leave Sheriff Greenleaf where he can't do any harm to us or himself."

Eva stole over an impish glance. "First I've seen anybody take a dive," she said.

CHAPTER SEVENTEEN

———

Gerald and I didn't exactly kowtow but we weren't above kissing ass in Sheriff Greenleaf's inner sanctum where the news about Old Man's murder had hit the fan. On top at that, Sheriff Greenleaf knew about Rod's prison escape and our trip to Mantis. His livid face contorted. Two deputies were guarding us. Our wrists and ankles were uncuffed but that was subject to change since Sheriff Greenleaf spoiled for the slightest excuse to arrest us and throw us in jail.

"Old Man left us to hook up with an army buddy at a bar. A couple of hours later, Gerald and I scooted back in Old Man's car," I said again.

Sheriff Greenleaf wagged a porky finger at Gerald. "Which bar?"

"Old Man didn't specify, did he, Frank?"

"Nope, he never did." I filed my thumbnail on the brass nail head trim.

"After leaving the bar, where did Old Man and this mystery army buddy go?" asked Sheriff Greenleaf.

"The Vietnam War Memorial up in Washington, D.C. Three friends who'd served with them in Nam are on that wall," I replied.

"Bull!" said Sheriff Greenleaf.

I glanced at Gerald. "Sheriff Greenleaf doubts Old Man's patriotism."

"Try to make allowances for narrow-mindedness," said Gerald.

Sheriff Greenleaf's chin jutted forward a quarter inch and his lips creased. "Nope sir, that ain't it. Your honesty is what I doubt. Johnson, you were in that motel room. Old Man was tagged by a twelve gauge. Twice. Two other men were found dead. Three, all counted. At point blank range. I want to know who unloaded on them and why."

I feigned shock, but the grief was authentic. "I was never in a motel. Maybe it was his army buddy who took off. I just don't know, sheriff."

"Bullshit."

Looking bored, Gerald weighed in. "Frank is on his uppers over this crap. Are we finished here?"

Sheriff Greenleaf bucked up from his chair. "Hell no, I'm not done! You're both lying."

"Hey, that's it. No more cooperation. If you ain't pinching us, we're out of here. Otherwise, I buzz Mr. Gatlin and we wait. Which is it, sheriff?" Gerald slid a cell phone from his belt.

The heroic deputy on our right decided to lunge for the cell phone. Gerald grabbed the deputy's wrist and twisted down hard. Emitting meek squeals, the deputy was a second from spending a lengthy stint in Intensive Care. His counterpart groped at his holster.

Disgusted, Sheriff Greenleaf waved off both his deputies. Then he turned back to me. "I've got my eye on you. Don't leave town."

"Is Dr. Thomas the only one making progress on the Jan Maddox homicide?" I asked.

"That's my jurisdiction, Johnson. Don't horn in on it. Now both of you clear out of my station house."

Outside on the dark street, Gerald spat. "You're right. The sheriff is a real shitbird. Where to now?"

"The post office," I replied.

We entered the lobby and Betty Maddox worked behind the beaver-board counter sorting through a canvas bin of envelopes and packets. Did she live at the post office? Agony over her cousin's death scarred her face in harsh lines that bracketed her taut lips. In a flash, I relived the moment I'd pocketed Old Man's dollar for taking on his case. Now it was a shame stick to beat myself with. I was a sorry excuse for a PI. I hadn't nailed his wife's murderer and only gotten my client killed. I toyed with the idea of new career options. My marketable skills quali-fied me for what kind of job? A flagman on an asphalt crew? Scrubbing pigeon droppings off park statues?

"March yourselves through that turnstile," said Betty. "This is awful. Tragic." We paraded in. Her posture stiffened as her moist, olive-black eyes fixed on me. "Old Man left here yesterday afternoon with you. Where you were bound, who knows? Boys will be boys even at Old Man's age, I reckon. You drove his Valiant back to town. The rear window was busted out and Old Man wasn't with you." Her voice rose an octave. "I know damn well you both were in that motel room. Now, for God's sake, please tell me what happened."

I summarized why we'd gone to Mantis, Virginia, how the fiasco at the motel had unfolded, and concluded by saying, "We'd no chance to muster a defense. Old Man diverted them long enough for me to take them out but I didn't stick around. Cops were streaming in. I apologize for leaving him but Old Man was dead."

"Cops are crooked the world over," said Betty with sympathy. "I've already arranged with the authorities to transport his body back to Scarab." She surveyed Gerald, approved of what she saw, and put out her hand. "Betty Maddox, Old Man's cousin."

"Gerald Peyton, ma'am. Deepest sorrows for your loss. I never knew Old Man, but if he was a friend of Frank's, then he was a friend of mine, too." They shook hands and exchanged soulful glances.

Betty's face relaxed. "Thanks for your eloquence," she said to Gerald. Then: "Frank, Old Man's A-frame will need cleaning out. That mess in the kitchen can't go a day more. Will you lend me a hand?"

"Just give me a holler anytime," I replied.

Gerald settled a hand on Betty Maddox's shoulder and squeezed. "Sleep easier about Old Man. Frank and I will make it right."

My nod was automatic, affirming only my grave doubts. We left the post office, Gerald's strides growing resolute on the walk up the brick steps to Scarab's Methodist Church. We went inside and our long shadows slid into the rearmost pew.

"What's the news here?" I asked him.

"Prayer," replied Gerald.

"Brother. What for?"

"To align yourself with God. Ask Him for a . . . "

" . . . a miracle," I said to end his sentence. "No love there."

Gerald scratched an ear. "Frank, you're five pounds of shit in a three-pound bag."

"Churches scare me pissless. That's all. Inside, I'm all torn up over Old Man."

"Hey, lean on me. You ain't too heavy," said Gerald.

"All right. Can you hurry it up any?"

"Too busy jawing with you. I haven't got started."

A dutiful but unchurched Roman Catholic, I sat there thinking that I hadn't been to Confession in a long time. What were the right words? Bless me Father, for I have sinned. I've smoked a few low rents but I've never buggered an altar boy. I guessed I'd spend eternity frozen in hell flames with a slew of guilty priests.

Gerald finally muttered his amen and we left.

The night-lit Chartreuse Ironworks looked foreboding as we pulled into the parking area. I saw behind John Wingo's trailer office a red cloud swoosh up where three hardhats grit-blasted a bridge girder and were accomplishing a lot more than we were.

"Let me talk to Wingo," said Gerald.

I keyed off the ignition. "He's long gone from here. I can guarantee it. Look, Forensics in Mantis will vacuum up a hair follicle or pull a plastic print off a soap bar. So evidence will put me at the murder scene in that motel room. Ballistics will tag the slugs to Old Man's .44."

"What did you do with the gun?" asked Gerald.

"Chucked it into an empty coal mine," I replied.

"Heads-up move. What now?" asked Gerald.

I thought for a moment. "I believe that Dot, Woody, Goines, and Wingo all belong to the Blue Cheer. They're all bloodthirsty racists. But who's left for us to question?" I answered my own question before Gerald had a chance to reply. "Nobody. What leads do we have? None. Add all that up, where do you get? Nowhere."

Gerald undid the door handle. "Hang in there. Something'll give."

As expected, Wingo hadn't shown up for work. The official reason, a night shift secretary informed us, was to use up his vacation time. A rough customer, she wore a seamless blue sweater with big armholes and a sweetheart neckline.

"Use it or lose it." She gave Gerald a lewd wink.

"Don't worry, honey. The tools in my shed are always bright," said Gerald.

She flashed him a raffish smile. "You got my phone number, tool man?"

"You in the book?"

"Top of page 34, first line."

Gerald smiled back at her. "'Page 34, first line' is now tattooed on my heart."

"Be listening for you," she said.

Our inquiries at the mini mart also proved futile. The new clerk acted surly. "T-shirts?" He parroted me. "The Blue Cheer? Really? Here? I haven't seen any."

"What dope are you on?" He didn't reply and I went out the door.

We departed and en route to my cabin talked about this and that back home in Pelham. Gerald gave me a rundown on who'd died, who'd been born, and who'd snaked whose old lady.

A queue of road signs at The First Primitive Apostolic Church spouted pious aphorisms. "Make Peace With God!" "Jesus Saves The Wicked!" "Man Proposes, God Disposes!" "Prayer Here Tonight!" None, however, said "The Blue Cheer Goes Down!"

While we bumped up my neglected jeep trail, a radio announcer advertised a blockbuster movie now out on DVD, the latest and greatest in electronic gadgetry. DVD, big screen plasma, HDTV, Web TV— what was the point of it all? Improving the technology didn't improve the content.

Seeing the vacant, murky cabin bummed me out. Gerald stalked out and, I guessed from all the noise, chopped up a cord of wood. I used the busted-up oak and poplar he brought in to stoke a blaze in the stove. A fifth of bourbon appeared out of Gerald's duffel bag and we were back in business. Gerald prowled the cabin floor in circles, stooping to throw the occasional hard look out the dark windows. He stopped in front of the bookshelves and ran a finger over my Golden Field Guides, holding his head sideways to read them.

"Swift digs here, Frank. Swift. L'il Abner and Snuffy Smith could start a commune. No TV, no Internet. What do you do for kicks? Watch porcupines fuck?"

"There's always the WWF Bra and Panties Matches in Huntington.

Or blowing some nose candy before setting off cherry bombs. For extra fun, I play old redneck comedy records. Get real, eh? What the fuck do you think I do?"

Gerald gave me an uneasy glance. "Okay, what's chewing at you, Frank? You look like hell."

"Well, get a load of me. I sold my trailer and left Pelham for a fresh start. Clean mountain air. Glorious Indian summer weather. Stupendous views. Cold country springs. Old Man and I stocked plenty of firewood. I have a library of excellent reads. I was in Hawg Wallow Heaven."

Gerald nodded. "Yeah, so what?"

"I was a happy hippy grubbing off the land. A few weeks more and I'd hunt up a job, start making bank, and keep myself in groceries. Maybe I'd work as a security guard. Then the other morning I woke up to my usual cornflakes and milk. Before it's tomorrow, some fool is launching shoulder-fired missiles at my cabin and two murders fall at my feet, including my only friend here."

"Four deaths if you add the two motel thugs," Gerald was quick to remind me. I hiked an askance eyebrow at him and saw that he was now sitting on the deacon's bench. "Shit, as the old mountain men used to say, happens, Frank."

"Are you ragging me?"

"Yep."

"Are you as sick of hearing me whine as I am?"

"Doubly so."

"Suggestions?"

Gerald resumed his prowling. "When the nail stops, grab a bigger hammer. Run it from the top. That first evening, you'd come in from chopping stove fuel and heard a noise in the sky. You sprinted out to the yard and looked up. Okay. Where was the Stinger fired from? Show me where you tripped over it."

As I routed out the Coleman lantern, the telephone jangled. Dreema Adkins at the forensics lab in Richmond delighted in my hickish "howdy" and my accepting her previous invitation to spend Christmas with her there in Richmond. She then sighed, not a good omen.

"I've come up with nothing, Frank. It hurts, too. Any latent prints or trace evidence on the Stinger motor case were destroyed. I couldn't raise any exterior stencils either. Honestly, I'm not sure what you expected me to find on it."

"You couldn't find anything?" I asked.

"Sorry. Now, I don't have any appreciable metallurgic expertise but the char and residue exhibit a clean, consistent burn. Oh, and a number was vibra-etched on the motor case's aft end near the lip. 312978."

"That'd be the manufacturer's serialization number." I jotted it down. "I know the Stinger was made at Hughes Corporation in Tucson, Arizona, and then shipped to Redstone Arsenal in Alabama. This wayward Stinger somehow then went on the black market to be snapped up by unsavory types with deep pockets."

I heard Dreema breathe hard over our connection. "Is time tight?"

"Very."

"You should take this to the Federal authorities. I know you must be thinking the same things I am," said Dreema.

"9/11?"

"Yes, this has terrorist written all over it. We've heard and seen the same media stories. Terrorists buying and smuggling in missiles. Maybe the government knows something about this one. Anyway, a Stinger's potential havoc is eye-popping. Planes are shot out of the sky. Dear God, my stomach is in knots . . ."

"It gives me the willies, too. But think it through with me, Dreema. If I came in now with what I know, they'd laugh at me. Test-fired Stinger motor cases are easy to lay hands on."

"They'd listen."

My common sense concerning the regime now in power thought otherwise. "They'd take me into custody. I'd be interrogated. Tortured. Any further fruitful investigation would stall."

"Even so, you should make a best faith effort," said Dreema.

"Maybe but I'll tell you what, for a 1980s weapon, a Stinger can still sting. Oh yeah, we built them too good. Rogue states with Stingers will terrorize the generations to come. No jet plane taking off or landing will ever be safe again," I said.

"Aren't there any available countermeasures?" asked Dreema.

"From what I've read, they're pretty expensive and ineffective. Electrical chafe technology derails the rocket's flight path. Fancy flares supposedly jam the Stinger's heat-sensing navigation. Even so, I'd never knowingly fly in an intended target plane," I said.

"Something I almost forgot." I could hear Dreema flipping pages. "I panned my loupe over every square inch of the metal's surface area. I did pick off three words stamped in miniscule 6-point letters on the forward end. The words mean nothing to me."

I heard Dreema flip another page of her notebook. I waited. And waited.

"The little letters spelled out three words," said Dreema. "The Blue Cheer."

A vapory halo surrounded the moon. The Coleman lantern reflected light off the red-eye shine of the 10-point buck eating crab apples near the cistern. Gerald hooted. "Hello, trophy city." The chagrinned buck flicked up its white tail and vaulted over the blackberry bushes fringing the woods.

Gerald knelt down to finger my Prizm's sliced tires. The image of Old Man waltzing around with the sugared gas tank sprang into my head. Instead of amusement, I felt an acute sadness.

"Could've been your throat," said Gerald.

"Let's press on," I said.

Gerald was adroit for an ex-linebacker. He crossed the ring of big boulders effortlessly. We stalked for more than a few minutes downslope by the lantern's light. Trout Creek came within earshot and I thought of the water burbling under Jan Maddox on the autopsy table. I tacked the red dot to my laser pointer on the rock slab where Old Man had rested the lantern. "I regained consciousness right about here."

"Lemme scope this out in my mind," said Gerald.

The lantern hiccupped and indistinct shadows swirled about us. Being marooned in this hollow wasn't an enticing prospect. Carrying Gerald's Browning 9 mil failed to give me much confidence. But I was feeling pretty giddy. The Blue Cheer's inscription on the Stinger and the vial removed from Jan provided the crucial missing links. Too easy and too handy clues, maybe, but I'd take them. All the bizarre and brutal events, I concluded, stemmed from this same hate cult.

"All right, I reconstruct the scenario like this. First, they sent up the drone. It was dusk. The shooter hunkered on the next ridge, waiting. Then he tracked the drone and fired off the Stinger rocket. It hit dead center," said Gerald,

"After I bumbled down here to see what was what, they socked me on the head. All right, then. We see it the same way. Good."

"But secrecy is important. That's why they tidied up afterward," said Gerald.

"A bunch of racist cutthroats blowing up stuff," I said.

"And killing defenseless women. They're cowards. That swings the advantage to us," said Gerald.

CHAPTER EIGHTEEN

———

The next sunup—it was Wednesday, if I believed my calendar—I lay awake in bed, blankets pulled up to my chin. The ceiling fan did a slow chop. A sleazy, cold sweat filmed me. Old Man, in my dream, had been screaming for me to shoot.

The bell of the shrilling telephone prodded me up. Betty Maddox snapped at me. "Do you have plans today, Frank? If not, please come help me clean up at the A-frame. I can meet you there. Bring Gerald. I borrowed a man's flatbed. We'll cull out the unwanted stuff and donate it to the Lady's Auxiliary. I already stopped Old Man's mail and newspaper delivery."

"Betty, do yourself a kindness. Give this a bit longer. Your nerves are raw right now," I said.

A sigh preceded Betty's softer voice. "The quicker, the better. I can't rest until I know their house is in order. And when that's done, I'll put the A-frame up for sale."

"For sale?"

I could picture Betty scowling. "I'm getting ahead of myself, which isn't like me. Moping has tossed me out of sorts but I'm getting it together, Frank."

"All right. What time?" I asked her.

"Say, nine-thirty. I'll bring the house key."

Gerald was squatting on the edge of the couch with a blanket draped around his shoulders like a shawl. "I was too lazy to start a fire and figured if I piddled around long enough, either you'd do it or the rising sun would warm me. I must be good because here you are."

"You must be." The stove door creaked wide and I built a teepee lay before striking a match to it.

"Who was that on the phone?" asked Gerald once thawed out.

"Betty Maddox. She's gung-ho to clean out Old Man's A-frame," I replied.

"That makes sense. She's being conscientious," said Gerald.

"Betty intends to sell it." I went to the refrigerator, draped my arms on the open door, and leaning, peered inside. "You like your eggs over-easy or scrambled, homeboy?"

"Neither. My breakfast is catered, courtesy of Old Granddad," said Gerald.

"Call him back. Make your order for two," I said.

"Does Scarab have a gym? I got a burn deep in my bones to go lift some iron," said Gerald.

I gave him an incredulous glance. "Even if there was a gym in Scarab, you'd come and help us move furniture, instead."

Purple grackles scattered aloft from a linwood tree as we rode into the yard. Betty's rumble in the flatbed truck charged up behind us. Intermittent drizzle on this overcast morning threatened to rain us out, a good excuse to cancel but Gerald had dissuaded me from phoning Betty back.

"She'll do it anyway. With or without you, she's set on seeing this through to the bitter end," he said.

Betty had tucked her gray-stippled, black hair under a scarlet kerchief. Her patched bib overalls fell loose, good for turning and twisting inside of, to unload a house. Height and sinewiness reinforced her youthful athleticism so that she was once a handsome woman who was still, well, quite handsome.

"Good morning, Frank. And Gerald." Betty bounced down from the cab cluttered with dog food bags. "Showers forecasted today."

"Ninety-two percent likelihood. If anything's rain damaged, I'll feel bad," I replied.

Shooing us up the deck steps, Betty nodded. "We'll pack boxes for starters. If the afternoon turns soupy, maybe tomorrow will be more cooperative. At least I can get started scrubbing on the kitchen floors."

Gerald sidemouthed to me. "Quit your gawking at the lady and stay on task."

Stepping into the A-frame, we were greeted by a hot, gamey stink. Goines had bumped up the thermostat. Why, I didn't know. Yellow crime scene tape still looped around kitchen chairs and numbered evidence markers dotted the floor tiles.

Betty's hand jerked in an emphatic gesture. "That godawful tape is the first thing to go."

"The crime scene should have been released back to its owner," I said.

"That's me. Get rid of it. That dreadful murder is history now," said Betty.

After detaching an end, Gerald spooled the tape into a lumpish ball. He blooped it over the wheelchair toward the wastebasket. Nothing but net. Jan's plants—coleus, shamrocks, geraniums, flowering aloe, and, I guessed, a massive crown-of-thorns—situated along the patio doors, had withered inside their terra-cotta pots.

"Dump those behind the woodpile," said Betty.

I stacked the pots, small on top of large, and tramped across the deck. The uncut grass felt plush and spongy. I stepped towards the woods and felt melancholic. Being here at the home of both murder victims, was it any wonder? I stopped at the forest's edge behind a bamboo trellis of climbing clematis and heaved the pots. They clomped against each other like dropped coconuts and fractured into shards among shrub clippings.

A cold rain hammered down on me. I cringed under my collared CPO jacket. I spat. Old Man and I had gone squirrel hunting in a copse of red oaks down the swale there. He preferred using a .22 with notched iron sights to a .410 because shotguns shredded the stew meat.

Remembering that detail made my throat tighten. The rain drummed down harder. Old Man and I would never go hunting again, but I couldn't cry anymore. They say rage is the flip side of depression. If that was true, then I'd flipped—a new ungovernable anger was shooting through me.

When I returned to the A-frame and went inside, Betty and Gerald were talking. Their tones were civil, even chatty, but while catching my breath, I detected an edge to their discussion, or at least on Betty's side of it. I went into the room.

"Lord, here's Jan's wedding gown," she said, from the loft. "Antique white, hand-beaded. Jiminy Christmas, I'd never believed such a thing was possible."

"Was it so terrible?" asked Gerald.

"Absolutely appalling. Oh, I know about high profile interracial marriages like Quincy Jones and Harry Belafonte. But even so," said Betty.

"Well ma'am, my thinking is you should marry the person you love and the rest of the world can go shit between their teeth," said Gerald.

"Are you married, Gerald?"

"Still playing the field, ma'am."

"Do you think it is a good idea for our people to marry theirs?" asked Betty, bracing her hands on the loft's wood railing. "I mean taking the long view into account."

"If you're asking whether I'm opposed to miscegenation, then my answer is no. I've dated white women. Not many, but a couple. Nice ladies, too, but I'm just as attracted to the sisters."

Wagging her head, Betty said, "Black men have always chased after the fairer skin, straighter hair, and thinner lips. They got a 'thang' for the white chicks. Don't you go and contradict me either, Gerald. I've seen the statistics. Old Man was just that way, too."

Gerald tapped the pencil eraser on the pad of paper. "I'm not disputing you, Betty. But I don't get my balls in a bunch at seeing a black man holding hands with a white gal. It's just not that big a deal anymore."

"You have the gall to make fun of me? I'm creaky and out of touch, eh?" Betty jabbed the coat hangar to punctuate her statement. "Let me ask you this . . ."

"Drop it, please, Betty. The inventory? We left it at three floor lamps. What else is there?"

" . . . why do you reckon Johnny Cochrane let Marcia Clark stack the jury with black women at OJ's trial? He was a sly old dog is why. The black sisters weren't looking out for their white sisterhood. Not in a million years. They took Little Miss Marcia for a ride, too. Sure, it was venom they vented but not venom at what had been perpetrated against another woman. Hell, no. It was venom against that blonde-haired, fair-skinned vixen, that Nicole Brown who'd seduced one of their own."

Gerald shot me a glance. "I've heard that same argument for years and it bums me. The Juice should've gotten the juice. End of discussion."

Not seeming to hear him, Betty went on. "At least Old Man was astute enough to stay childless. I'll give him credit for that much sense."

"You're damn strong in your dislikes," said Gerald.

I let my eyes drift upward from the old issue of *Shotgun News* on the kitchen floor just about the spot when Jan had lain sprawled where I'd cut her down. "Were you opposed to Old Man's marriage?" I asked Betty quietly, stepping into full view.

Betty froze for a second. She licked her lips and then bit the corner of the lower one. "Well, of course, I didn't spell out my reservations to them. I haven't a cross bone in my body. They had their own lives to live. What's more, I loved them both the same as I did anyone else in our family."

Looking over at me, Gerald spoke fast. "Betty was speaking in the larger philosophic sense, Frank. I dig where she's coming from and wouldn't read anything too serious into her remarks."

Betty seemed almost bitter. Seeing the collapsible wheelchair now on the sofa, I asked, "How was Jan injured?"

Betty narrowed her eyes at me and lowered her voice. "Rambunctious. Tripped on these damn stairs one morning. Cracked her spinal cord. But let's not speak any more about it. I'm getting upset."

Gerald winked like after a lot of beer in a bar and passed by me on his way out the patio door. I had a similar yearning to go out for a nip.

Then I recalled Jan telling me a mysterious illness (a virus?) accounted for the wheelchair and wondered who was lying. For now, I'd let it ride. "Old Man said this was the Maddox home place. Did your folks have the deed to the mountain?" I asked.

Betty toddled down the loft stairs. "Indeed, yes. Our folks were dirt-poor sharecroppers from Jackson, Mississippi. They migrated north to

Akron and toiled in the rubber factories making tires. When that went under, they came south. Scarab had a bonanza of mines and coal was dirty but profitable. Land went clay-cheap. Dollar and a couple cents an acre. They slapped together Sears & Roebuck kit houses. Old Man had to demolish his parents' house here to clear space for this A-frame. Ripped out my heart."

Betty bent in the knees to retrieve an African-American quilt from the floor. Its design incorporated garish meteors, comets, Zodiac signs, and shooting stars while a black Jesus, crucified, anchored the design's center. "My Grandmother Clarissa stitched this quilt. She was a genuine artist."

"It shows, too," I said.

"Jan had the nerve to stow it inside a cedar chest. This quilt is a museum show piece. Meant to be seen and admired," said Betty.

"Could the sunlight have bleached it?" I asked.

Betty folding it up said, "It's of little consequence now. I've reclaimed the quilt as a Maddox family heirloom."

The morning rain had slackened, as had our vigor to tackle the housecleaning project. We decided to bag it for the day. But my suspicions, like my eyes, had fallen on the outspoken Betty.

CHAPTER NINETEEN

A souped-up Jeep Cherokee convertible sporting a white roll bar and whip aerial rambled up Old Man's lane through the treeline into view. Its driver, lanky and young, vaulted out of the bucket seat as my eyebrows V-ed in anger. The driver, in tasseled loafers, slopped over to the deck's bottom step to confront us.

"Roy Pinkerton." He was proud of the press credentials he flashed at us.

Apprehension clouded Betty's features. "You left a message on my answering machine."

"Righto. Old Man sicced me on Sheriff Greenleaf who's been sandbagging Jan's homicide investigation. We were a team. He had some more dirt for me." Roy sprayed spit at us, nothing intentional but wet just the same.

"That source is gone. Your big scoop died with him," I said.

"Two murders, twice the news. Ms. Maddox, you're beholden to carry through what Old Man started," said Roy.

A testy frown etched Betty's handsome face. "Out of the question. I don't know anything. I'm sorry, son."

His head tilted down, Roy swiped one loafer on his chinos, repeated the same trick with the other loafer. He counted the freckles on his knuckles for a moment, then said, "I investigated a certain lead of my own. Did you know that a private license worked for Old Man Maddox? Now, the Virginia Department of Criminal Justice Services told me Virginia has no reciprocity agreement with us. Here, a Virginia licensed detective is *persona non grata*. Now any ambitious state auditor would delight to know what I do. It'd score him or her a plum promotion. Huh, Johnson? Is that news fit to print, sir?"

His smile, growing into an officious smirk, provoked me to say,

"Gerald, escort Betty out to the flatbed, please. Roy and I will be here a minute."

Grinning like the butcher's dog, Gerald took Betty's elbow and once they went around the corner, my hands rifled out to clamp on Roy's coat collars.

"What the f—?"

Forefinger at my lips, I officiated. "*Sh-h-h*, Roy. Don't talk. Listen. One word printed about Ms. Maddox or me and you can take your teeth home in a pocket."

Roy Pinkerton smirked more. Whunk! I armbarred his mouth hard enough to knock out the loose spit. His teeth shook in their sockets and his misshapen head drooped in a backward arc. Blood daubed his lips and chin.

"Enough," said Roy. "I-i-it'll be as you say."

"Good. Sorry you ran into that damn tree limb, too," I said after him.

Roy staggered over to sit in the Jeep Cherokee. He piloted down the bend and out to the state road. I sighed. What story might clatter off the local presses was anybody's guess, but if I'd persuaded him, the ink-shitter would pursue his Pulitzer Prize on someone else's back, instead of breaking ours.

So, Old Man's threat to Sheriff Greenleaf about tipping off the media was legitimate. He'd never told me. Thrill kills boosted newspaper circulation. Now with Old Man's murder on top of Jan's, rife rumors and shabby speculation were no doubt sailing through Scarab at dizzying rates. That only proved I was right all along about Scarab being a dirty little town. My powerful impulse to get out of town returned.

Might Betty's real estate broker get with my pitch? I wondered. FOR SALE: One cedar log cabin. Furniture & appliances convey. All expected modern amenities: running water, electric, flush crapper, A/C, washer & dryer, smoke detectors, and woodstove w/four cords of oak. Seller will accept best offer. Caveat: Buyer must supply own quaint charm. Seller is fresh out.

"Your tires need replacing," said Gerald.

We now bumped into a sharp turn pulling to the tar-top road where

Betty, in the flatbed truck, lumbered ahead of us toward Scarab. Gerald ferreted out a bourbon bottle and indulged a late morning nip. "Your Prizm's newer than this junker. More dependable, too."

"I say no to swapping out cars. For sentimental reasons, which I'm sure you understand, we'll stick with the Valiant."

"Fine, buckled up in either is equal torture for me. Detroit has yet to build a big crate to accommodate us big men. What now?" asked Gerald.

"I've been thinking. There's this granny lady, Hattie McGraw, who knows Dot Christmas and Woody Sears. She's our best shot at picking up their trail again," I replied.

"Is she at home now?" asked Gerald.

"I doubt Hattie McGraw ever leaves her mountaintop," I replied.

"So, Dot and Woody have bolted. Wingo has vanished, too. Deputy Goines, your good buddy, jetted off to Montana to hunt elk. Some driver brought those two assassins to the motel in Mantis. Wherever the Blue Cheer's hideout is, it's cramped and crowded," said Gerald.

"What do you think about our odds?" I asked.

"I don't think about it. You shouldn't either," replied Gerald.

On the verge of noon, we scooted along a maze of orange clay roads to conquer Hattie's mountain. The girl, hair red and willowy as ever, teed off on the golf balls. I admired her stick-to-itiveness. Once her supply of golf balls was depleted, she'd scurry into the stand of persimmons and gather up her stock in a copper wok. Then she'd take more practice swings. I waved at her but she only stared after us.

We trekked up the switchbacks in stunning time and barreled along the plateau. Gerald's hands pushed up against the roof headliner to minimize his head smacks. My brain, one big bruise, throbbed. The tires clawed to stay on the rut's upper bevel. We persevered to see Hattie's yellow daisy meadow today dotted by purple ironweed. The domestic fowl, like on my previous visit, squawked to alert Hattie about our arrival.

Gerald spat. "Infernal birds. Eggs and eating are all they're good for."

"We'll chill here for a little," I said.

Hattie, after a while, walked a ways out from the cabin. Sunlight caught her leathery expression and you had to wonder what she pondered standing there statue-still. Eventually an arm arose from underneath a fuchsia shawl, a gesture of welcome. We hauled out of the Valiant. A down-reaching path took us to her. The chary birds gave Gerald a wide berth as they'd done with Old Man.

"Who comes? Speak clearly and loud," said Hattie.

"It's me, Mrs. McGraw," I replied.

"Missus was my grandma's name. Hattie is mine. Who is your side-kick, Frank? It isn't Old Man, now is it? Wait, come and sit."

Her slat-back chairs were arranged in a triangle. A red-checkered tablecloth fluttered through the crack in her rear plank door. The smell of smoked ham made me think of lunch.

"Self-introductions go quickest. I'm Gerald Peyton from Pelham, the same flypaper town as Frank's in Virginia. We go way back. I'm here helping him out."

"Old Man is dead. Two thugs crashed into our motel room with twelve gauges barking. We were still half-asleep," I told her.

Hattie's arthritic fingers intertwined and her sad regret grew palpable. "Old Man is dead? Cut down? Didn't I predict it? His wife, Jan, and now him. I've never seen such violence. Who's next? Are you marked for death, Frank? What happened to these gunmen?"

"Frank waxed them both, then scrammed before the deputies swooped in. That's not for public consumption either, ma'am. We're going after Dot Christmas and Woody Sears," said Gerald.

Hattie's face showed disapproval and I offered a hasty explanation. "Gerald is a bail bond enforcer. His job is the search and capture of outlaws."

"I know what a bail bond enforcer does. If you've searched their home and workplace, I've no further ideas where they'd lay low." Hattie's hawk talons for a hand gestured behind us. "There are scads of hollows in that wild woods. Take your pick of which one to look in."

My disheartening vision had us searching an infinite maze of rabbit paths. "Do they have a favorite hidey-hole?" I asked.

Hattie's forehead wrinkled as a brass-banded watch flopped on her lowering wrist. A blind lady's ornamentation, perhaps? "They could be anywhere," she said.

I had an insight, perhaps a fluke, but I stuck with it. "When Old Man and I were up before, you told us about a family Klan cemetery."

Gerald, his glasses off to clean on a shirttail, stopped. His eyes enlarged.

"Bremo's Promontory over in Curtis County. It's a spry romp off the hard surface and these days lies in rank weeds as well it should be. I don't go there," said Hattie.

"Remote, isolated, and forgotten. Could be the Blue Cheer's hide-out," I said.

"Don't go there," said Hattie.

"Never mind. I'll put that weight on my shoulders. Sketch us a map, ma'am. I'll guide your fingers to fill in the landmarks," said Gerald.

A bit later after talking, Hattie said, "Oh, set down. Eat you some supper."

Gerald and I said together, "Yes ma'am."

We ate sliced smoked ham, out-of-season ramps, home-baked bread topped with white clover honey, and drank gallons of chicory coffee. Gerald couldn't cram it in fast enough or stop heaping on the compliments.

"You all stay safe," said Hattie, as we left.

"Holler at you later, ma'am," said Gerald.

My foot rode the brake down Hattie's mountain. "Oho!" Gerald pointed. The girl with the red-tussled hair chunked a posthole digger into the orange clay by the road bank. Hattie had given the girl's name as Edna. Nipples beamed like big mocha brown eyes under the sweat-sopped fabric of her Charlie Daniels T-shirt. A mailbox mounted to a pointy post and a crowbar lay by a doffed sweatshirt. Edna hiked up a palm: halt. We did.

Gerald rolled down his window. She leaned her arms on the sill and balanced her chin on her knuckles. Closer up, she looked older if not wiser. "What you gaping at, Homer?" Her question wasn't accusatory or puerile, only curious.

"You, my dear lady. Frank is enthralled by your unsurpassed beauty. No question," replied Gerald.

"Don't try and bullshit me. You've been up to Miss Hattie's, I expect. That's twice I know about. Why?"

I spoke. "She's assisting us."

"How might that work?" asked Edna.

"We're looking for Dot Christmas and Woody Sears. We're busy putting out the word that Frank Johnson and Gerald Peyton want them. Bad," said Gerald.

"Dot and Woody, oh yeah. They're the devil's spawn," said Edna.

"Do they come up here much?" I asked.

"Sure, if they ain't off grunting," replied Edna.

"Grunting?"

"Vibrating earthworms out from the dirt to sell at bait shops," said Edna.

"Have they been up lately?" I asked.

"Not for a while. Screwy thing, too, being as October is the best month for bagging pine duff. I may as well tell you, since almost everybody knows. Dot and I were once an item. Of course he went and did me bad. When I was with his child, he didn't step up to be a man. It popped out stillborn. Dead of a broken heart, I expect." Edna's hand nudged away Gerald's head. "Quit fondling me with your eyeballs, Homer."

"Yes ma'am." Gerald chuckled but her sad story left me grimacing.

"Now Dot made money hauling that steel. As many nights as he was gone, those high rise welders might've erected the second Empire State Building, but we'd have heard about it by now if they had, I expect. One thing about Dot—his hatred of black folks is legendary," said Edna.

"He's one super bad dude," said Gerald.

"Did Dot ever mention a family cemetery?" I asked.

Edna closed one eye, thinking. "An old one in Curtis County."

"You've been a big help. Thank you, Edna," said Gerald.

Edna gave us a slack-handed wave as I agitated the road gravel. In high spirits, Gerald cracked up laughing clear out to the paved road where I put us south, the way Hattie's map showed, to Bremo's Promontory in Curtis County.

"Yes sir, marriage is in my cards," said Gerald.

"Don't hurry so. It's far overrated," I said.

Hattie had us streaking through the stoniest terrain ever gouged by the glaciers during the Great Ice Age. Wednesday was getting away from us so I mashed the motor and we tackled the first summit. The Valiant's six-banger wheezed and bucked but we overcame the hump. The Doom and Gloom (news and weather) over the radio sounded the same as yesterday's.

We came to the bottom and skirted a sludge dam impounding the runoff from coal processing. Sloped embankments looked black-slimed and a raunch smelling between days-old tuna and burnt sulfur buried in our sinuses. It reminded me of Scarab. POSTED signs at the gate warned off intruders like do-gooders and crusading journalists. Ill feelings existed between the locals and the coal company.

Blasting in the mines had knocked the water from folks' wells and fly rock dashed out house windows. Moreover, the coal company left behind shaley rubble, slate detritus, and gob piles to create a wasteland rivaling Death Valley. Big Coal, what a sweetheart.

Cliff Waldron came on the radio, his singing voice mellow. "Blue-grass belongs to the people," said Gerald.

"Everybody, everywhere," I said.

Somebody's beltware beeped. It wasn't mine. Gerald picked off the number from the pager. "Damn, this is like being hooked to a leash." He unclipped the cell phone to call the number. He offered his client a lame excuse for his absence and then went into receive mode. Angered about forfeiting a bail, she demanded instant results. Gerald gave her assurances that she was a valued client but she wasn't having any of it.

"Yes, Helen Ann. I'm keenly aware of the one-year deadline on bail skips. We still have us some time, right?" Her screams hurt even my ears. "Yes, I'll jump right on it," Gerald lied to Helen Ann. "Gimme his last known address. Las Vegas, right. You have a nice day, too." He patted shut the cell phone. "That lady tries to run my life." His voice rose into a comical falsetto. "Gerald, go here, go there. Gerald, do this, do that. Gerald, Gerald."

"I'll pay you for your time today," I said.

"Nothing doing. This gig is steady enough. Morons trying to outfox the law throw me lots of business," said Gerald.

My eyes rolled with a half-head turn. "Behind us under the seat you'll find a shotgun pistol. I'm still mending from its kick but you might do better with it."

Gerald, allured by his new plaything, missed the giant hemlocks in bog-ridden basins. My mind ranged out and joined another traveler. My cousin Rod Bellwether guided by the Polar Star had to be hitch-hiking along New England's lesser routes. Would truckers take pity on the fugitive? Company rules spoke against it. Truckers only stopped for bums in Red Sovine songs. No sweat, though. Rod was wired to survive. How would he do it? He might sneak into a four-car garage and bridge the starter to a sleeping Yuppie's Lexus. He might hijack a Chevy Suburban from a soccer mom topping off her tank at a self-serve gas pump.

Vague details of Rod's murder arrest filtered back to me. One eye-witness, a jobless parolee detoxing in a halfway house, had fingered Rod from a six pack: a photo array of six headshots, five of which were beat cops, the sixth being Rod. The parolee had seen Rod bugging out of his house near the time of Kathy's death. That'd been another strike against Rod, along with the partial print on the Gerber knife. Plus, Rod did resemble a thug from the Screen Extras Guild. The local jury, swayed by the evidence amassed against Rod, found him guilty as charged and awarded him the death penalty.

A pistachio green pickup with fart-can exhausts blitzed up to dog our bumper, then hit the hammer lane. The good-natured driver waved back at us. Next, a Caddy towing a trailered Jet Ski went around us and after we passed by some hayricks, I pulled off to the shoulder and hopped out to answer a call of nature behind some briar bushes. Before leaving, I went around to tighten all the lug nuts with a spanner wrench in the likely event we needed to tear ass off Bremo's Promontory.

CHAPTER TWENTY

―――

Hattie's memory guided us to three roads, each bumpier and narrower than the previous one. The glen we wanted lay tangled in belt-high yarrow, mullein, and bull thistle. We reached the clearing and the Valiant scuttled about quarter way across before the weedy jungle checked our progress. We fumbled out to go it on foot when a covey of quail exploded into flight. Outlying oaks and pitch pine soon funneled us into arboreal shadows. Whooping, Gerald shagged a fruit-bearing branch.

"Paw-paws. Yeah, boy."

"Tastes like fried chicken?" I asked.

"Better." Gerald's clasp knife cut off a slice. "Here, sample some hill-billy caviar."

Eaten out of hand, the yellowish pap tasted close to muskmelon. The paw-paws had gray-brown scaly bark and the fruit was shaped like a small cucumber. You just never knew when they might come in handy. Around a stag horn sumac patch—its slender red leaves accented by frosts—we found a faint trail, witch hazel bounding either side. I was reminded of Old Man's witch hazel aftershave. We still worked together. I took some comfort in feeling that way.

We skirted the wreckage to a plane crash marked as "# "on Hattie's map and my imagination ran rampant. Rustling fabric. Gruff murmurs. Men in white gowns hoisting pine-knot torches in the gloom. The unruly group swelled before a rostrum backlit by a bonfire. A lynching bee! The Exalted Cyclops tied seven knots to a noose and flung the rope up over a branch in the gallows oak. Visceral shrieks pierced the night world. I halted and exhaled to shake off the eerie vision.

Gerald, his face shiny with sweat, breathed in spurts. One boot drudged before the other. Troubled eyes lifted. From here on, our going was almost straight up Bremo's Promontory. "Great. Now the real work kicks in," he said.

"You climbed the Washington Monument. This isn't half as steep and not near the same elevation," I said.

Gerald ass-planted against a boulder. "Woodsmen bring a canteen of water. But we ain't woodsmen, are we?"

"A cold country spring waits at the top," I said.

"You lie, too," said Gerald.

A flapping noise directed our gazes skyward. A brace of turkey vultures, buoyed by thermal currents and luffed by high winds, patrolled for dinner.

Gerald sniffed an armpit. "Did we lose our deodorant?"

"Let's look alive," I said.

This time Gerald led off. The struggle upward was bad enough but we also battled ticks, chiggers, and black flies. Bossy wrens, in the hawthorn shrubs, scolded us; a barred owlet heckled us. I skidded downslope but luckily my boots landed on an overhang. I climbed on, grabbing at tree roots, grapevines, and anything attached to the cliff-face. I couldn't believe enthusiasts did this for sport. Gerald grunted uncomplimentary adjectives about my manhood,that I pretended not to hear because under duress, the big guy was just venting.

Hattie had an unerring impression of a stone manse that her folks called the Baylor Place. We found its shallow foundation mounded under Virginia creeper and trumpet vine. I went over and saw that slate shingles had sealed the cistern's hole. After resting, we hooked and crooked our way higher. I gripped a cat briar and squawked. I scraped out stickers with my Buck knife, wishing for a pair of leather gloves. I finally reached the ledge where Gerald was smoking a cigarette.

"You still trust that blind crone?" I asked him.

"Hattie wouldn't lead us astray. Duck down here. See, on this side of that chestnut? Daylight. We're almost at the top."

"I see night is falling. Fast. We didn't pack any flashlights."

"Suck it up, Frank. We'll travel by celestial navigation."

The weather had washed some grave markers into a gorge behind us. First on our waffle-bottom soles, then on our rumps, we slid down to where the grave markers assumed lumpish shapes in the failing daylight. A recumbent lamb crowned one while a chubby cherub lolled on a second. Scrunching closer, Gerald lit his Zippo to read partly eroded inscriptions, birth dates early as the 1830s and deaths late as the 1930s. Many stones bore the surnames Christmas and Sears. Those pale gowns were once again within me. The ghouls "assembled in Klonovokation," to use their rhetoric. Their rope snaked up; their hangman's halter dangled down; their condemned man's shrieks chilled my marrow. I had to stop this blood horror acting out in my mind.

"We've seen enough here," I said, shaking.

Gerald ignored me. "The cemetery must be above us."

"Do you see any old skulls?" I asked.

"No skeletons were washed down here. Even manmade lakes, flooding over graveyards, don't flush up buried bones."

"That's useful to know, Gerald."

We climbed up the ravine and saw a wrought-iron fence boxing in grave markers tilted at unnatural angles. A derelict pine cross, facing east to each day's rising sun, guarded the cemetery. Taking into account the plot's disrepair, we concluded that the last caretakers came before FDR.

But now audio enlivened those torchlit images in my mind. "Grand Dragons, and Hydras, quiet please. We are convened here in morbid affliction and bereavement. Our prayers are offered in the name of the valiant and venerated dead . . ."

"The Klan still haunts this damn mountain," I told Gerald.

"Shouldn't I leave my calling card before we go?"

"Come again?" I asked.

Gerald's thumbnail flicked a match head. Fire spurted from it. The summer drought had left the ridge's vegetation a tinderbox. "They came to burn crosses in my ancestors' yards. Now I come to torch their cross. That's the unholy gospel according to Saint Gerald. Fair is fair."

"Hey, don't bullshit about that." The back of my wrist restrained him. I couldn't read in the more-dark-than-light moment how serious he was.

"No bullshit, Frank." Gerald's match didn't waver. "Too much for you? I'll spot you a ten-second head start. Ten, nine . . ."

I lit out. Raced like nobody's business. My boots thudded over sticks, once stomped in and out of a groundhog hole. The curvy path dipped at the mesa's rim where I threw a glance back over my shoulder before my descent. Fire, towering fast, ravaged through the fence's wrought-iron pikestaffs to engulf the gravestones. Breezes fanned its greedy heat and when I visualized the mob, now, their white robes slithered off to burn in the inferno. Naked men—fair-skinned scarecrows, really—danced and hollered at fiery devils for mercy. But there was no mercy to give. The gallows oak burst into a big canopy of flames. Falling, the burning oak tumbled on the old rugged cross.

The clomps behind me were Gerald's. He shouted out a command. "Scat!"

We scrambled down the path, smoke hounding us. We romped by the Baylor Place. I staggered, rolled, and jounced. Gerald flopped down on his ass, skidded past me, laughing his fool head off. My hands and feet propelled me over rock and rubble and I did the crawdaddy crawl to the bottom of Bremo's Promontory.

It was a few minutes after ten o'clock Wednesday when we crossed Scarab's corporate limits. My headlamps were creaky fingers parting the curtains for our third act, whatever that was to be. The radio soothed us, or I should say me. Gerald snored under the latest issue of *Penthouse*, a blonde showing a vapid, come-love-me smile on its front cover.

DJ Eddie Stubbs, the forty-something blade-thin fiddler for the Johnson Mountain Boys, served up classic bluegrass on WSM beamed out of Nashville. Johnnie & Jack did their tuneful, sincere 'Ashes of Love'. I could relate to its sentiment. Any love here had burned into ashes.

I was glad to hear some local boys represented. Bea and Everett Lilly, natives of Clear Creek, West Virginia, near Beckley came on. Bea, playing rhythm guitar, sang lead. Everett, on the mandolin, harmonized in a tenor. Everett back in the early 1950s had recorded with Lester Flatt, Earl Scruggs, and The Foggy Mountain Boys.

Yawning, Gerald lifted his head from the space between the seat and door. "Did I doze off on you?" he asked. That got us to talking. We were of two different minds. I added the hillside cemetery trip to our string of flops while Gerald put a more positive spin on it.

"Sure we can't put our finger on one credible lead, but we had some trip," said Gerald.

"Going anywhere with you is some trip," I said.

Gerald drummed his knuckles on the dashboard. "What did I do to earn this grief from you? Lighten up, huh? We heard the fire whistles go off."

"From now on you keep that Zippo in your pocket," I said.

"Yeah, sure."

I braked at the mini mart lot beside the gas pumps where consumers had the convenience to wand in a credit card and key in any quantity of gasoline. Real money need never grease palms. Our digital age is a little too slick. Gas fumes blended with the wood smoke in my clothes and hair. Baleful visions and voices on Bremo's Promontory had dissipated from my mind.

I breathed a little easier.

Squeezing the gas pump's handle in a tired stance, I couldn't help but next wonder if all the Peytons—Gerald in particular—ran just a gear short of insanity, the same one I ran in.

"I'm off to take a leak," said Gerald.

"Jolly for you. Pick us up a couple of sixes, huh?" I called after him.

Left to right, my radar tracked for any sign of local law enforcement. I knew Sheriff Greenleaf was flinging a fit but I'd let him stew. The power tin-badge sheriffs wielded in jerkwater towns boggled the imagination. Common sense told me not to jerk them around too much. I wondered if they turned a blind eye to cults like the Blue Cheer.

The gas pump clacked off and I rehung the nozzle.

"Stake your eyes on this," said Gerald behind me. I saw him hook both thumbs toward a yellow T-shirt he wore over his work shirt. A walking fish swallowing the word DARWIN divided the slogans, "The Blue Cheer!" and "God Is A Lie!".

"Where did you get that?"

Gerald gave a chuckle. "The gal at the counter sold it to me."

"How?"

"I asked her. She fell all over herself waiting on me."

"Don't all ladies? Show me."

We trooped into the mini mart's warmth. The girl, one knee flexed on a stool, folded back a well-thumbed issue of *Seventeen*. "Sexy, shiny how-tos," its banner touted. Bangs shortened her forehead and she wore her own hair in a top pile. A demure navel below her midriff showed a barbell piercing. She was some lucky dad's handful. Her snug jeans were embroidered down the outside seams. She took an extra second eyeing Gerald before speaking, her folksy twang punctuated with bubblegum snaps.

"Yes, sir?" The girl spun her straw-yellow hair on her index finger.

"Another T-shirt, if you please. Red, too. Right, Buster? Tell the young lady about it. Red is your color and nothing else will do," said Gerald.

I nodded, yes indeed. We followed her down the aisle between refrigerated beer and breakfast cereals. The girl undid the padlock on a gray steel door.

"Is this the last one you'll be wanting?" The girl yanked the light switch string.

"That's it, right Cousin Buster?"

"That's right," I said.

"The unreal extent I go to for our customers," said the girl.

"You deserve a raise," said Gerald.

"Ha. You ain't just whistling Dixie," she said.

The pasteboard carton containing the Blue Cheer T-shirts sat just inside the doorway by a stack of pirated porno tapes. The box's mailing label had been hand-printed. The girl knelt on one knee, her top front spilling loose, intent on ferreting out a red T-shirt. The upper hemispheres of her breasts curved under a beige cotton bra but before I could scope any further, the front door snicked open and shut and a large lady entered the mini mart. The girl's head swerved.

"Leah? Where are you, dear girl? I'm late and apologize. Billy got bucked off his ATV, banged his head and took seven stitches. He looks like Frankenstein without the neck bolts. Didn't knock any sense into him, I'm sorry to say."

"Hi, Mary Jean. These customers asked after those T-shirts, the walking catfish jobbers."

Mary Jean let out an exasperated moan. "No, Leah! Those aren't for sale. I've told you a million times."

Mary Jean stormed at us, the purple pants suit shimmying on her Sumo wrestler frame. She tugged the bottom hem of Gerald's T-shirt. "Remove this, sir. You can't leave the store wearing it. This is a mix up and I'm sorry as all get out. You have a refund coming."

Gerald stiff-armed Mary Jean, who was clearly crowding him. She regained her balance after tripping into the lunch meats counter. Again she came at him but he sidestepped her flailing arms.

"Gimme that T-shirt. I don't want to rip it off you," said Mary Jean.

"Lady, this is mine," said Gerald.

Mary Jean clicked her tongue in reproach. "By orders of Deputy Goines, it is *not*."

"Why?"

"He didn't give us a reason. He's the law around here and doesn't have to."

"Peyton, P-E-Y-T-O-N. That's me. I bought two of these T-shirts. Tell Goines if he wants them, come and get them. I'll be reachable. Go call the motherfucker. Tell him any time."

We paid and exited while Leah and Mary Jean chattered in testy murmurs. In the car Gerald asked, "Did you pick off the name and address on the box label or were you too busy gawking down Leah's blouse?"

"It was Goines," I replied.

CHAPTER TWENTY-ONE

My cabin's electric heat ticked in the baseboard radiators and for a change we couldn't see our breaths. The ambush at the motel fresh in our minds, Gerald pulled the first watch. He arrayed the shotgun pistol, bourbon, and a new deck of playing cards on the coffee table, a home project I'd built out of particleboard.

My happy pills went down the hatch and I hit the rack to enter Wednesday night's dreams. Before long I was riding an escalator up to the "Whites Only" Department. A girl on the down escalator locked eyes on me. Waving, she threw me kisses until my ride ended and I Velcroed on a fat bulletproof vest. Quasimodo-like, it rode on my shoulders. I lumbered on and as the hump grew heavier, it undid my joints. All at once, Tommy guns poured out hot metal darts. Shot through-and-through, I caved to my knees, screaming. Old Man ran up, laughing.

Gerald poked my shoulder. "Your turn. We don't want the boogie man to eat us."

I arose from the bed still dressed. I stretched under the ceiling fan's slow chop and poked out front. Wonder of wonders, Gerald had deigned to build a fire in the stove. The coffee was percolating.

"I got this now. Stretch out on the couch and catch some sleep," I said.

"I'll wait up with you. It'll be daybreak in a few minutes. Chess before breakfast?"

Gerald had dribbled watered-down booze into the shot glass set and we ripped through a game, the jiggers tossed back in rapid succession.

"Check," I said at the penultimate move.

Gerald killed the final toddy, the white's king. "Checkmate," he said.

Laughing, I slipped him some hand skin. "Well fought. Where's your T-shirt?"

"Hanging on the gun rack with yours. Can you feel it, Frank? We're a frog's hair from cracking this nut. The Blue Cheer is finished. I'm amped!"

"Slow down, hoss. Once this breaks, I'm bringing in the cops," I said.

"In that case, I've got a contact with the West Virginia State Police. Lieutenant . . . lieutenant . . . starts with an 'L' . . . Logan. Mary Logan. I helped her out on a drug case. We busted a pack of mules transporting blow through West Virginia on their way up to hub cities."

"All right then, we can call Lieutenant Logan when we're ready to move. One thing more, Gerald. Nobody can die. Nobody. I'm still wrestling with nightmares from our last dustup with those Neo-Nazis. I wake up with my heart in my mouth and my brain on fire. Never again, I've sworn to myself. Never."

"You take it too serious. Those Brown Shirts bastards died as they lived. Violence begets violence, quoted verbatim from the Good Book," said Gerald.

"No matter, preacher. We play by the rules this time. Are we in sync on that?" I asked.

"Whatever you say." Gerald wiped out two mugs. Beer frothed gold suds into both. "Here you go, I fixed your breakfast," he said.

"Thanks but I better not. Pardon me while I call Gatlin, another of my adrenaline whores," I said.

After downing both beers, Gerald tapped out a cigarette, blazed it, and palmed the Remington 20. "Gatlin is the main man. Meantime, I'll go learn how this sweet baby shoots."

Not yet six a.m., Gatlin, already in his office, took my call. That never ceased to amaze me—a billionaire hard on the job when he might be entertaining beautiful women aboard his yacht. Different strokes. His inflection rang with that hyped-up pitch that I'd learned not to trust.

"When do you get an answering machine? Did you quell that mess at Bitterroot Prison? Have they apprehended your cousin, Rod?" he asked.

"No, something else is hotter than that." I fed him all the latest news. Breathing heavy, with the barest interruption, he listened.

"Gerald set the cemetery and mountain on fire? I have never defended a grand arson case. I wonder how I would finesse it . . . oh, never mind. You say you laid hands on the T-shirt. Ergo, the Blue Cheer is no will-of-the-wisp. Now go on offense and smash these fifth columnists."

I held the telephone a little away from my ear. Go on offense? Against whom? My boss man had lost it. "Suggestions, Counselor?"

"You should take on one of two fronts. First, Old Man's cousin, Betty Maddox. Her motive for selling the A-frame this soon sounds suspicious. I believe it warrants further scrutiny. Does she stand to profit from Old Man's estate or his life insurance? Why did she oppose his marriage to Jan?"

"Yeah, okay. I was thinking much the same thing. What else?"

"That ambulatory squid design that you described intrigued me. So, I asked myself, Robert, what does it signify? My golfing pal is a retired prison psychologist. He kept hundreds of tattoo photos because once you go to prison, they own your skin. That reminds me of—"

"Tattoos?" I knew tattoos detailed a con's pedigree. They showed if he was a veteran, a sailor, or had any gang affiliations. Tattoos also showed where a con had served time and who waited for him on the outside.

"Yeah. You heard me right. Tacs, or tats, or ink," Gatlin went on. "My point being once I detailed this particular one to Dr. Hanson, my golfing buddy, he immediately knew its meaning. Our assumption about an Aryan Brotherhood or White Supremacist gang, it turns out, is off-base."

"How?" Asking that was my undoing. Gatlin, like any lawyer, took tall pleasure to explain things in excruciating minutiae.

"Hanson first educated me about Aryans and their endemic tattoos. You might find on them a swastika embossed with a three-leaf shamrock. That's Irish, see? Within each shamrock leaf, you'd see 666."

"Yeah, they give us green Irish a black eye," I said.

"Other tattoos will tout SWP that stands for Supreme White Power . . . "

"The walking fish tattoo?" I urged him.

"Didn't I still have the floor, Franklin? As I was saying, the fish with legs should have been self-explanatory. It symbolizes how we evolved from the deep blue sea by following Darwin's theory of evolution."

"Darwin?"

"Precisely. The Blue Cheer is an atheist cabal. It holds that any notion of a Supreme Maker is a cockeyed fairytale. Not a new phenomenon, I grant you, but this group is ultra radical. A different focus than the Aryans, but their venom is as toxic. I know a lady—a formidable lawyer, too—with the Southern Poverty Law Center. They've tried for years to build a solid case to sue the Blue Cheer into bankruptcy. Their leadership, however, is too cunning."

"Atheists?"

"You heard me correctly. The Blue Cheer opposes mongrelizing the races, especially black on white. That right there provides a motive for the Maddox homicides. I can't expound on their dogma or speak their argot, but they're born killers so stay on your guard against them."

We rang off. I plunked down on the sofa and went on a mental Easter egg hunt. Where had all the walking fish logos appeared? One place struck me—the fire tower! A fish had been scrawled on its concrete footing. Prickly sweat nettled my backbone while I recalled the man in a red cap throwing potshots at Old Man and me. My fist whapped into my palm.

Andes!

He had to be mixed up in the Blue Cheer. I had to verify it for sure. Racine University's Admissions Office, found through the still reliable Directory Assistance, was in the Mossburger Building. I ginned up a ruse and placed the call. The young lady would love to aid a FBI investigator. My businesslike cadence snookered her or maybe she just didn't care.

"You're striking out," said the young lady in her likeable drawl. "Our computer lists no Andes, first or last name, as a candidate in our MFA program. Sorry, sir."

"Go back," I said. "This particular student withdrew due to some unforeseen difficulty. Say, he went broke. Had writer's block. Got pissed off with jaded New York agents and mega-publishers. Does any ex-student fit that mold?"

"Sorry, doesn't ring any bells. Perhaps your guy was a squatter. That is to say he quote, informally audited, unquote a writing professor's classes without paying tuition."

I acted surprised. "That goes on?"

"All the time. Writing professors flatter hangers-on to pack their classrooms. A full peanut gallery puffs up their fragile egos." The young lady laughed a little as if a former classroom groupie herself.

"How far back have you researched it?" I asked her.

"Eight years."

"You hit any records yet?" I asked.

"Nope. Do you have any more information about Mr. Andes?" asked the young lady.

"Yeah, he crowed about polishing off a Master of Fine Arts thesis. A crime novel of one stripe or another."

Her amused snicker came in an offhand way.

"I don't recall the title. Wait, yeah I do. *Bringing the Heat*," I said.

"But a crime novel? Not here, sir. Racine University is literature-minded to its core. No MFA candidate in their right mind would dare to fob off a genre novel. No thesis committee would sign off on it. At any rate, no Mr. Andes surfaces. Should I keep digging in our paper files? I can call you back by the day's end, sir."

"You've helped me more than enough already."

Andes, a compulsive liar and smooth operator, had duped me with his story of being a graduate student. Our next course of action was evident: hump on up to the fire tower and give it a thorough going over. Gerald, out back, was busting up a box of 20-gauge shells. His rounds were chewing up an old cherry tree stump that I'd been meaning to dynamite out of the ground.

He aimed the shotgun pistol with one hand. An empty shell spat out, landing beside twenty or so others littering the crabgrass. Just then, in rear profile, Gerald was a facsimile of Old Man. Their heights were approximate. By far younger, Gerald looked several pounds heftier and thicker through the neck and shoulders. Both men stayed loyal and fearless, why I valued their friendships. Gerald was always up for anything, which is why I felt better about our coming out on top. Two more gunshots pounded the stump.

Slivers of wood and bark kicked up. Gerald ejected the clip and dealt me a sheepish grin. I'd call it firing range practice but to him it was playing around. I moved from the sunny porch into the early morning's penumbra.

"Big problems?" asked Gerald.

I balanced my hams on my heels, cowboy-style. The plastic shotgun shell felt warm in my hand. The smell of burnt cordite burned in my nose. "No, the opposite. Our big break, maybe. We better run it down."

"Spill it," said Gerald, all grins.

I hit the highlights of Gatlin's lecture on tattoos and atheist hate groups, then tacked on my own ideas about the fire tower and Andes' mythical higher education.

"Andes had a good reason to lie," said Gerald.

"Unquestionably. Three guesses what for and the first two don't count," I said.

Gerald nodded. He didn't need to say it, but he did, anyway. "The Blue Cheer." It wasn't a question.

"That's my working assumption," I said.

"Did Andes strike you as flaky?" asked Gerald.

"Opinionated, always. Arrogant, you bet. But a kill-crazy nut? No, I never suspected it. He has these weird eyes, one black and one blue gazing not at, but through you in this Charles Manson stare."

"And you say the Blue Cheer are atheists, not racists?"

"Gatlin's of that mind. But does it much matter?"

"Fuck, no. You're just hairsplitting. One is as bad as the other. So, what now? Do we drive up to the fire tower?" asked Gerald.

"Not with Andes still here watching us like the Sphinx. We'll take up an axe and chainsaw, then light off on the pretext of cutting firewood."

"Man, I already love it."

We cached the handguns under our coats. No telltale lumps appeared. I put on a camouflage vest. I shouldered the double-bladed axe and a coil of manila rope. Gerald, hamming it up, put the chainsaw on the chopping block, unscrewed the gas cap, and gave it a sniff. The tank was dry. He found the gasoline can and filled the chainsaw's tank. We also took the gas can with us into the woods furthest away from the fire tower.

Once in the cedars' foliage, I sketched us a map in the dirt. It looked confusing. I drew up the layout again, only simpler. Gerald approved it and we struck off in the Thursday morning cool.

We blended into the woods as stealthy as we could. My camouflage vest was loose leafy greens over brown. The ski mask hiding my pale face was hominy-hued. Gerald wore a faded brown windbreaker and cloroxed blue jeans with ripped hems. His nutmeg complexion didn't require a ski mask.

Six steps in front, Gerald cut with lynx-like surety over spongy pine needles. He was Old Man's protégé prowling the Mekong Delta, the mud slopped up to his knees under the flame trees. More perturbing to think, perhaps, was that he was the incarnate of Old Man's avenging angel. We ditched the chainsaw with the gas can and rope inside an elm's hollow trunk but retained the axe. We didn't gallop straight uphill to the fire tower but instead crept along the gravelly ravine to Trout Creek.

I jumped. It was only a sapsucker chiseling on poplar bole: *rat-tat, rat-tat, rat-tat*. Gerald, flexing his eyebrows, grinned at me. We pressed on. Scuppernong grapevine, tupelo wood, and maybe kudzu wove an impenetrable thicket, but we were tenacious. The natural screen heartened me, but it slowed our progress. We hacked away branches and made little detours. Downwind, I whiffed wood smoke and wondered who'd have a fire going out here.

Water trickled over the craggy limestone falls. Gerald's hand directed my eyes to a homemade deer stand wedged in a willow oak's groin. He performed a charade, putting his fingers behind his ears that I guessed to be antlers, and firing an imaginary rifle. Right, a few minutes after dawn, deer season was now official. The hunter, struck with buck fever, didn't man his battle station. Had he fallen off the deer stand and broke his fool neck? No time to check, we soldiered on.

Gerald, using a fallen log for a bridge, spanned Trout Creek. Wary of tumbling in, I followed him. Safely. Were hostile eyes glued on us? Gerald withdrew the Remington 20 from under his coat, toyish-looking in his hand but still lethal. My fingers squeezed the Browning 9 mil's grips. Crossing Trout Creek, my property boundary, had upped the ante.

Memories of Old Man and I dodging flak from the red-capped shooter preached caution, but didn't we pursue an always elusive quarry? I shivered at a mental image of Jan Maddox swinging on a green nylon rope and then and there, I promised myself this: Never mind what frustration and no matter what effort, the Blue Cheer was going down. Gerald's lips thinned into a slash. He felt it, too. I guided us to the fire tower's rear. Dogtrotting, we crested the knoll. The hemlock matting muffled our footfall like racing in doeskin moccasins. We emerged from the woods into the clearing's sunlight and approached the fire tower.

Somebody had erased the Blue Cheer's logo off the concrete footing. Gerald didn't waste time. He clutched the lowest crossbar and leveraged himself up to the ladder. A 360-degree scan encountered no danger. I handed him the axe. If the trapdoor proved stubborn, he could smash his way through.

I stayed below on the ground. Should Gerald draw fire, I'd rake out a fast barrage as he hightailed it down. We realized before its execution that our plan was reckless—a popgun 9 mil was no defense against assault rifles. Gerald's large man agility astonished me. He wiggled up the ladder at breakneck pace, the axe handle clanging against the steel derrick. Once aloft, his palms smacked against the trapdoor.

Gerald bawled down to me. "It's nailed shut. Is Andes barricaded inside?"

"Hardly. I bet he nailed down the trapdoor, then crawled out a window to reach the ladder. The skinny bastard could do it," I said.

A derisive noise. "I ain't crawling through any windows," said Gerald.

"Just chop yourself a hole. That old wood will split up."

A vehement snort. "If they open up firing, gang way. I'm coming down. Fast."

"Work the axe, not your gums. I'll keep things tight down here," I said.

I threw a hurried glance toward the nearby woods. Gerald hooked a knee through the uppermost rung and transferred weight to his other boot. He took a couple practice swings. Satisfied with his range of motion, limited as it was, he swung the axe. Its steel blade glanced off the wood.

"Is that all you brought?" I said to taunt him.

Gerald reared the axe back and hurled it. Its resounding whack bit deep into the wood. Echoes hopped off the treetops. My oily thumb snicked off the 9 mil's safety. Three successive thwacks ruptured the trapdoor. I put down one knee and braced my arm against the tower's leg. Bullets could fly from any direction while Gerald chopped away. The first hollow thunk told me his axe blade had busted through the trapdoor. He swung smaller strokes to enlarge the crack into a serviceable manhole. Splinters rained down on me.

"I'm done," said Gerald, after a short while.

"10-4. Should I stand sentry down here?"

"With that racket, even the dead know we're here. Shinny your butt on up."

After re-stashing the 9 mil in my waistband, I chinned myself to the lowest crossbar and went up the ladder, my eyes shut to forestall the twirling in my head. Touch of vertigo. I wormed through the manhole and found Gerald rummaging through shelves. His shotgun pistol nudged aside rusty cans.

"What's in here? Myrrh and frankincense?" Gerald lifted a pine box's lid. But only mouse turds lay inside it. Dried asters in a tinfoil-wrapped demijohn and greasy wads of paper torn out of the yellow pages gave the space a hoboesque look. "We're batting a perfect zero, Frank."

Biting my lips, I deliberated on motive. Why had Andes lied about his enrollment at Racine University? What thread, if any, linked him to the Blue Cheer? Where was Andes when each Maddox was slain? Did he even have an alibi? Nobody was now at the Maddox A-frame and the tar-top road was a bleak, blue ribbon.

"Didn't you tell me this forest is posted?" asked Gerald.

My hand swept around us. "Yep, both sides. It's part of a national park. Andes worked as a volunteer here."

"Andes lived the life of pharaohs. Up here grooving on nature, munching on vitamin C, and shitting in a chamber pot," said Gerald.

"It appears he took that off, too," I said.

Gerald's boot scraped away floor debris. "He pretended to grind out a novel on a laptop computer and fed you that hogwash about graduate school."

"And I bought it, too. Let's go to Scarab and chat with our friendly sheriff," I said.

CHAPTER TWENTY-TWO

The copper steeple came into view first, triggering a memory of Zelma Roe's flock shouting their prayer service hallelujahs. Old Man had urged me to take measure of Zelma and I'd balked. Why? Same old apathy? Angry, I stood on the accelerator. The Valiant's indestructible engine bucked and its tailpipes belched out banners of stinking black smoke.

Gerald scowled, waving his arm to dispel the scorched metal smell coming from under the hood. "You'll seize up the pistons, Frank. Slide it on over. Better check this out. Something's wrong."

"It just needs oil," I muttered. "Old Man keeps cans in the trunk."

I grated slowing tires over the red stone gravel. Gerald and I climbed out. The First Primitive Apostolic Church, pristine white, gleamed at us. Serene for prayer, it was a refuge to soothe beat-up bones, and I ached all over. Russet chrysanthemums and tawny nasturtiums bracketed the cinderblock porch. It was a picturesque chapel. Think Norman Rockwell. Think L. L. Bean catalog cover art. Think Thomas Kinkade. Think why was the damn nightlight over the entryway left burning?

After propping up the hood, I tried to undo the oil cap and fricasseed three fingers on its hot plastic. The short hairs on the back of my neck stood up. Something about the nightlight burning rang false. I keyed open the trunk and rummaged through crates of junk to find road flares, parachute cord, a bent hooligan bar, a surveyor's perambulator, and enough other stuff to call Old Man a genuine pack rat. The one prize I didn't find was the one I was looking for.

"Nary a drop of oil," I said to Gerald.

Gerald turned and pointed behind us. "Might be some in that tool shed."

"Cool. What can we score for a breaking and entering?" I said.

Gerald didn't bite. "In a pinch like this, I'll risk it."

"Then go ahead. I've had my fill of jails."

"Let's skip it, then. We'll thumb a ride into town," said Gerald.

"Wait a second." Hadn't the A-frame's porch lamp been left burning, too, Jan Maddox swaying inside, dead on the end of a rope? The eeriest case of déjà vu sent a shudder through me.

"You got the heebie-jeebies?" Gerald asked me.

Squinting, I saw something drawn below the light fixture by a bug zapper. It couldn't be. Walking nearer, I craned my neck and squinted harder. It was, though. I swallowed back my fear. Some creep had etched a walking fish using black Magic Marker on the white clapboard. The Blue Cheer! "Inside, Gerald." My head jerked towards the church.

Gerald hustled over to me. "What's up?"

"This light's on. Somebody's been here and gone."

"Or not," said Gerald.

Our steel flew out. We flanked the door, pressed flat against the sun-baked clapboards. They warmed my lower back, hands, and rump, but not my blood. Gerald stretched and his fingers jiggled the knob. Swinging hinges creaked an invitation that we accepted.

"Cover me," said Gerald.

I tipped my chin at Gerald. Semi-crouched, he curled past me. I scanned the roadway left to right and the coast was still clear. I trailed him inside. He crouched behind the rearmost pew and secured the left side. Kneeling, the 9 mil in my fists, I staked the opposite side. My fingers sweated. My heart beat harder.

The door clicked shut behind us. The red neon tubes above us in the steeple purred as the crucifix came alive. Blinks adjusted our vision. The mustiness made me sneeze. Gerald winced. I hazarded a glimpse up the center aisle where the three-tiered altar descended to a knee-high railing. Sunlight through the stained glass windows diffused reds with blues over greens. I heard drips. I smelled blood. The drips grew louder. The blood smell grew stronger. Gusts whipsawed through the louvered steeple; windows clacked in their jambs.

Gerald hissed over at me, "*Pssst.* Don't freak out on me."

I let out a hard breath. "We're not alone."

"I already know that. Do you see any rooms up front?"

I checked up the center aisle again. "The pastor's study, off to your left."

"Listen, I'll move ahead. If even a June bug farts, you grease it."

Gerald duckwalked to the side aisle, his head tucked low. He sprang into a mad dash up to the front. The 9 mil in my upright stance swiveled above the pew like a turret gunner. Finger on the trigger, I stood ready to deliver a fatal strike. Alas, no June bugs farted. But so far, so good. Gerald occupied the altar.

He executed a series of deft maneuvers around corners and behind walls and cleared out the altar space before snapping on the light switch. Fluorescence gleamed off Zelma's shut door and the altar buffed to a burnt yellow. At Gerald's go-sign, I sprinted up the same aisle he'd taken and joined him behind the altar. We signed all our communications and, at Zelma's closed door, repeated our side-by-side tactic.

Gerald jerked the lever handle. The hinges, this time oiled, were compliant. I peeped inside. A fresh chitlins smell overwhelmed me. Nausea socked me low in the guts. I gawked. Zelma Roe's death had been vicious.

Zelma, behind her glass-topped desk, greeted us, her three eyes peeping from under her bangs. The nightshade blue of her two natural eyes clashed with the third's meat-red color. A .25 or .32 caliber—the favorite of pro assassins—had punched a hole mid-center of her forehead. A blackish residue of cordite rimmed the hole.

A space heater cut on to rattle away and I kicked it off. I struggled to focus. Procedure. Had the murder weapon been ditched nearby? I felt too numb to search for it. My eyes cut to Gerald, also transfixed. I pummeled my fist on a sash and raised the window. Refreshing air swooshed into the study.

I heard my veins suck dry. They collapsed. I stared closer. Knots of blood stained the beige carpeting. Zelma's necklace was a razor slice curving from ear to ear. Gray gristle and bone slivers protruded.

"G-g-god Almighty." Gerald's jaw dropped.

Blood doused the pockets of Zelma's blouse. It also speckled her Holy Bible and reading glasses on the green desk blotter. Incisions cut up her abdomen. The batik print skirt was slit up the middle, and down there was lots of blood. I averted my gaze.

"Th-th-this ain't right." Gerald, his glassy eyes now on me, snarled. "Hear me? It ain't right."

"Who?"

"Who? You know who. Untie that flag and let's get her covered up. Christ, her body is still warm. For fuck's sake, the killers must've lit out minutes ago."

Detaching the flag, I felt, with every pulse, more depleted and punchless. Enough death. Enough. A gold chalice on the altar contained waxy wafers for the Black Sunday Communion. My tongue tasted like wax. I spat.

"It's time to pull the rip cord, Gerald," I said, entering the study, the flag in my hands.

Gerald's large hands clamped my shoulders. He shook me hard. My teeth clicked. "Huh? You say we back out of this shit? That what you're telling me? Snap out of your funk. Am I getting through, Frank? If you don't wake up, you can kiss death row hello. Rod and you can tap out messages there through the plumbing. You with me?"

"A-a-aw right," I chattered. "Turn me loose." From here on, I'd never steel my nerves but rely on my MP training or something instinctual.

Gerald snapped his head. "Frank, outside. Quick."

We retraced our steps down the aisle and out the church doors. We halted at the road. No getaway car disappeared into the distance.

"With that much of a head start, we'd never overtake the killers. Let's snoop inside more," I said.

We returned to the pastor's study. After swaddling Zelma with Old Glory, Gerald parted the mini-blinds and turned on a brass floor lamp. "Dear Lord," he said in a coarse voice. "Frank and I ain't greedy. One clue will do us. One big one. We'll mete out the justice. Amen."

I didn't bother to respond. My gloved fingers inched out desk drawers, the top one first. Gerald took apart the filing cabinet. Papers flew about us. We went at it like that while Zelma, putrefying under Old Glory, threw out a mausoleum stink. I found the usual stuff crammed inside desk drawers: church memos, a paid gas bill, a ruler, rubber bands, correction fluid, and an envelope of clipped store coupons. The bottom drawer, spacious enough to suspend hanging folders, contained Zelma's red knit scarf and stocking hat. Underneath them—yes!—was a dog-eared journal.

I let my eyes skim over the choppy sentences describing Zelma's service for the Lord. She visited the black lung hospice in Scarab, delivered hot suppers to shut-ins, and honchoed a library van visiting outlying towns. Charities and good deeds filled her days. A vibrant lady I'd never meet was gone. Despite a stab of misplaced loss, I pushed on reading.

Zelma was also politically engaged. The Blue Cheer first bobbed up two months ago in her entries. My fingers turned the page. I was keen to learn more about Zelma homing in on Scarab's underbelly. She packed plenty of grit. Indignant and standing tall in the bully pulpit, she lashed out, condemning the Blue Cheer by name. Protective churchgoers cautioned her outspokenness but it was too late. Trouble came fast when word reached the Blue Cheer. Zelma Roe became a marked lady.

Badgering telephone calls, she wrote, escalated into physical threats. Zelma complained to a largely indifferent sheriff that struck a chord in me. Leery to implicate church folks, she discontinued her protesting sermons and hid her anxieties from them. She also befriended Jan Maddox. Their dinner engagement back in the summer, which Old Man had referred to, was mentioned. A few days later, it seemed, she decided to share her torment with her new friend Jan and then swore her to secrecy.

"What's that?" asked Gerald.

"Zelma's journal. Read it for yourself." I handed the journal to him.

Breathing hard, Gerald got the gist real fast. "It says Zelma talked to Jan Maddox. But that's as far as they could take it."

"But we're taking it all the way," I said.

"Fucking-A." Gerald removed books shelves and one by one riffled through their pages. "Dear lady preacher," he said in a sober mutter. "Speak to us."

Irritated, I frowned at him. "Quit with the mystical crap, okay?"

A scrap of yellow legal paper trickled free of a prayer book. Cursing,

Gerald bent over to retrieve it. "What the . . . ho, ho, eat crow, Frankie my boy. Eat crow. The lady preacher does speaketh. Here's a map, no less."

"Gerald, I'm warning you—"

"—I shit you not, my favorite turd."

I crowded his elbow and also examined the scrap of yellow legal paper. The same bold script as set down in Zelma's journal labeled the drawn-in roads. One road curved up to the fire tower and from there, a dotted line marked a windy footpath through the boonies to an asterisked destination—"THE BLUE CHEER COMPOUND!" A shorter jeep trail snaking in from a tar-top road to the same destination was unknown to me.

"It's easy now to fathom why they killed her. Yes sir, if this is genuine, the truth is simple enough to understand," said Gerald.

"It's in Zelma's handwriting. What she knew about the Blue Cheer could cook their goose," I said.

"Ain't it the truth." Gerald grinned at me. "Now we'll cook their goose."

A fatalistic calm soothed me. At last, I had a glimpse of our nemesis or at least held in my hand convincing proof of their existence. I returned Zelma's journal to the same desk drawer and closed the study door after us. "The Blue Cheer did this murder and they're finished. Are you up for this?" I asked.

Gerald braced his butt against the altar railing and folded his arms over his chest. "Let's step back and look at this objectively. We're two soldiers armed with cap pistols. I'd say that's suicidal."

"Is it?"

"For the sake of argument, let's suppose I have a violent felon to go round up. What do I do? Well, let me tell you. First off, I assemble a veteran posse. Vets I know to be solid in a jam. What I don't do is go at it single-handed. We strategize a plan, strap on body armor, and bust in armed to the hilt. Anything less—well, like I just said—is suicide."

"Wrap your mind around this. We don't have the time to enlist a private army. We move now because the Blue Cheer must know we're closing in," I said.

"Your decision is made. What the fuck can I say?"

"Up at the cabin is a .243 rifle. It has a Bausch & Lomb scope. One ammo clip," I said.

Gerald's forehead wrinkled in wry humor. "That's all you got?"

"All right then, I think it's time to call in your state cop buddy."

CHAPTER TWENTY-THREE

———

To kill two birds with one stone, I risked telephoning Betty Maddox. If she was one of them, the Blue Cheer, I'd hear it in her voice: a guilty hesitation, a stuttered syllable, or a curt gasp. If she wasn't one of them, I crossed my fingers in hopes that she could find us some heavier armament. My twisting insides rebelled but I braved venturing inside the pastor's study.

I slanted my shoulders away from Zelma and breathed through my teeth to blunt the stench. It tasted even viler than it smelled. My shaky fingers found Betty's home number listed in the white pages. Her reedy "hello" gave me the jerks but I went ahead and told her where Gerald and I were and what we needed.

Incredulous, Betty asked, "Swoop in on them?"

"It's doable," I said.

"It's iffy, I'd say, Frank. For the time being, let's pigeonhole that plan. They murdered my kin. Now who else do you say is dead?" asked Betty.

"Zelma Roe," I replied, eyeing the grotesque blood-shot flag.

"Our Holy Roller preacher?"

"Butchered like a shoat hog." I followed my gut instinct. Betty was no joiner with this hate faction. Besides, this conversation had to end fast. "We need more firepower."

"What?"

"Guns. Bigger guns," I said.

"Right. In Old Man's trunk. Poke along its edges and tip up a corner. The floor panel should pop free. Take a look under it."

"Will do."

"Mr. Johnson, don't hang up. I want in on this. Don't tell me no. Ladies volunteer for the army nowadays. They ship overseas to fight beside men. A mite grayer maybe, but I'm gutsy enough. You owe me."

"And put more lives at risk?" I said.

"Then I best bring in Sheriff Greenleaf," said Betty.

Gerald would bitch, but what choice did I have? "See you in a few minutes."

"I'll be right there," said Betty.

Near noon, the sun burned at its hellish zenith. I hiked around back of the church where Gerald had coaxed the Valiant to hide in the hollyhock hedgerows. A flagstone walk led to a small cemetery of lopsided, brown slabs. Again I wondered how gravediggers excavated holes in this rocky terrain. Dynamite? Jackhammers? The venerable pick and shovel?

Cell phone in hand, Gerald said, "Logan has signed on."

I jabbed in the trunk key. "Was Logan agreeable?"

"With a little persuasion, yeah. She blew her stack until I gently reminded her that she'd earned those lieutenant bars on my shoulders. Well, sort of. Anyhow, I leaned on her guilt."

Gerald started to explain the owed favor but I wasn't listening. "Hey, you hear that?"

The colicky engine had to be an ancient John Deere tractor: *tut-tut-tut-tut, tut-tut-tut-tut.* We face-planted to the dirt.

Gerald poked me from behind. "Is the church door closed?"

"Yep."

"Did you turn off the porch light?"

"Uh, nope."

"Smooth move."

The John Deere tractor hauling a wagonload of firewood took an eternity to chug by us but the pace in Scarab, I'd learned, could be a sluggish one. But our luck held firm. The tractor chuffed out of audible range, and we hopped up, dusting the dirt off our fronts.

"Old Man's trunk has a cubbyhole," I said.

"What's inside it?" asked Gerald.

"I dunno. Betty didn't say." I went over and keyed open the trunk.

We pitched out rags and crates to empty the trunk and Gerald's knuckles tapped and his fingertips probed. A snag of wax cord by a taillight pulled out the trunk's bottom panel. Flanking the spare tire, swaddled in black plastic, two long guns were clipped in place along with a flat of shells.

I silently thanked Old Man and, I swear, he growled at me, "Go kick some ass, babe."

Gerald shucked off the black plastic. A pair of 12-gauge Remington 870 shotguns, a big hit with the brotherhood in blue, were chambered for 3-inch shells and the red rubber butt plates only sweetened their value.

Gerald loaded the artillery and we planned out how to conduct an advanced reconnaissance using Zelma's hand-drawn map. Lieutenant Mary Logan meantime rode a fast horse. Betty glided up in a lipstick-red Monte Carlo, the model and shade that held sway over mature ladies. We clambered inside, she gunned the gas, and her tires raked up the red stone gravel.

"Suck a right at the fire lane," I said. Gerald hulked over the front seat, his muscular arms stretched out to drum his fingers on the dash-board. "Park behind the fire tower," I went on. "We'll hike in the long way through the boonies. It's safer."

"I wonder how Zelma found the Blue Cheer's lair," said Gerald.

"Zelma probably followed one of them and drew up the map. With her friend Jan dead, she had no go-to person. Too bad she didn't know about us. Things then snowballed fast and before she knew it, her life wasn't worth a slug for the same reason as Jan's," I said.

"They knew too much. We'll get to the fucking bottom of it," said Gerald.

"That ain't just hot air, hero," I said.

Betty straightened her kerchief and her anger vented. "Utterly un-thinkable. It's Jasper County, Texas, all over again. The next thing you know, they'll come to lynch us upside-down from the tobacco sheds."

Gerald grunted.

I'd no comeback. Misery cramped my mid-section as lurid pictures of our last tangle with the Neo-Nazis writhed in my mind. Gerald, of course, had been in the thick of that fight along with his younger brother, Chet. Seeking relief, I tried adopting a carefree attitude like Old Man, the tenderfoot, in Vietnam. It didn't mean anything. Death and life, pain and sorrow, murder and depression, all of it meant nothing.

Then our possible options ticked off in my head. A: Sheriff Greenleaf had to be in the Blue Cheer's pouch. Nix that idea. B: Lieutenant Logan was two hours off, but bringing what? Not the 101st Airborne Division. No, just one skeptical but able state cop in a CV cruiser. C: I could sit pat until the Blue Cheer came along to put a cap in my ass. D: I might commit *hari kari*. No, ours by default was the most expedient decision and any further ambivalence about it invited disaster, too.

Betty gave my knee a maternal pat. "You buck up. Old Man told me about you. Frank Johnson, he said to me, is my best friend in the world, but you know what, Betty? He sometimes makes me want to scream."

Gerald chipped in his two cents. "All we got, Frank, is each other and right now."

"Heavy, man, heavy. Park us on the far side of the fire tower. We'll pick up the right trail down in the trees," I said.

Betty crossed the split log bridge and made the final turn between the sassafras shrubs. She parked by the fire tower, a rustic sentinel that had outlived its importance. We piled out. The fire tower's gaping trapdoor attracted our gaze.

"Could a spy in the sky be following us?" Gerald asked me.

Splintered wood crinkled underfoot. "Now how likely is that?" I asked.

Gerald clasped the lowest rung and hauled himself up. "We've got to know." He started to climb. At the quarter way mark, his head cranked sidewise. "Hear that?" he bellowed down to us. "I'm drawing heat. A gunner out there toward the treeline." He did a down periscope and his lips formed a roguish grin I knew so well. He rubbed spit on the raw blisters the rusty steel had grated off his palms. "All because we're out to spoil their fun. Damn."

"I didn't hear any shots," said Betty.

"Why stick around? Let's break for cover," I said.

"There it is," said Gerald.

I sprinted, leading with my waist, my camel legs putting down long, distancing strides. Betty fell in behind me and Gerald folded in behind her, his twelve gauge covering our asses. We halted at the wood's edge, puffing for breath. Serious doubts racked me. The shooter's high-power rifles would trounce our short-range shotguns. On the other hand, if engaging in any close-in brush fighting, we'd fare much better.

The pathway's source on Zelma's map was a defunct Buick Skylark latticed over with grapevine and Virginia creeper. Picking up the path's track from there wasn't as apparent. We paced over a search grid. My eyes forged lanes of sight through the shadowy forest but I found no markers. Tree trunks, thick and thin, hampered our search. We also kept a sharp eye out for the shooter. Gerald moved further out and I waved Betty over to scout along the wood's margins.

In a short bit, Gerald loped back to us. "The trail must be a series of chop marks about yay high." His flat hand rested at eye level. "The first mark I found didn't click. Twenty feet more, a second chop mark was more than a coincidence. Then I connected the third to the fourth chop mark. They run south to north like the trail sketched on Zelma's map."

"Lead on," I said.

"Ambush?" asked Betty.

"We'll move in single file. Go slow. Expect the unexpected. Any strange noise, fire heavy and hard, dive for cover. Watch each other's back," said Gerald.

"Lead on," I repeated.

It was slow going. Gerald paced off the correct distances between the subsequent chop marks. We skirted a column of lichen-clad, red boulders, a rock formation noted on Zelma's map. Our trek dipped from virgin oaks into a stand of hemlock and aspen. Old gypsy moth defoliation let in a nuanced sunlight.

The 9 mil poked into the crook of my back. My hold on the pump twelve gauge didn't slacken. My tongue wadded into a piece of steel wool and I couldn't work up any spit. *Kik, kik, kik! Kik, kik, kik!* A pileated woodpecker's outcry scared me to throw my shotgun to my shoulder pit. Betty hid a smile.

We pitched into a wilder, higher province where bear scat and deer rubbings grew more frequent. Lactic acid seared my calves and thighs as we followed the blue paint bars now marked on rocks. At a creek, Gerald removed his sunshades to ride upside down on his mesh hat. If the Blue Cheer had half a brain, their outposts would've engaged us by now, but they had no brains so we soldiered on.

We heard them before we saw them. Boisterous yells, metal clanging against metal, and a motor backfiring. We descended into a straight-away through a shallow, hardpan valley. Two mountains intersected and the fold created an excellent defensive position.

A twelve-foot chain link fence crowned with four strands of slash wire enclosed their palisade. A no-man's zone bulldozed out ten to twelve feet buffered the fence. Loose greens over browns of camouflage cloth formed an immense canopy that thwarted aerial detection. Betty hid while Gerald and I collected information along their perimeters. Once we finished, we reunited to compare notes.

The bulk of their infrastructure was a work in progress. A long, ramshackle structure clad in green vinyl served as a barracks and the outbuildings included ammo dumps, a commo bunker, a mess hall, a shower facility, a rifle range, and a few other sheds. They'd roasted a pig in the smelly barbecue pit within the past few days.

I'd spotted the signature "walking fish" banner flapping under the Stars and Stripes on a bamboo flagpole. The jeep trail, also bulldozed as shown on Zelma's map, ran into the twin gates on the south corner where a vacant sentry box made of framed-in 2x4s stood. A well-drilling rig sat near the gate, suggesting that these subhumans thirsted for something other than blood.

"Manpower?" I asked.

Squatting, Gerald flexed on the balls of his feet. "I saw signs of activity. Whose land is this?"

"It's national park land but you won't run into wood rangers way back here. A bear hunter who has wandered astray, maybe," replied Betty.

"Signs on the chain link fence say 'U.S. Government Military Facility. Top Secret. No Trespassing'. That tends to dampen any hunter's inquisitiveness," I said.

"But what is their head count?" asked Betty.

"I saw enough bunks to house a militia only they must all be AWOL," I replied.

"Well, I saw four. One taller than the rest has these weird-ass eyes. The dumpy dude with scraggly sideburns they called Goner or Goines. I didn't catch the names for the other two. They're busy beavers filling up sandbags near the barracks," said Gerald.

I knew them all. A fighter's adrenaline juiced up my nerves. Dot Christmas and Woody Sears. Goines. Andes!

"Below the barracks is a heli-pad. Their chopper is probably fueled, so I'll hobble that first," said Gerald.

"What about the authorities? Shouldn't we wait on them? Call them?" Betty took out a cell phone.

Gerald gave a discouraging headshake. "Too damn little time. Lieutenant Logan is still booking over the Interstate. You can hardly get a signal up here. I already tried."

I didn't respond. I was too busy wondering how you capped an adrenaline gusher inside you.

"Let's hit them before any others pull into the gate," said Betty.

For once, our roulette wheel hit a premo number. No high tech motion sensors or surveillance cameras stationed along their perimeters announced us. No pit bull terriers barked at our hostile scents. We melted into evanescent green shade within spitting distance of the compound's fence. We poised there, ready to strike first. Our success depended on the element of surprise.

CHAPTER TWENTY-FOUR

Our battle plan was a gem. We'd creep to the chain link fence and slink in under a culvert on my sector. Then, we'd isolate each of the men to overwhelm and tie up with a gag. That done, we'd move on and defang the next bastard. Too often such optimism is naïve.

Ferreting underneath the chain link fence was the easy part.

Betty was the last through when a fusillade of automatic rifle fire blanketed us. We dispersed as in a jailbreak, each vaulting for the nearest hard cover. Mine was a berm of white masonry sand. Gerald toppled over a concrete mixer for a shield. A shade to the right, Betty lay prone sheltered by stacked bricks.

I crawled on my elbows along the sand pile and sneaked a careful peek from the side. Gunshots had tapered off. Snipers lurked up in the unfinished barracks the length of a football field away. A human form, holding a rifle, shifted. I pulled back. The next hail of gunfire strafed us, rounds zeroing in hotter and closer. Thrashed-up sand dusted my head. Gerald swapped volleys off his shotgun with them. Our lack of cover in front made any advancement sure death. Survival might boil down to simple math. Could my 9 mil outrange my twelve-gauge shotgun? I whipped through a clip but no way was the 9 mil any more effective.

Andes, by this time, was astute enough to grasp their weapons superiority. During a lull I spotted the four men dismount from the barracks' rafters. The last man down lowered a weapon. Their new ground-based strategy became obvious to me. They'd outflank us and after sealing off our lines of retreat, hover outside our kill zone, and plink us off one by one.

"Come to papa," said Gerald.

"Fat chance. Listen." My whisper came out as a dry-throated rasp.

"They're on the move. All that's left, they figure, is rubbing us out piece-meal."

"They're pretty much right," said Gerald.

"What's on your mind, Frank?" asked Betty.

"Move wide right before they can slip behind us. The construction materials will give us some cover. Pin them against the fence."

"And make them beg for mercy," said Gerald.

A herd of T-Rexes would have had more stealth than Andes, Goines, Woody, and Dot. We heard their hollers and cloddish boot thumps. An ejected clip clinked from a rifle. We moved out, dodging behind sawhorses, concrete bags, and a gasoline generator on our desperate gamble to push them into the chain link fence.

Goines barked out orders. But dissent arose in the ranks.

"Double time!"

"Damn it, I'm doing the best I can."

Andes' voice cut in. "Shut up and soldier. Point man, have you established contact?"

"Nope. Let me get a better look."

"No! Maintain marching!"

Betty's attack angle was shortest. Old Man's shotgun pistol in her hands was a blunderbuss. Gerald sprinted to draw even with her but arrived a second too late. A lank figure in combat fatigues stomped around the corner. The last thing Woody Sears expected was to hear a shotgun cock.

"Drop it!" yelled Gerald.

Woody, by reflex, swept up his rifle. Screaming, Betty discharged a round. She missed. I was stunned. At that close range, how could she? Gerald shouted out. A distraction. Woody's aim was slapdash. I next saw Gerald dash off a round that knocked Woody flat. His boot heels flew up like blank flashcards. He was out of the fight, dead.

Andes hollered. "Who was shot?"

"I don't know. Where's Woody? Woody!"

"Woody?"

"Woody's dead. I shot him," shouted Gerald.

"Is that them? Where are they?"

"We're being shoved into the fence, stupid."

"Run for it!"

I did just that. I heard the chain link fence behind the ammo dump jingle. I saw, from the corner of my eye, Gerald stopping to drag up Betty. She appeared unhurt and fell back. The chain link fence rattled louder. Somebody was scaling it and my last dollar went on Andes.

A shotgun pumped out thunderclaps. Gerald, I glanced back to see, had gotten the drop on Dot Christmas and Goines. Neither bundle recumbent on the ground twitched. Andes, my prey, was a hell-for-leather chicken. He'd left the seat of his pants on the uppermost strand of slash wire. He also outdid me at fence climbing. I scaled up the chain link okay but my straddled legs snagged on the top strands. It was like dry humping a chainsaw. The razors' edges nicked near my crotch fabric.

Gerald huffed towards me. "You going after Andes?"

"Uh, as soon as I finish up my self-vasectomy here."

"Ouch. How did you do that?" Gerald grabbed his fingers through the chain links, dug for a toehold, and powered up to me. He held down the slash wire strands. I wiggled free and dropped over the fence to land on the other side, elated.

Gerald handed my twelve gauge and a clutchful of shells over the fence to me. "Happy hunting and good shooting. Betty and I will head back to lead in Lieutenant Logan. Man, she'll flip over this. Totally flip."

I nodded my approval and lit out. Andes enjoyed a good five-minute head start on me. Wouldn't you know he'd bolt? The Blue Cheer's leader had a yellow streak. I cycled a fresh shell into the shotgun's chamber. A crisp walk took me into shady hawthorn and alders. Think what you will but stalking a subject through woods trumps any meanness that urban streets can dish out. Having done it in both environments, I compared street smarts to woods smarts.

Plunging into a deep woods like this one brought more details to sweat. Echoes carried. Shadows confused. Ambushes waited. The quarry wore no hunter orange. The hunter if not on full alert at all times became the hunted.

Woods, though, gave me one distinct advantage over city concrete:

cutting for sign. I wasn't a Mohican brave but Andes put down tracks even Jose Feliciano could read. Andes' footprints, in mud, slew outward and his retreat bordered on headlong panic. I moved at a steady jaunt, picking up and putting down my feet on slightly bent knees. Having gained my second wind, each breath wasn't a life-sustaining gulp and my lungs were no longer on fire.

Twilight ceded to darkness. Mountain by mountain, the blue ridges accepted the night's cold mantle. Trees barricaded me. Laurel branches slapped my cheeks, keeping me alert. As anticipated, fagged legs soon slowed Andes. The obvious hadn't occurred to him. If I were in his shoes, I'd entrench in a spider hole amid this second growth and poise my rifle's forestock on a swatch of club moss. I'd center the crosshairs on my pursuer's heart and wait for the optimum second to trip the trigger.

Andes followed the valley path for the greater part of an hour. The bulk of a cliff pressed in on my right. He doglegged left near a series of old trenches, a northward turn that stumped me. Granted, he was in full flight but a wild hair wasn't the reason for the turn. No, Andes had a destination in mind. A safe house maybe? Laying siege didn't appeal to me. My stomach rumbled on empty and dinner came when pawpaws dangled just within my reach. My fast thanks went to Gerald. I scurried on and downwind caught a helicopter blade's hollow *chop-chop-chop.* Just as quick, it slacked off in the dark hush.

The twelve gauge shotgun grew too heavy. I ejected its shells and buried it in a crevasse under sprigs and acorns, then pocketed the shells. The Browning 9 mil was now my only ally. I picked up my pace, growing confident that I'd soon overhaul Mr. Andes. We moved along the crest to a ridge.

I navigated through the murk by touch, my fingertips grazing against the intractable surfaces of bark, rock, and leaves. I'd pause every so often, straining to hear Andes snapping a tree branch or cursing a stubbed toe. I was grateful that darkness diminished a sniper's opportunities. But not so fast, Johnson. Andes might pack night vision hardware, devastating with moonrise soon on the way. I felt sheepish stupidity. My boots crunched over pebbles and I stayed keen to the slightest alien sound. A clattering sound petrified me. Then I relaxed. A buck scraped its antlers on a sapling to remove its velvet.

Where was Andes? Had I lost him?

I flumped down on a turtle-backed stone and enjoyed my first sit-down since exiting the compound. My radium-tipped watch dials glowed at eight o'clock. I estimated my three hours travel averaging three miles per hour. Nine, maximum ten miles east, then we made the cutoff north. I hadn't the foggiest notion where his cutoff led. No man-lights glinted and a chilled wind bit into my face. Glittery stars limned the horizon. Moonlight gave objects shadows.

I jogged on, rested again, listening sharp. Andes had eluded me in the dark. Then he committed a cardinal mistake. The scent of tobacco drifted over me on the night air. I looked for the cigarette's giveaway ember and within steps my vigilance paid off. Concentrating on the cigarette's fiery tip, I crept up on the unsuspecting Andes as he languished against a tree trunk. I snatched Andes' collar and crammed the Browning's muzzle into his side. "Move and I'll blast you," I said.

Andes' head jerked. Cigarette sparks spattered. "Johnson?" His high-pitched voice sought reassurance. "That you?"

"Smoking is dangerous for your health. Hands on your head." I hitched up Andes' automatic rifle and sidearmed it in the direction of a rockpile. The rifle landed with a crash that triggered a noise like a castanet. Frisking him, I confiscated a clasp knife and a three-cell flashlight. They'd come in handy for what lay in store.

"This is it, Andes. You talk. I decide if I kill you. We flying straight?"

Andes' swallow was audible. "How much do I tell you?"

"Every nitty-gritty detail," I told him.

CHAPTER TWENTY-FIVE

But Andes and I got off on the wrong foot. "Johnson, I ain't breathing a word to you about jack. I'll die first," he said.

His machismo was worth a throw of the dice. The upshot, however, was predictable. I didn't relish the old CIA trick as much as I'd wanted to. The Browning's steel backstrap whacked his skull. Andes hog-grunted and fell to his knees. I took his point—he did pack enough brass to play a hard case.

I could beat him into road pizza and never learn squat. Miles from nowhere, my taking him off at the head was doable. I'd plead self-defense and Gatlin could pry any homicide rap off me. Nope, I'd better not. The flashlight beamed over his bloody crown.

I handed Andes my red sweat rag. "Here, wipe your face." I shed my hold on him.

"You caught me. But anything can happen on our tramp through the dark boonies. Anything," said Andes.

My muscles tensed. Andes' larynx at my Buck knife's tip bobbed in a gulp. "You'll talk. Loud and clear. Or I'll cut it out of you," I said.

"I ain't saying a word," said Andes.

Just then, another propitious castanets' rattle vied for my attention. Rattlesnakes!

"Cut me and be done with it," said Andes.

Old Man's uncle's antics on his private snake-infested ridge inspired me with an outrageous idea. "You'll talk. There are religious ways to make you," I said.

As I hoped, that lit a fast fuse under Andes. His lips tightened into a gash. "Stick your lousy religion."

"Brother Andes, I heed only the Holy Ghost. No mortal, you see, opposes it." I tilted my head keeping one eye on him. One hand gestured as I belted out the kind of howls made when passing kidney stones. Such fluent glossalia, speaking in tongues, proved persuasive enough.

"Shut up," said Andes, his voice cracking.

"No can do. The wonder working power spurs me to holler His glory." Even shriller gibberish cribbed from my Holiness Church-going days flowed out. An eye on Andes, I faded a few paces to the rockpile.

"Quit talking this crazy shit," said Andes.

"A disbeliever, are you? I'll prove I speak the truth. Kneel, evildoer."

"Kneel? That's crazy talk," said Andes.

"Kneel. It's a concession of subservience." My hands dislodged a slab off the rockpile. My shrewd glance flicked down with the flashlight's beam. Coiled timber rattlesnakes were tempered by the autumn's chill and I snatched the thickest viper behind its arrowhead snout like Old Man had told me. Knots of reptilian muscles squirmed in my hands.

Face pale, Andes flinched. "I don't want that thing near me." I stalked over and my weight bulled him down. Legs buckling, he collapsed to the ground. I clutched a shock of his hair and lifted Andes to his knees. His upraised hands made for flimsy shields. "Stop . . . I hate snakes . . . stop," he said, whimpering.

"Hark, Brother Andes. This rattle is a sign God is displeased. Repent." I did a snake-bit jig and spouted more gobbledygook. He bought it all, now, backwoods preacher speech and all. Once I'd brought in the rattlesnake, the act had really gotten under his skin.

"Goddamn you!"

"What? You disparage the Lord's name," I said. The enraged rattlesnake, its length-shaking rattle deafening, stoved its pointy tail into Andes' mouth. "Grovel, Brother Andes. Repent and grovel as the serpent does."

Andes spat out a scream. He roared on and on. His face contorted. I released the overwrought rattlesnake, tangling into his lap. The aroma of urine hit me. Andes sniveled. "Don't kill me. Please, Johnson."

Psychological warfare, you had to love it. I relented long enough to grill him with my questions. "The Blue Cheer. Who are they? What's their objective?"

Andes sputtered, slapped at the lethal rattlers. "They'd kill me if I said anything."

"I'll kill you now," I said. The rattlesnake's slashing fangs snicked Andes on the wrist. He brayed out. The snake poison was diluted, half-hearted. He'd live, I prayed. "I want answers, Andes. No let up until you talk."

Andes kicked. "I'll give it up, just lift this snake off me."

I grabbed the rattlesnake behind its arrowhead snout.

"The Blue Cheer denounces the pious drivel these TV evangelists espouse . . ."

"Skip the propaganda. Who killed Jan Maddox?" I cut in.

"I dunno."

"Liar. You're the culprit. Admit it. You tortured that ravaged woman. Mutilated her. Deny it, I'll pound you to pulp." I slung the rattlesnake sailing through the air to land in its rubble kingdom. My toe banged Andes in the ribs. Something cracked. It wasn't my toe.

But then Andes sprang up at me. I dodged his tackle and my punch caught him in the guts. He faltered on stilts for legs. But he wasn't going to punk out on me. He renewed his charge. Shifting, I parried his right cross, feinted left, and pirouetted to slap a hammerlock on him.

"Fess up, Andes. Tell me how you do it. First, you rough up the victim. Kind of like this, eh?" I wrenched his arms, the ball of his humerus a tweak away from dislocation. A new agony heightened his screeches. "It's a pity I don't have a Taser like the one you used on Jan Maddox. Sing out Andes. I'll tear out your arm. Club you to death with it."

"Jan and Zelma. They were on to us. I don't know how," said Andes.

"Who killed Jan Maddox?"

Vomit bubbled at his mouth. "Goines. Put it on him," said Andes in hoarse quavers.

"He sicced the two kill-crazies on us in the motel?"

"Yeah, Goines. Who shot them? You?"

"The pleasure was all mine. But now Gerald has popped Goines

and your two homeboys, Dot and Woody. Why shouldn't I pop you?"
I kneed Andes away from me. His maniac outbursts tapered to dismal
groans as he sucked at the snakebite.

It was just as well. I'd heard enough to last a lifetime. Running the
flashlight around us, I found the sweat rag and slit it down the middle.
I bound up Andes' hands and ankles, then settled in, stranded this
Thursday night on a godawful mountaintop with a self-styled Anti-
Christ. It depressed me.

Our campfire's flicker gave off meager warmth. Betty loomed large in
my ruminations. The morning we spent cleaning out Old Man's A-
frame had revealed her outspokenness about interracial marriages.
Missing Woody Sears with a shotgun blast at short range back below
caused me to doubt her loyalty. Were Gatlin's suspicions about her in-
volvement with the Blue Cheer right? Andes' escape attempts intruded
on my thinking. His persistence on rolling over and wriggling off into
the wilds forced me to pin his ass between four big rocks.

We could've, I supposed, scrabbled back through the moonlit forest.
But I wasn't taking the chance and if I didn't kill Andes now, then the
taxpayers of West Virginia could foot the bill later. No, I'd bring him
back alive. I wasn't in the martyr-making business for hate groups.
Noisy rattlesnakes in the rockpile spiced up our evening and Andes
remained pinioned between them and me.

To while away the hours, I attempted off and on to chat with him.
Not all of my questions were answered, but then they seldom were.

"Who shot at us at the fire tower?" I asked.

Andes trained his eyes, demonic in the firelight, on me.

"Andes, you either answer me or give Mr. Rattlesnake a blow job.
Which is it?"

"No more rattlesnakes."

I shrugged. "Some like the meat. Cooked, it tastes like chicken. But
you'll eat yours raw."

"You fucked up our big mission," said Andes.

I tossed another branch on the campfire. Sparks flew up. "It's
finished. You lost. Now, who shot at us?"

Andes gazed off into the darkness, his natural habitat. "Woody or Dot, maybe both halfwits."

"That's more like it. Your gig in the fire tower was the perfect cover," I said.

"I should've let you drop through the trapdoor that first day you climbed up to visit me."

I grunted. "Who did the surgery on my car tires?"

"The same halfwits," replied Andes.

"If the Blue Cheer is so hush-hush, why did you sell T-shirts at the mini mart?"

"Goines was hoping to recruit some fresh blood. I put the kibosh on it."

"And I suppose we'll put the Jan Maddox and Zelma Roe homicides on Goines since he's dead. Right?" I said.

"True enough," replied Andes.

I flung another broken branch on the fire and more sparks sheeted up. "You're a lying crock. No matter. Doc Thomas has enough trace evidence from each crime scene to prove you were there."

"Evidence? Goines was the investigating officer. I assure you, there's not one scintilla of evidence to incriminate us," said Andes.

"H'm. Goines purged the evidence locker? I should've known." I felt bummed until I recalled a certain detail. "Don't get too cocky." My hand patted at my jacket pocket and I took out Andes' clasp knife to show him. "There's my proof. I bet Zelma's dried blood is in these fittings and under the nacre grips. Your rifle will go back with us tomorrow for ballistics analysis. Guess what's the kicker? Exhibit A, the green nylon rope you used to hang Jan Maddox. Goines never vouchered it. You see, your murder weapon is still lying in the bottom of a wastebasket at the A-frame. Right where I put it."

"Bullshit," said Andes.

"Yep, I cut it off Jan Maddox myself. Now I'm no Dr. Henry Lee at interpreting DNA, but I do know about Locard's Exchange Principle. That says a palm print or something of yours rubbed off on the rope. You're toast," I said.

"You're bluffing. We were overzealous good ole boys playing soldier on government property. That's our worst offense. Whoop-dee-doo. Eighteen months probation and five hundred hours of community service spearing gum wrappers on a nailed stick. On Christmas Eve, I might end up serving meatloaf to toothless winos and crack whores. But I'll survive."

"You'll do a heavier penance than that. Give me the straight skinny on the Stingers," I said.

Andes played it cute. "Stinger rockets? None. I promise you."

I shunted around to heat my cold rump at the fire. "Andes, you're one tough cookie but I've no compunction to kill you here."

Andes garbled an obscenity about my mama. My Buck knife came out. I went over, flipped him, and cut off most of a shirtsleeve. Square-knotted together, the cloth strip made a nifty gag that brought me some peace. I stayed awake through the night.

Near moonset, I decided that before too long I should drive up to The Wall in Washington, D.C. and find Old Man's army friend, Lucas Tackett, the Golden Gloves champ from Georgia who'd stepped on a Viet Cong land mine. I'd try to track down any soldier from Old Man's military unit who'd made it back on The Freedom Bird. We'd raise a beer to toast Old Man.

CHAPTER TWENTY-SIX

———

Ragged clouds showed in the mauve dawn sky as I crouched, staring at the heap of cold campfire ashes. I'd outwatched the night. Andes didn't move. A disturbing thought came and went about the drunk CPO who'd killed my parents. They'd been at the wrong place at the wrong time. Timing was everything. Like now it was time for us to get off this damn mountaintop. I kicked Andes awake. He snarled at me. I had a laugh at his pathetic bravado.

The pink morning star had fizzled out. We filed off the ridge at a snappy hike, almost a jog. I didn't bring down any stone tablets but Andes went manhandled in front of me. I took off his gag until he popped off again about my mama and I was only too happy to leave him muzzled.

Andes continued acting uncooperative. Underneath a horse hornet's nest, he stumbled and sprained his ankle. Wary, I stepped up. He whipsawed a leg around to knock out mine but I dodged him. His second antic was even less original. He broke into a canter straight through a willow copse. I chased him down and held the 9 mil far enough away from his hand so as not to leave any powder burns, and shot him. He bellowed and gripped his injury that bled like a stigmata. I felt lousy but it gave Andes something else to occupy his attention besides attempting to escape.

Gerald's paw-paws made for a good breakfast.

"I don't eat hog chow," said Andes before I wadded the rag back in his mouth.

We breezed into the Blue Cheer compound within a couple of hours. Andes pinned his maimed hand under one elbow to stanch the bleeding and gaped at the vast difference one long night had wrought.

Law enforcement types bustled everywhere. The compound's twin gates were chained open and state police cruisers, red-blue roof lights activated, lined the primitive road. Man, it fired my blood to set my eyes on them. I tallied up ten radio cars before the Mobile Crime Unit and HAZMAT vans shuttled around them.

Uniforms and bomb-sniffing canines were clearing out the various buildings in the compound. The Army had dispatched three HVs manned by soldiers in SWAT combat rig. Two technicians, wearing headsets, swept the packed clay ground with doughnut-head metal detectors while a third videotaped the entire compound with a digicam. I saw National Park rangers huddled in an animated knot and a couple of mechanics performing a flight check on the chopper.

"Quite a comedown, huh, Andes? Your day of reckoning is at hand. This is where it ends, see? Stick that in your crime novel," I said.

Andes' red-veined eyes bulged as he muttered oaths. I ignored him.

Lieutenant Logan had reacted with due force. In these post-Osama days, the Terrorism Threat and Incident Response Squad had been rallied. I breathed in relief when I turned over my prisoner to the state police officers who seemed to assert jurisdiction at the compound. Andes, a multiple killer-in-cuffs, fidgeted in a state police cruiser that keened away with two escorts to the state road and on to his fate in Wheeling. Just before disappearing through the gate, he screamed and spat through the rear window at me, his face contorted with hatred. That got a laugh from me.

A forensics technician bagged and tagged Andes' pricey automatic rifle and clasp knife. She never smiled. Nobody, in fact, smiled. Another clean-cut police cadet, all of eighteen I supposed, guided me into the unfinished barracks where Gerald, his hand propped on a steel bunk frame, talked to a state trooper.

"Hurray! Our main dude has returned." Gerald put on a boyish grin before making our introductions.

Lieutenant Mary Logan accepted my hand and brusquely shook it. Her uniform was a crisp forest green and her lieutenant badge, nameplate, and shooting medal were all gold. The silver rank bars on her collar were the ones Gerald had mentioned. On closer study,

I felt certain he'd overblown his importance in her attaining them. I associated her sober demeanor with police officers of great integrity and a low bullshit tolerance. Her gray eyes bored into me.

"I was telling the lieutenant here that Marshall's Thundering Herd looked awesome on TV," said Gerald.

Sniffing, Lieutenant Logan pulled out a notebook and pen. "Plenty of thundering herd right here," she said.

"Now Mary, we only reported what we'd encountered," said Gerald, his tone placating.

Her voice stiffened into a more official one. "You should have waited for the West Virginia State Police. This is our jurisdiction, not yours, Mr. Peyton."

Her abrupt formality also put me on guard. I had no trouble picturing us rolling out of here in a rear cage, hands tethered behind us. Striving for credulous, Gerald put up his palms. "What better choice did we have, Mary? They started to move and we were on the brink of some more big trouble. Then they saw us and started firing. Self-defense was our last resort. Huh, Frank?"

My nod affirmed his blatant lie that just might wash in these post-9/11 days.

"Okay, Gerald," said Logan a little less harshly. "We'll take down your version of events, but you'd better stick around real close. There's to be no more cutting loose from you or Mr. Johnson. If so, I'll jail you both myself and throw away the key. My work is already cut out when I go to explain this to Department HQ. My colonel will go ballistic."

My breath rushed out. "It's all good," I said before Gerald could talk again and goon up things. "From here on out, we'll play it straight with you."

Gerald and I moved to stand just outside the barracks' entry. I ensured that we were beyond inquisitive ears and asked, "Okay, who all died?"

"Woody Sears, Dot Christmas, and Deputy Goines," replied Gerald.

Goines was dead. I again breathed out in relief. "Where's Betty Maddox?"

"Beats me. When I got back from boosting you over the fence, she'd already gone. I hiked back to the fire tower and her Monte Carlo had disappeared. I met up with Lieutenant Logan and company on the state road and guided them back here on the primitive road by using Zelma Roe's map. We arrived in the wee hours."

"Damn flaky way for Betty to act," I said.

"Could be it was too much for Betty and she freaked. She acted jittery," said Gerald.

I scanned around us before asking, "Were any Stinger rockets recovered?"

"No. A few full-auto AK47 rifles, RPGs, flash bang grenades, and small arms. Enough armament to titillate the ATF crowd. What were these damn Stingers for?" asked Gerald.

I flexed my shoulders to work out the tightening muscle spasm. "Andes had to be plotting a showstopper. He was smug about the Stingers last night."

Authorities came and sequestered Gerald and me. We sat at a cafeteria table inside a dingy room off from the barracks' sleeping quarters. A framed copy of the sniper's creed hung on the paneled wall. I got up and turned the creed around to face the wall. We stretched and scratched. Uniformed figures paraded in, all of them lobbing important but repetitive questions at us. Except not much more was left to go on the official record.

I suggested they go at Andes by using a rubber hose to loosen him up. Bad joke. Once again, nobody smiled. They were a humorless, racheted down bunch of do-gooders. As well they should've been, I supposed. I'd worked with such conscientious investigators in the MPs. They finally told Gerald and me that we were free to go but to stay reachable. We rode away from the compound in a state police cruiser, Gerald grinning at me.

CHAPTER TWENTY-SEVEN

———

We trifled away the time under the tan retractable awning in front of my cabin. I'd wolfed down three tuna fish hoagies, Abe's lunch special, with Rolling Rock, God's champagne in the green bottle. I'd arranged for a tow truck to transport the Valiant from The First Primitive Apostolic Church into Scarab for garage repairs.

I slipped in a bluegrass CD of the O'Quinn Brothers. Whistling out of tune, Gerald organized his gun cleaning materials on a thrifty newspaper picked up at the mini mart, then cycled the twelve gauge's pump to shuck out all its shells. He wetted the bronze bristle brush with Hobbes #9 gun solvent, poked the brush down inside the bore, and scrubbed away, spraying solvent and lead fouling out its muzzle. I enjoyed shooting guns, but not cleaning them.

Gerald's glance included me. "You didn't brief Sheriff Greenleaf. Is he in league with the Blue Cheer?"

"He could well be," I replied. "You've got to understand this investigation will take the Feds some time to sort out. As their scope expands, they'll root out other Blue Cheer members in hiding. But Andes won't cut a deal and snitch. He's too hard core, too stupid. I'd say that Dot Christmas, Woody Sears, and Goines manned the trenches and they may've known about their day-to-day operations. But they were ignorant about any grand strategy."

"Uh-huh." Gerald threaded two cotton patches through the eye of the aluminum rod and saturated them with Hobbes #9. He made one snappy pass through the bore. "It's peculiar how the T-shirts disappeared from the mini mart. They're probably destroyed by now."

"Our two are safe enough. Those and the Stinger motor case will go to Lieutenant Logan. As will Zelma's journal, along with the pieces of green nylon rope." My gaze fell on the Prizm still dry-docked on its steel rims. "Now if we could only track down the Stingers."

"For shits and grins, let's suppose I'm Andes and we'll role-play it. All right, my summer stint in the fire tower is finished and I'm ready to boogie. Everything of value is tossed down to stow inside my car and I mothball whatever's left."

A little perplexed but indulgent, I played along with Gerald. "On the way out, I fall by Frank Johnson's cabin to explain what's up. I'm off to the university and ask him to keep an eye out for any trouble at the fire tower. Johnson, the dumb cluck he is, swallows it hook, line, and sinker."

"Wait. Back it up." Gerald oiled inside and outside the shotgun and wiped it down with a chamois cloth. "Let's say I'm still stuck with a raft of Stingers. Where do I cache them? Screw my car trunk. They're too heavy, on top of that being too risky." He chambered a fresh shell. "Car? Say, I bet I know where the Stingers have been stockpiled."

I returned his stare. "I'll bite. Where are they?"

"Come on and I'll show you."

The fire tower's stickman shadows heralded us hiking up from the woods. This afternoon's trip had been a timesaving straight down and up the mountains. We returned to the path leading through the forest to the Blue Cheer's compound. I saw the junked Buick Skylark intertwined with grapevines. A hog block V8 engine under the Buick's cavernous hood once powered it. Ridge-runners a few generations ago had gunned their muscle cars to transport illegal white lightning out of the gnarly hollows before cannabis cultivation and crystal meth labs took over as the new local underground economy. The Buick, examined up closer, disclosed certain artificial aspects.

The grapevine was a fake with its natural looking leaves made of a silken material. Its jungly growth obscured the Buick's windshield and undersized windows. A brown sealing wax attached the vines to the glass. The scarred up hickory and aspen tree trunks suggested that the old Buick had been recently towed and purposefully lodged in the handy thicket. A light bulb blinked on in my head. I now followed

Gerald's line of thinking on where to find the Stingers.

"Watch out for booby traps?" I asked.

"Why? Anything explosive would touch off the Stingers. Besides, Andes wanted quick, easy access to his babies," replied Gerald.

We tore into our search. Gerald ripped away clingy plants and stems from the cracked windows. My Buck knife cut through the plastic plant stalks. Andes' hidey-hole, an ingenious one, used cardboard with camouflage markings to blot out the window glass. We tugged on each of the four door handles and found Andes' treasure trove. He'd removed the Buick's front and rear seats to stack the pine transportation crates lengthwise. He'd even hollowed out the trunk to accommodate extra pine crates. Grinning, we lifted off a pine crate from the top stack.

We used a left-behind pinch bar to prize off the lid. Gerald whistled at seeing his first Stingers. Two, nestled inside the crate, had been repackaged from their original containers. I went through a factory inspection on one rocket and noted the manufacturing date stenciled on its body made the Stinger an early model. Still I knew by seeing the signs of refurbishment that the batteries had been replaced along with the coolant in the sealed tubes. Deterioration, then, wasn't a factor in limiting the Stinger's ruthless destruction.

"Imagine what one of these babies can do to an aircraft," said Gerald.

"It staggers the imagination," I replied. One of us at each end, Gerald and I repacked the Stinger crate inside the Buick.

"We'll call Mary Logan and get the Feds up here pronto," said Gerald.

"And we ain't moving an inch until they arrive," I said in a grimmer voice.

CHAPTER TWENTY-EIGHT

———

Late Friday afternoon, Gerald packed his duffel and returned home to Pelham after his tenacious client, Helen Ann, had issued her final ultimatum. While we were replacing the slit tires on my Prizm with new ones the garage had dropped off, he talked to her on his cell phone. Then he disconnected and rested a hand on my shoulder.

"I gotta blow home, Frank. My boss lady calls. But it's all over, so let it be. Hear me?"

"All right then," I said.

Gerald gave me a funny look. "Three funerals in two days. That's a lot to sweat. Will you hold up?"

"Don't worry, man. I've already decompressed."

Gerald sniffed. "Do you smell smoke?"

"It's just the woodstove backing up," I replied.

"If you want to bullshit or anything, just hit me on the hip. It's not too far for me to come back," said Gerald.

"I'm good. I'm okay. Go take care of your business."

Gerald, three hours later, boarded a Greyhound at Scarab's Main Street depot and rode the dog west over the Allegheny Mountains to Virginia. I wished I was on the bus, too. Just back from dropping Gerald off, I was alone in my cabin but not for long. An edgy rap came at my door. Odd, I hadn't heard a motor grinding up my lane and I wasn't expecting any company. I cradled the twelve gauge in my elbow, strode over, and cracked open the door. It fell away. My mouth sagged. Rod Bellwether, my castaway cousin, brushed past me on his way into my cabin.

"Hey, Frank," he said, flumping down on the sofa near the woodstove. He looked gaunt, unshaven, crazed, and dangerous. "You ready to do me some good? Like we go and tree a cold-blooded killer?"

"Rod, how long have you been hiding out in my woods? I've smelled your campfire smoke more than once," I said.

"From the thirteenth of never. I came to talk about Kathy. But first, do you mind putting up that damn twelve gauge?" said Rod.

I leveled its chokebore muzzle straight on Rod's chest and his eyes didn't waver. "How did you escape from Bitterroot?" I asked.

"The old-fashion way. I bribed a dirty guard. Look, you're making me paranoid."

The shotgun's muzzle never flagged. "You did kill your wife, the hardhearted little fuck that you are. Kathy died at your hands. Yep, the jury nailed it right. You made your daddy proud, too. You make me want to puke. But guess what? You're headed back to the rat cage, boy."

Rod stirred to lift himself up from the sofa, saw my shotgun, and thought better of it. "Says who?"

A maddening rage poured through me. My knees felt unsteady. "Says your phony alibi. After all this damn time, it finally hit me. Every killer makes at least one stupid mistake. Now I know yours. It's like the prison bull guard told me, you can't read a Pop Tart label. You couldn't be out fishing, sipping whiskey, and reading the Sunday funnies the morning that Kathy died. Why? Simple. You can't read. Or write. You had to dictate your letters in prison."

"I can make out small words," said Rod in defense of the stupid lie. "Now hold on here, Frank. Think motive. Why would I kill Kathy? More importantly, once out of Bitterroot, why would I circle back to see you?"

I did a Sydney Greenstreet shrug. "I could care less why. Maybe you get off on antagonizing me like when we were kids. But Warden Breeden can send a wagon here in a matter of hours and I've got nothing but time, Rod. Time to be rid of your ass, once and for all."

"Wait. I can beat this rap. Gatlin can—"

"Gatlin isn't defending you. Forget about that idea. You should've kept your ass in gear, cuz. To you, everything is a game. But you've no chips left. I've called them all in."

Rod bucked off the sofa and rushed at me. I saw the Gerber knife slicing into view, the same type blade that had shanked his wife. Tripping a step backward and sensing that I was off-balance, I swung up the shotgun. Its walnut stock whipped in a savage arc and smacked against Rod's skull. He sank to the floor. I stood there stewing over him. What pissed me off the most was his playing me for a fool.

Later, after uniformed officials hustled Rod back to Bitterroot State Prison, I scratched my name off Warden Breeden's shit list and breathed a little easier.

Saturday was Old Man and Jan Maddox's funeral. As befit the somber occasion, I dressed in black denim jeans and a navy blue jacket. I also took along the 9 mil. The dawn was gray. The mangy skies, muddy roads, and greasy mist depressed me. My eyes hid behind willow smoke sunshades and I moved on my first three alcoholic crutches into the day.

I arrived fashionably late and lagged near the chapel's doorway. My deceased friend was a respectable draw as most, if not all, of Scarab's folks were in attendance. I marveled to see that the Blue Cheer's hatreds held no sway over these good townspeople. I didn't sign the register. Dr. Thomas asked if I needed anything.

"Only a refill," I replied.

"Me, three," said Dr. Thomas, his slur noticeable.

We tiptoed downstairs to the quiet autopsy suite below the funeral home where he scared up a fifth of Wild Turkey from inside the autoclave. I felt relieved to be drinking it and not their toxic home-brewed moonshine liquor. Dr. Thomas told me an off-color joke featuring lollipops, an electric toothbrush, and a blonde bimbo. I'd heard it before but this rendition still invoked a rib-cracking hilarity. He showed me an old sheriff's badge, his livelihood until he'd earned his college degrees and joined his family funeral business. We adjourned upstairs.

An elderly lady wearing a leopard-print pillbox hat ended the funeral service by reading a passage from *Love Story*. A swell if corny gesture. There wasn't a dry eye in the chapel, mine included. I served as a pallbearer and fell in queue with the lemmings' procession, our headlights turned on. A retired African-American sergeant major played a moody chorus of 'Amazing Grace' on the bagpipes at the gravesite and then left in a bat black limousine.

I loitered in back behind the awning and faux patio grass where Betty Maddox came trolling for me. Without a word, she marched me up front like a show horse to claim one of those chairs reserved for the immediate family. She and I were the only ones seated there. I thought about her running off on Gerald at the Blue Cheer compound but I kept my mouth shut. I visualized Gerald gunning down Goines and the others that helped to console me.

I didn't feel closer to Old Man lying there inside the knothole maple box. He went out, I liked to think, like a good soldier. Old Man had brought back his inner demons from Vietnam, only they'd never roared out. He'd probably told me more about his time in Nam than anybody else but I couldn't recall any of his stories. I wondered if anyone had thanked him for his service. I hadn't.

The preacher recited a Psalm and when the buzzing crowd thinned out, Eva, the attentive autopsy assistant, steered me past their excavated graves and between the granite headstones. The turned earth smelled moist and fecund. She ran me home. I was in no shape to drive myself. We filed into my cabin. While I babbled on, she gnawed the pink portion of her lips and listened. She nodded a lot. Maybe smiled. Eva had to split and pick up her dad, a sloppy drunk, working at the ironworks. I put the 9 mil away.

On Sunday I rested. Listened to Ricky Skaggs. Read Charles Williams. I saw a black bear behind my cabin. I drank like a fish.

Monday was The Reverend Zelma Roe's funeral service. I started off better by parking my Prizm on the street and hobbling into the chapel a few minutes early. I was also sober. Dr. Thomas, sickly green in complexion, nodded at me and hurried off to greet the organist. We'd depleted our stock of good jokes and bourbon.

A skull-faced preacher had driven over the ridges from Elkins on the hot afternoon. His canned elegy—the ashes-to-ashes and dust-to-dust one—gave us a good, cathartic cry. Like the Maddoxes' service, Zelma's was also a closed casket. Hers was a powder blue steel casket topped with a funeral spray of yellow gladiolas. A few curiosity-seekers probably left disappointed. I skipped the graveside prayers and can't say who went to the cemetery. I heard that Abe's threw a big bash afterward.

CHAPTER TWENTY-NINE

Awaking the next morning on the cusp of the DTs, I quit drinking cold turkey, a knack the Black Irish carry in their genes. What else needs saying? Greenleaf, running unopposed for sheriff, lost to a write-in campaign for Dr. Thomas of which Eva, a few church ladies, and I were the chief instigators.

Roy Pinkerton and the other news media wrote up Gerald, Betty, and me as heroes but I never read a word about it. Gerald, pleading self-defense, wasn't charged in absentia for killing Woody Sears, Dot Christmas, and Deputy Goines. I drove up to visit Hattie McGraw on her mountain but her cabin sat empty. I also didn't see Edna practicing her golf swings.

Events turned surreal when I took a telephone call from the CIA in Langley. A resonant male voice asked me pointed questions about Old Man's death but I had a few questions myself. With neither of us giving up any answers, we reached an impasse only resolved by hanging up.

The target drone I'd seen obliterated in the sky, from what I could piece together, was a gas-powered propeller jobber that some outfit down south sold for a couple thousand dollars. Remote controlled from a box, it taxied off 25 feet of runway, say, like down the fire tower's lane. Andes and the Blue Cheer probably stole it out of a contractor's ware-house. I thanked the salesman for his help.

More than curious, I phoned Lieutenant Mary Logan at the Elkins Troop Headquarters. She was out and I left a message. After three unsuccessful tries, I stopped calling her. A tight lid was kept on any information about the source for the Blue Cheer's Stinger rockets. They'd been stolen or bought from somewhere. I wanted to dismiss the possibility that the theft had occurred here in the Lower Forty-Eight but a persistent doubt lingered.

Prosecutor Irving, the very same day Greenleaf was unseated as sheriff, declined to prosecute and rescinded all the charges against me. Dr. Thomas returned my Kel-Tec 9 mil confiscated on my false arrest by the late Deputy Goines. Finally it came time for me to leave Scarab. Winter fast approached. I left feeling dispirited, but I'd intercepted the Stingers, sabotaged the Blue Cheer, took out Goines, and jailed their leader, Andes. A lot of bang for the buck Old Man had paid me. My tryout as a mountaineer, however, had proven an unglamorous bust.

I first contacted Gatlin, like any unemployed slob would do, to beg for my old job back. He was overjoyed to hear about my homecoming. An affluent client in Middleburg was suing her husband for infidelity. Sex pictures, the down and dirty kind, were essential. Man, I couldn't wait to load up my 35mm and bust my tail again for Gatlin.

I packed up the Prizm and at the first curve dipping away from the cedar log cabin, I squirmed around to take one final, parting look. It threw me lots of memories. The richest were those afternoons Old Man and I had cut up oak into fire logs. The bourbon whiskey we'd shared had been unforgettable, too.

Old Man and I had been friends. We all have so damn few, too. Well, I'd miss him but my stomping grounds were with Gerald Peyton, his brother Chet, Gatlin, Doc Edwards, and the rest in Pelham, Virginia. Not here.

Later I'd have to make that pilgrimage to The Wall in Washington, D.C. and spend Christmas in Richmond with Dreema Adkins, my favorite forensic scientist. But for now, it was time for me to go home.

I dropped by the Scarab Bank and cashed my jailbird check for $44.28. It didn't bounce so I had gas money to make it home. One block over, Betty Maddox loitered outside the Scarab Post Office, a hand shading her wary eyes as I shunted to the curbstone. A car key on the ring in her other hand tapped against a hip. I stretched out of the Prizm as a battery of mixed emotions beset me. I did and didn't want to leave town. Betty stayed put and I walked over to her. Slow.

"Leaving us high and dry, huh?" said Betty.

"Yeah. Sort of how you left Gerald and me at the Blue Cheer compound," I said.

Displeasure coarsened Betty's handsome features. "Like I told you before, Frank, I panicked, hurried back to my car at the fire tower, and drove straight home. I was a wreck. It took me hours to settle my nerves. I haven't slept in nights. How can you blame me? Anyway, didn't everything turn out okay?"

"You'll keep me informed about my cabin?" I asked.

"I already agreed to it. Who knows, maybe my realtor will sell both properties to the same buyer. Meantime, I gave Old Man's Valiant to Eva. She's a nice girl. There's more. The park service, I hear tell, is razing the old fire tower."

"Good-bye and good riddance. Plan on my return to Scarab whenever Andes goes to trial. I'll be tapped with a subpoena. Won't Gatlin love making that trip again," I said.

Betty's smile was sad like Old Man's but she wasn't Old Man. "Better lump in John Wingo the ironworks director, too. The cops apprehended him early this morning up in the panhandle."

"Glad to hear it." After a small pause, I spat out what was really on my mind. "You never liked Jan Maddox did you, Betty? You know what I figure? I figure you called Andes and the Blue Cheer after talking to me at her church that day. Andes knew when to climb up into the barracks' rafters and waylay us once inside the compound. You had a cell phone. There's more stink, too, my nose tells me." I conjured the image of a seedy motel room. Old Man shotgunned to death in his bed.

Betty's eyes fell into a blank stare. "It's over, Frank. Let it be."

"All right, then. I'm not big on stirring it up again. I just know what you did," I told her.

"Good-bye, Frank," said Betty.

Having settled that, I folded into my Prizm and drove away. Slow. Scarab was a town like that—it pissed you off. But I hated leaving feeling so damn beat down. I went past the Hubcap Madonna, past Sheriff Greenleaf's office, past Dr. Thomas' funeral home, and finally past the Chartreuse Ironworks.

As a cold mountain drench set in, I turned on the radio. Dr. Ralph

Stanley keened the lyrics to the ballad, 'Rank Strangers to Me'. You know the stanza where the singer travels back to his old home place in the mountains and nobody, even loved ones, recognizes him? Well, those lyrics choked me up inside.

The windshield wipers flapped back and forth as my eyes wetted. At first, I tried to shake it off, tried to steel myself. I sniffed and wiped at my eyes. I only teared up worse. Bluegrass music, especially the traditional hook-in-the-heart songs, can do that to you.

I turned off the radio.

Acknowledgements

Many diverse people contributed to this book's inception.

Thanks go to the engineers and scientists at Atlantic Research Corporation in Gainesville, Virginia. My eyears there as a technical writer drafting SOPs for manufacturing Stingers seeded many of the ideas grown here.

LEOs on The Real Police Law Enforcement Resource message board fielded my cop-related questions. In addition, the Military Police Homepage message board provided background material.

Other helpful people interviewed are cited:

Tom Caceic and the Shawnee Gun Club for pointers on firearms.

Mike & Cora Tervo for stays at their place in Romney, WV.

Dolores Davis and Chris DellMea for their knowledge on coal mines.

Larry Maynard for environmental insights.

Rick Broussard at Aerojet Composite Models for explaining target drones.

Forrest Brandt, 1st Lt., OIC at "KLIK," AFVN, for musical tastes in wartime Vietnam. Briane Turley, Ph.D., West Virginia University, described Appalachian cemeteries.

Rosi Smith, Southern Poverty Law Center, for confirming their suits against hate groups.

Holly Farris for her professional background as an autopsy assistant.

Joyce Payne and Wise County, VA Chamber of Commerce for local color.

Greenbrier Chamber of Commerce for bluegrass musicians native to West Virginia.

Don Hill and Early Valiant Barracuda Club as well as Peter Morthen at R&S Valiant Club in Australia for assuring me that vintage Valiants are still very much road-worthy.

Landon Noland for comments about his job in the bridge building industry.

For criminology assistance from interviews, thanks go to:

Ed Uthman, M.D. (Forensic Pathologist, Houston)

James Kaplan, M.D. (West Virginia Office of the Chief Medical Examiner)

Lt. Joe Parsons and the West Virginia State Police

Nancy Chatlak (Circuit Librarian, 1st Judicial Circuit Law Library, WV) and Rosalie Henke (Deputy Clerk, Circuit Court, Ohio County, WV)

Terri Helmick, West Virginia State House

Whatever technical goofs are my own fault, not theirs. To those whose inputs somehow evade my failed memory, I hope an apology will suffice. The Hattie McGraw character was inspired by Eudora Welty's photograph, "Blind Weaver/Oktibbeha County" (1930s). My "Vietnam War Memorial Triolet" originally appeared in Troxey Kemper's *Tucumcari Literary Review.*

Key research text sources included:

Michael Baden, M.D. and Marion Roach, *Dead Reckoning: The New Science of Catching Killers* (New York: Touchstone, 2001). Describes autopsy details in humane, humorous terms.

Chris Baker, "Community Development and the Prison Industry in Rural Appalachia," *Mountain Promise* (Brushy Fork Institute, Berea College, Kentucky) Summer 2002, Vol. 13 No. 2. Discusses a perhaps circumspect way to revive slow regional economies.

Dickey Chapelle, "Water War in Vietnam," *National Geographic*. Vol. 129, No. 2 (February 1966). War correspondent's pictorial essay on early defensive war.

Dickey Chapelle, "Helicopters Over South Vietnam," *National Geographic*. Vol. 122, No. 5 (November 1962). War correspondent's coverage of the chopper war.

Vernon J. Geberth, *Practical Homicide Investigation* (Baton Rouge: CRC Press, 1996). Bible for criminal investigation. 'Nuff said.

Joe Heim. "The Old Country: DJ Eddie Stubbs Won't Let Nashville Forget Its Roots." *The Washington Post*, July 27, 2003.

Kenworth Trucking Press Release. "V. Van Dyke Tethers Two Kenworth T800s Together To Handle Huge Load." June 19, 2002. http://www.kenworth.com.

Amelia Kirby, "Prison-Industry in the Appalachians," *Digress Magazine* (August 1998). Describes her eerie visit to Red Onion Prison's "Open House" before the first inmates arrived.

Discography of the Osborne Brothers. Osborne Brothers Homepage. http://www.osbornebros.com

Wallace Terry," *Bloods: An Oral History of the Vietnam War by Black Veterans.* (New York: Random House, 1984). A classic on the black war experience I reviewed for *The Roanoke Times & World News*.

Tending the Commons: Folklife and Landscape in Southern West Virginia. The Library of Congress Online. 9/29/00. Tons of anecdotes and lore captured in audio files from mountain people.

Biography

Ed Lynskey was born in Washington, DC and lives in that area. He is married to Heather. He has worked in the defense industry, including eighteen years on the development and production of Stinger missiles. His crime fiction has appeared in *Alfred Hitchcock Mystery Magazine*. Other work has appeared in the *Atlantic Monthly, Washington Post*, and *New York Times*. Other novels in the PI Frank Johnson series include *The Dirt-Brown Derby, Pelham Fell Here*, and *Troglodytes*.